Vultures

Book 3

Laura Mae

Vultures is sequel to *Fliers* and *Sparrows*.

You can find this book on Amazon, Barnes & Noble and other sources listed on her website.

www.lauramaeauthor.wordpress.com

Vultures by Laura Mae

Edited by Sarah Jane Day

Cover art by Angie Alaya

www.lauramaeauthor.wordpress.com

This is a work of fiction. Names, characters, businesses, places, events, locales, and incidents are either the products of the author's imagination or used in a fictitious manner. Any resemblance to actual persons, living or dead, or actual events is purely coincidental.

First Edition

ISBN: 978-0-578-38535-8

Chapter One

Waves of electricity slowly made their way out of Sydona's system. She stuck to the floor like a paralyzed victim. Every minuscule thought infiltrated her mind, leading up to that exact point. She thought she was ahead of him, but he had always been in the lead. Malik had too many eyes. As large as the Sparrows' rebellion appeared, the Vultures tripled them. Would it always be a losing battle no matter what she did? She hated thinking that way, but her current position left her no alternative.

Peeling herself off the white marble floor as her body felt somewhat normal again, she examined her surroundings. She wiped her face of tears and sweat. She was eager to see her father. A pounding heart leaped out of her chest as she stood up and pressed her hands against the plastic prison wall. In another cell, he sat across from her on a cot as thin as paper.

"Dad!" she cried, pounding a fist on the plastic. The smooth, rigid surface didn't budge. She pounded until both of her hands tingled.

He rose to his feet, shuffled to the wall, and pressed his hands against the plastic. She noted his trembling chin, but ignored it as it would only cause her to break down. She couldn't afford to use up any more energy. She had to focus.

Ian spoke, but even in pure silence, she failed to hear anything at all. His voice was so mellow to begin with, she didn't expect to hear him. She shrugged her shoulders to show him she wasn't able to understand. The father and daughter stared into each other's eyes, somehow trying to communicate telepathically. Sydona observed his condition. His skin appeared darker, just like he told her in the letter. The wrinkles in his face had deepened and the hunch in his back seemed worse than before. He shouldn't be in there. She still couldn't understand how they found him. Only the Sparrows knew of the island. An uninhabited island at that. Barely anyone else in existence knew of it.

His fragile hands slid down the wall and he turned away. A chin that once trembled was at its lowest point, fusing with his neck. Sydona perked up and pounded the plastic again to show him she wasn't done. She would never be done looking at her father, her last living relative on Earth. And he was trapped there because of her.

Unable to communicate effectively with her father, she retired to her so-called bed. She listened to her breathing as she stared up at the white ceiling with an overly exposed fluorescent light fixture. The intense buzzing sound gave her something else to focus on. Her heart steadily beat within her bruised and damaged chest. One by one, her friends' faces came to the forefront of her mind. She wondered if she would ever get to see the people she grew so fond of again. As Raoul's face came to mind, so did Jubilees. Only a week or so ago, she was taken by Natalia. His niece was only four years old, the same fairy they had a Vila Prah for the day before they left. What would Natalia do to her? She had only just learned how to fly.

Just then, someone appeared behind the wall carrying a metallic tray. It was Natalia wearing an outfit just tight enough to expose her stomach and cleavage. Her hair was pulled into a small twisted bun, while her makeup was fresh and heavy. A long chain with a dragon charm hung around her neck, but it didn't seem to match the rest of her ensemble. Sydona accidentally caught her eye, and Natalia winked quickly. Her heart gravitated to her throat, and it made her want to vomit. She had no idea what Natalia was doing there and feared the absolute worst. The Vulture accompanying her wore all black, making him look more sophisticated than Jones. The copper taste of his blood still lingered in her mouth. The tray she carried had a glass of water, an apple, and what looked like a sandwich. Despite how much she despised Natalia, Sydona's mouth watered. Natalia stood behind the guard as he input the code next to her cell that glowed red. As the door slid open, he instantly pointed the gun at Sydona. Cautious, she sat up in her cot.

"Down boy," Natalia barked with a smoky voice and snapped her fingers.

"But the doctor said—"

"Does it really look like I care what the doctor said?" Natalia dropped the food down on the nearby bookshelf and pivoted back around to the guard. She grabbed his groin and leaned in closer to him. Natalia's back was to Sydona as she whispered in his ear. Judging by his face, it was something dirty. Whatever she said worked. The guard lowered his gun back to his side. Natalia locked her eyes on his, and he bit his lip as he left the cell. He must have realized how ridiculous he looked. When he took his post near the door, he cleared his throat and broke eye contact. As Natalia turned to face Sydona, her expression melted into a disgusted scrunch.

She leaned into Sydona. "That man has *the* smallest dick I've ever squeezed."

Sydona answered with wide and confused eyes.

Natalia took a minute to look around the trashed cell. "So, what the fuck happened here? You on your period, too? I think that road trip synced us up."

"What do you want?" Sydona asked, changing the weird subject.

"I don't want shit, niña. John told me to bring you some food so you don't starve to death. Would that really be such a bad thing?"

Sydona's jaw tightened. "I'm not hungry."

"Let it rot, then." Natalia grabbed a piece of the broken chair and examined it, admiring the sharp point. "This what you was gonna use to kill him?"

Sydona glanced away. She hoped by not answering she would bore Natalia into leaving.

"It's not bad, really. You gotta do it in his sleep, though. If you *really* want him dead. No defense. Unaware. It's *so* much more satisfying when you catch 'em off guard."

What the hell was that supposed to mean? Was that her plan for her—to come down and kill her when she was sleeping? And the way she said it worried her. It was as if she had done it before, killing the unaware. Sadistic. But at the same time, she had a point. Sleeping makes a person innocent and unarmed. Guards didn't surround Malik in his bed, did they? She could find that out for herself.

Natalia tossed the stake to the side and sat next to Sydona. Sydona instinctively bounced away from her and halfway off the edge. "I remember when this place used to be crawling with you freaks. Crying and begging to let them go. Like, *all* the fucking time. It was so goddamn annoying." Natalia grabbed the apple off the tray and took a bite. She continued with a mouthful. "I used to do this thing where

I would see how long it would take to get their eyes to change from purple to brown. Turns out, it doesn't take that long." She laughed, spewing bits of apple. "But the *real* challenge was getting them to change from green to brown. My record was a minute. It was this teenage boy who was such a little prick. *He* was my Everest. I finally got it when I figured out that fliers don't necessarily need fingernails. When I got the pinky off, they turned brown *real* quick!" She laughed so hard she practically choked.

Sydona's fists vibrated with anger, and she knew her eyes would be blazing green if they could still change.

Natalia turned to face her. "I can't do that with you, though. You're defective. Shame." As she took a few more bites, she let half eaten fruit fall to the ground. "Well… it's been *nice* talking to you."

She turned to leave, but Sydona couldn't hold back. She still had questions.

"How'd you find Theodore?" she asked.

Natalia flipped back around, turning on her heels. "I'm sorry, who?" she asked with the biggest smile.

Sydona could tell she had been waiting for this question, but she didn't care. She sprung up and closed the distance between them. Her face was inches away.

Natalia stepped back and chuckled. "He came to *us*, puta. Like a lost little puppy."

"W—Why would he do that?" She furrowed her brows.

"Fuck if I know. He was homeless, and smelled like shit. He wanted to go somewhere he could stay and eat. Fucking pathetic. Get a job, right? But just as I was about to set my boys on him and put him out of his misery, he said *your* name. Said y'all were friends and sold weed, like a couple amateurs." She laughed and shook her head. "Anyway, I decided to spare him like the generous person I am and told him that if he could lure you to us, he'd be set for life. Dumbass agreed almost instantly. It was his idea to set the trap."

Sydona stood dumbfounded, trying to understand her story. "Theo wouldn't do that... He wouldn't hurt a fly. There's no way he would set up explosives."

"I'm not letting that fucker take my idea! The dynamite was all me. He just found the location and stole a department store mannequin. Everything else was me. Pshh," she said with an eye roll at the end.

"Theo killed himself right in front of me! Shot his..." Sydona paused and shut her eyes. "You did *that,* too."

Natalia shrugged. "Looks like I did the world a favor, then."

Sydona couldn't hold back any longer. Her shaking fist burst from its cage and landed square in the middle of Natalia's face.

Natalia fell backwards, and blood began to leak from her nose. "Excellent!" Natalia said, wiping her face and biting her tongue between her grin. She quickly recovered. Within a second, she tackled Sydona and slammed her against the wall. Natalia wailed her fists at Sydona, but she took equal shots back at her. Natalia's necklace swayed around. Sydona snatched at it. She was eventually able to grab it, but Natalia yanked herself backwards and forced it out of her hand. The spikey wings sliced into Sydona's palm. The yelling and screeching bounced against the plastic walls until the guard barged in and plucked Natalia out of the brawl. He shoved her back into the hallway and blocked the doorway, refusing to let her back into the cell.

"What the f— I wasn't done yet!" she screamed.

"Orders are not to hurt her. Not even *you!*" he retorted. The plastic wall glowed crimson again as the guard locked it back up. Natalia fixed her hair and glared at Sydona. When Sydona flashed her a sideways smirk, Natalia stormed off, the guard trailing behind.

As soon as they left her sight, Sydona flopped down on the bed. Her entire body ached, and she arched her back in pain. The news about Theodore rushed back to her. Why had she never come back for him? He was so desperate for *something* that he turned to the N.F.A. She could have prevented his death, his messed up life, all of it. Tears welled up, but they retreated as she heard a sound coming from her father's cell. He was hunched over on his bed, coughing. It was so loud it brought a sinking feeling to her stomach. Was he sick?

"Dad," Sydona said out loud to herself. Once she noticed him coughing harder, she panicked.

"Hey! Hey!" she yelled and pounded on the wall as hard as she could. Her eyes darted from her sick father to the edge of the hallway, hoping to see someone who could help. Even if it happened to be the crazy woman. When no one appeared, she grabbed the tray, flung the food off, and threw it at the plastic door. She slammed the metal against the plastic so hard her ears vibrated with a high-pitched ringing. Still, she kept going. After a solid minute of relentless pounding, it was useless. Her father soon held up his hand and stopped coughing. Sydona let out a heavy sigh. Her fists relaxed. Sweat drenched her entire body. The cell felt as if it were growing smaller with each shaky breath.

What would happen if he wasn't okay? The doctor needed them both alive, didn't he? Why wouldn't someone be down there to make sure they didn't try to kill themselves? There were no cameras or buttons or anything she could see to ensure nothing happened.

Not much time passed until she noticed different people walking down the hall. Doctor Malik. Again. This time, he had just one other guard with him. He wore a white lab coat over his suit and propped himself up with a cane that featured a bronze eagle head.

A wide grin was plastered on his face, like she was a present he'd been wanting to open all December. The guard opened her cell and directed her out with a simple head nod. Malik stood still in the hallway as he put handcuffs on her. As it clicked, she took a step, but the doctor stopped her. Sydona stumbled and flinched her head backwards. He then pulled out a metal, flat ring from his pocket and pulled it open. Malik snapped it around the light brown line circling her wrist, and her heart wanted to explode.

"No, no, please..." she pleaded softly. As much as she wanted to fight, she didn't have much left in her. Her stomach suddenly felt completely empty.

"Don't beg, Miss Wilder. It's unbecoming," he cautioned.

The sight of the bracelet forced flashbacks of Eagle Lake, and the memories made her lightheaded. She didn't understand why he bothered with the cuff if she couldn't fly. But she thought it was best not to ask. Malik took the lead, and the guard walked behind her. They made the long walk down the corridor, the same way she first came in with Natalia and Jones. She took a lasting look at her father who stood by his plastic door. His eyes were red and watery, and his face more worn than ever. She needed to tell them about his condition.

"My father is sick. He needs help!"

The guard shoved her forward.

Sydona stumbled. "I'm serious! He's coughing *a lot*."

"He's old, that's what old people do," said the guard, unconcerned with her father's fate.

Her teeth clenched. "Where are you taking me?"

"We're going to administer some tests," Malik replied.

"What tests?"

"Shut the hell up," said the guard with enunciated syllables.

Before she could retort, Malik spoke. "Now, now, Corry. Is that any way to speak to our guest?"

She narrowed her eyes at the fact he regarded her as a guest and not as she would describe it: a prisoner. Corry backed down and never said another word. As they kept walking and she was able to calm down, she wondered if she should tell him she wasn't able to fly anymore. Maybe that would push him over the edge. Maybe he would end his own miserable life over years of failed research. It was a morbid thought, but it made her smile.

What would he do if she didn't do what he wanted, though? Just kill her? She bit her lip. The last time she did something he didn't like, he electrocuted her and took away her ability. Killing her would be the next step, right? Or something worse. She was too nervous to say anything, so she walked in silence as they left the facility and went outdoors.

The first rush of crisp air embraced her senses, and she inhaled it deeply. Staleness from the prison below quickly dissolved. Her focus was renewed in the fresh, ocean air, and she slowly observed her surroundings. Veering to the left, they walked to the mansion on the hill sitting upon the one-hundred acre location. The house more than doubled the size of her sky blue Victorian. She thought her house was large, but this one was obnoxiously big. Floor-to-ceiling windows covered most of the walls, making it feel as if the room opened up to the outside world. It had multiple levels and even half levels, raising it about three stories high. The landscaping around it was impeccable with not a single leaf out of place. Things that could be symmetrical, were.

A complex of two-story buildings caught her eye in the distance as they proceeded up a large flight of bleached, concrete stairs. It looked similar to an apartment setup with cars parked on the cozy street out front. But they couldn't be normal apartments. In such close vicinity, they had to be part of the complex and not a separate neighborhood. They were on a peninsula. The only logical way Doctor Malik could do what he did without nosey neighbors, was to also own those, too. She wondered who, if anyone, lived there.

Malik slid the glass door open for them, and her bare feet sunk into the lavishly soft carpet. White was a favorite color inside the mansion as well. She imagined slamming Malik's head against a window and staining the carpet red, just to add some color. Every inch of the place was flawlessly designed with blues and whites. She still preferred blood red. It was the back of the house, and they trekked through the living room with twenty-foot ceilings. Windows stretched just as high, letting in the constant Californian sun. She actually admired that detail. Even though the mansion was large and bright with several, high-tech electronics, it somehow still felt homey.

After passing by the kitchen with an island, trekking upstairs and then down a hallway, they entered an office. It was covered floor to ceiling with bookshelves. Ladders were placed along the shelves to reach the higher books and the only window occupied the space behind the desk. The aroma of wood hit her in the face as if she were in the Amazon. A gold bust was displayed behind glass on a shelf, but she didn't know who it was. And on top of one of the few bookshelves that did not touch the ceiling, was a magnificent broadsword mounted proudly to the wall. This was his sacred place, his sanctuary.

Corry stood by the door in case Sydona tried to escape, while Malik made himself comfortable on the shiniest leather chair she'd ever seen. A sleek computer that would make Giovonna envious sat on an oversized, mahogany desk. Sydona stood in front of his desk where another two shiny leather chairs sat, waiting for something to happen.

"Sit, sit," the doctor spoke, waving his hand out over his desk. "Would you like some tea or water?"

Sydona hesitantly sat on the edge of the leather, with her handcuffed hands placed on her lap. "I'm fine."

The doctor removed his glasses, placed them on his desk, leaned back and began with a long exaggerated sigh. "Well, Miss Wilder, it certainly has been a while, hasn't it?"

Sydona gave a slight nod and swallowed.

"No need to be nervous. I just want to talk. How are things?" he asked, tilting his head. As if he were a high school guidance counselor.

"Uh..." she uttered, stunned by the question. They weren't friends, not even in the slightest. Why would he ask such a trivial question?

"I apologize. Poor choice of words. Let me ask this instead..." He leaned forward in his chair and intertwined his hands on top of the desk. "When exactly did your eyes change color?"

The edges of Sydona's lips curled. "When do you think?"

"Eagle Lake?"

"After you electrocuted the hell out of me," said Sydona and made a slight lunge forward in anger. The doctor's eyes shifted to the guard behind her as if stopping him from intervening, then focused back on her. His bushy eyebrows furrowed and he adjusted himself in his seat. "That's impossible, Miss Wilder."

"Obviously not," Sydona sat back and glanced away from him. His staring was beginning to rub her wrong.

He then stretched his hands out and observed her hands. The brown line on her wrist peeked out from beneath the bracelet, and he grabbed it fiercely. He rotated her arm around to examine the scar. "Your eyes were the only thing affected, yes?"

Her jaw tightened, and she snatched her arm back. She refused to give him the satisfaction of a "yes". He needed to feel how she felt. The shock of it.

Malik sat back, tilting his head the other way in a different manner. Not in a curious way, but more of an accusing, suspicious way. "Natalia informed me that she saw you in the sky."

"Well she lied to you."

He shook his head and pursed his lips. "I don't believe you."

Her heart pounded. "If I could fly, I would have gotten here much sooner to kill you."

He threw his head back in laughter and pushed his chair back. "Lovely. Let's test it then, shall we?"

Sydona's stomach sank. "What?"

"I need to make sure you're not lying to me too, Miss Wilder."

He seized her arm, nails digging into her skin, and forced her to her feet. "Why would I lie about this?" she protested.

"I can do many things, young lady, but one thing I cannot do is read minds. In order for me to truly know, I need to test it." He put his glasses back on. Sydona was about to say something when he walked right past her and whispered something to the guard. Corry nodded, grabbed the walkie on his hip and left the room, shutting the door behind him. Malik stood next to the door, waiting in silence.

"Where are you taking me?" Sydona demanded.

Malik stayed silent and peered down at his gold watch to pass the time. Soon, the guard reentered the room and whispered something else to Malik. He nodded and announced, "very good! Come along then, Miss Wilder."

Sydona clenched her jaw in frustration. The doctor led the way again, and the guard took his place behind her. After Malik locked the office, they made their way down the long hall and left the house the way they came. She glared at the back of his greasy black hair. His pace quickened as he showed them past the garage prison and to a cliffside jetting out over the vast ocean.

He pivoted around, and his copper, dead eyes snapped onto hers. The wind picked up in the higher altitude. Her short blonde hair whipped around her face, while the gust only moved a single black strand above his eyes. He strutted over and pulled out a key from his pocket. After unlocking her handcuffs, he threw the key at Corry and then pulled out another mechanism that unhinged the metal bracelet. It was hard to see exactly what it was he used, but it looked something like a bent paperclip. He then let go, stepped to the side, and held his arm out toward the ocean. The cliff dropped away to violent waves only fifty feet from where she stood.

"What?" Sydona genuinely asked.

"Fly," he said, voice stale.

Her stomach twisted. "I told you I can't."

"I said *do it*," Malik raised his voice.

"No, I'll die!"

"Then I'll know you weren't lying!" he screamed, spraying saliva into the air.

Sydona shook with anger and confusion. Did he really want her to jump off a cliff? Why couldn't he just believe her? What would she gain from lying about it? And what was to stop her from running the other way?

"We don't have all day, Miss Wilder!"

"No! I'm not jumping off a cliff!"

"Yes, you will. And you'll fly."

"I won't!" Her anger quickly turned into tears.

Malik dropped his head and shook it back and forth. He made quick strides back over to her. His nose almost touched hers. His breath reeked of menthol and old coffee. He whispered, "Here's the deal. You do this, whether you can fly or not. If you don't, I won't hesitate to hurt your sick father. If you can fly and fly away from me, same outcome. I need to see proof, Miss Wilder… I need to see it!" He paused to compose himself and fix his hair. "You only need to fly for a minute and circle back. Then we can go about our day."

A huge lump formed in her throat and body surged with rage. She hoped the Sparrows would be there at any second to save her. Willow would come in and do her thing and shoot him in the head like she almost did once before. Or Knox would fly in from nowhere and take him out with a single blow. But no one was coming. They probably couldn't get within a mile of the place. And leaving would only endanger her sickly father more. Sydona finally nodded reluctantly at him. He stepped back to give her space.

Sydona took in a sharp, deep breath, blew out, and burst into a sprint. The edge of the cliff got closer and closer as her heart beat faster and faster. It was like she was being forced to commit suicide. Her lungs felt tighter the closer she came to the edge. The patch of grass turned brown, and soon her feet and body hung in midair. For a single second, she truly felt like she was flying. But it quickly ended as gravity took over, and she plummeted toward the rocky waters below. She braced herself for the unforgiving waters and forced her arms and legs into a pinpoint. Eyes squeezed closed as she readied herself for her demise.

"I'm sorry, daddy…" The wind tore the words from her lips, and she wasn't sure if she imagined herself speaking.

In an instant she was consumed by the ocean. Despite it being so close to the shore, her feet never touched the bottom. The waves were forceful, and she felt as if she were in a washing machine. Salt water invaded her nose and mouth and crept into her lungs. She was a game to the sea as it pushed and pulled her along, trying to see how long she could last before it consumed her. Her head broke the surface. A huge gasp of air filled her lungs, but then the current dragged her into the depths. Just as she thought she might be able to swim her way out of it, one vengeful tide slammed her into a large rock, and she felt the immediate sting of death.

Chapter Two

RAOUL

Raoul sat on the end table between the two beds of the hotel room. A cartoon on the television kept Devon, Silas, Jet, and himself preoccupied. Raoul had never really sat and enjoyed an entire show, and he wanted to watch until the very end. After the show ended, he flew up to stretch his wings. Completely unaware of what occurred in the past thirty minutes, he glanced around the room and squinted his dry eyes.

"Where's Syd?"

Silas left the comfort of the bed to stretch his back and tend to his injured leg. "She's outside, talking with Gia."

Raoul flew to the sliding glass door and pulled back the dense, rust colored curtain. He noticed a phone wire leading outside, and the phone sitting on the table, but Sydona was nowhere in sight. "Did she come back in?"

Silas wandered over to look out with him. "Maybe she went for a walk?" He slid the door open wide, and Raoul flew out ahead of him.

A sound like a disconnected line beeped from the receiver, which hung over the edge of the mesh table by its spiral cord.

"Something happened," Silas said as he observed the small patio. Raoul felt it too.

"What's going on?" Jet announced as he came to look with Devon.

Raoul's gut told him something wasn't right. Sydona wouldn't just leave without telling them, and the phone off the hook made him uneasy. He flew up to the second floor where the rest of the group was staying. He banged on their glass door as hard as he could. Knox eventually came over and let him in.

"Hey, Raoul!" He greeted him with a smile.

"Sydona up here with you guys?" he asked as he buzzed around the room, searching in the bathroom and under the bed.

Willow chuckled. "I don't thank she's under the bed, buddy,"

"I can't find her. I can't find her." he mumbled out loud. His heart pounded in his ears.

Avani spoke up. "Chicano, calm down. She's prolly just out for a walk or somethin'..."

"No! She wouldn't leave without telling us!" he yelled, his heart thumping fiercely.

A loud knocking on the door stopped the talking. Harold opened it cautiously. Silas pushed it open further and limped into the room, out of breath. "D—did you find her, Raoul?"

"Sydona? No…" Knox scratched the back of his neck. "What the hell is going on?"

Jet spoke from the doorway in unison with Devon. "She's gone."

"Syd's missing?" asked Avani with wide lilac eyes.

Willow shook her head. "She ain't gone; she's gotta be somewhere. Come'on, I'll help ya find her."

Raoul nodded, squashing his fears down. Willow's cool tone helped calm him, and he buzzed around the room to search for clues.

Devon spoke up, his voice small and high-pitched. "She wouldn't just leave us, would she? She's our family."

Jet patted the boy's back. "We'll find her, don't worry."

The comforting words didn't help, and he began to sob in the middle of the room. "I miss my mom and dad!" He cried and wrapped his arms around Jet's waist. Jet stood still for a minute, unsure of what to say and then bent down to hug him. Raoul heard Devon's muffled words in Jet's hoodie, "I just wanna go home…" Jet squeezed him tighter.

Raoul flew over to face Devon. "Hey, we're going to find Syd. I can promise you that, okay? And yes,

we are all family and will be here for you always."
He smiled with a wink, and it made Devon laugh.

Devon pulled away from Jet and wiped his face
with his glasses still on. "I—I think I heard Syd
on the phone earlier with Gia. Maybe she knows
something?"

"Yes!" Silas exclaimed. "That's a great idea,
kiddo! Let's see if we can find something."

Devon's smile widened, and everyone praised
him, lifting his spirits right back up. Raoul noticed
Jet in the corner, less than excited. But before Raoul
could ask him anything, the group headed downstairs.

Raoul dove from the upstairs balcony and flew
right to the phone, which was still outside, before
everyone else even left the room. When he landed on
the table, he noticed a sliver of yellow paper poked
out from under the phone. He grabbed it with both
hands and beat his wings to help him pull it out.

"Silas!" Raoul yelled. "I think this is Gia's number. Can you call her?"

Without hesitation, Silas dialed her number,
while also bringing the phone back inside. The rest
of the group began to trickle into the hotel room.

Silas placed the receiver to his ear, and when the
ringing on the other end stopped, Raoul flew up to
the receiver to hear what was being said.

"Syd? Syd is that you?!" Giovonna's voice
rushed out.

"No, Gia. It's me, Silas," he answered.

"And Raoul!" Raoul yelled.

"Oh my God. It's so good to hear your voices! But... where's Syd? What happened?"

Silas replied. "That's why we're calling. Did you happen to hear anything? Before she stopped talking?"

"Uh, well, we were in the middle of talking when I heard Sydona make a weird noise and then nothing. In the background sounded like a woman. She called her a puta. Whatever that is..."

"A puta?" Silas twisted his face. Raoul caught Avani's and Knox's reaction to the word. It then seemed very clear who was involved. Only Natalia would use a word like that.

"Yeah. What happened to her, Silas?"

"Not sure, but we think it involves Avani's sister, Natalia," Silas answered. Knox nodded his head heavily up and down, and Avani smacked him.

"Avani has a sister?! What do you think she did?"

"Natalia works for the doctor. There's only one place she would've taken her..." Silas's words faded off, and he removed the receiver from his ear and gripped it tighter. His eyes squeezed shut, and he swallowed hard. He returned the phone to his ear. "We need to find her."

"Oh no..." said Gia. After a long pause she spoke up again. *"Come get me. I want to go with you."*

"What?" Silas asked with a slight laugh at the impulsive decision.

"I want to help you find her. I need to make sure she's okay."

"Gia…" Raoul said as he and Silas exchanged looks.

"Please, Silas!"

Silas replied. "We can't come get you, Gia. We would be backtracking. And, not all of us can fly. My leg—"

Willow pushed her face closer to the phone, causing Silas to crane his neck away. "Yeah, sorry, baby girl; I ain't flyin' anymore on this trip. I tried it, and I am *done*."

"Willow? Oh my god! Willow the Widowed! I've missed your voice so much!" Giovonna said much louder.

"I've missed ya too, pumpkin. But we can't go back; we're too far now."

Raoul watched Willow's face. It suddenly turned pink, and her eyes glistened. She really cared about Giovonna. They all did.

"Okay then. I'll come to you," she said confidently. *"Where are you?"*

Raoul flicked his wings. "You're coming here? It will take too long, Gia."

"No it won't. I've actually calculated it out. If I can force myself to fly roughly sixty miles per hour, I could make it there by morning."

"Morning?" Silas asked with raised eyebrows.

"You'd be flyin' all night. You'll exhaust yourself," Willow said.

Silas added. "Plus, it's dangerous. It's like midnight right now."

"You guys can argue all you want, I'm coming. Gimme the address."

The three collectively sighed. Raoul felt the situation was all too familiar. It was just like back at the diner when Sydona told her she wanted to go alone, and Giovonna insisted. Once she got something on her mind, nothing could stop her. Even now that they were closer to the doctor's headquarters, she wouldn't take no for an answer.

"Take the I-80 west until you start seeing mountains. We're at Three Peak Inn. Room 12," Raoul said.

Everyone in the room glared at him. "What? She's family. She's coming with."

"What about your folks, hun?" Willow asked Giovonna.

"Screw 'em. You guys are more important."

Raoul's chest pounded. Her words made him feel warm but also broke his heart. Were her parents really that bad? What if they put out another search for her? But it felt wrong to not have her as part of the rescue mission.

"We could all get a good night's rest while we wait for Gia, and that way we'll be fully refreshed to get Syd back. Yeah?" Raoul said confidently.

Giovonna answered, *"Perfect. Willow, I have my beeper. Let me know if anything happens. Otherwise, I'll see you guys in a few hours!"*

"See ya real soon," Willow said. Her voice was gentle, but Raoul could tell she didn't really want her to come. Perhaps because of how dangerous it was. She'd be safer at her own home.

"Can't wait! Bye!" Giovonna said quickly.

Silas hung up and glanced over at Willow. "Guess we wait 'til mornin'."

"Gia's coming back?" Devon spoke up from the twin bed.

Jet rubbed Devon's head. "I guess so. Let's get you ready for bed, okay?"

"We'll go back upstairs then, sí?" Avani nodded.

Knox agreed. "A good night's rest isn't a bad idea."

"How are we supposed to sleep with Syd missing?" Silas said shortly.

The group stayed silent, and Raoul could almost see a dark cloud hovering just below the ceiling.

"We have to keep the faith," said Raoul. "Syd and I have a deep connection, and I know she's still alive. I can feel it."

"Amen, Raoul," said Willow, tears welling in her eyes. "I'll be sayin' a prayer for her tonight, an' I expect you all to do the same. She'll be back with us before ya' know it."

Raoul glanced at Silas who lay on his side of the bed and draped a jacket over his face. Avani made a point to hug Devon before she left, and she whispered something in his ear that seemed to cheer him up.

As the rest of the group left the hotel room, everyone got settled underneath the sheets. But Raoul couldn't sleep. He felt his blood pressure rise the more he realized his best friend was completely alone with Vultures. With Malik. And the fact it happened right under their noses. Maybe if he hadn't indulged in a silly cartoon, all of it would have been avoided. He couldn't bear to sit back and relax again until she was found.

He fluttered over to the tiny bathroom and landed on the sink. Turning the handle, he warmed up the water, then plugged it up. The oval sink filled with water, and Raoul jumped up, turned his back to the water, and landed on the surface with his toes pointed up. Water covered his ears, and he closed his eyes. Shaman Faro's words entered his mind, and he repeated them over and over in his head.

"Imagine the water as a sponge. Let the emotions that flow over absorb into the basin. Look at it around you, look at it from above. It cannot control you. You control it. Now that the water holds your emotions, allow them to drain. Wash them away.

"Remember: everything happens in the universe for a specific purpose. We are not meant to understand but to accept that which we cannot change."

Raoul took several deep breaths as he held onto the Shaman's words. Focusing only on the water surrounding him, he allowed his anger to seep out and suddenly felt a weight lifted. He swam to the edge of the sink and pulled the plug. Raoul watched the water circle into a small tornado down the metal drain. Lifting his chin and exhaling, he then made a soft makeshift bed on the table between the beds and was finally able to fall asleep. He knew once he woke, Giovonna would be there, and they would find Sydona again.

The next morning, Raoul was the first one up.

Skipping his usual stretch, he curled up on his towel and lay there, waiting for someone else to wake. The sun rose over the mountain peaks and flooded through their curtains. Giovonna hadn't made it yet. His leg shook anxiously. Did she get lost? Did she even leave her house, or did her parents stop her before she could? And more importantly, was she going to stop somewhere to get fruit?

At last, two gentle knocks rapped their hotel door, and his red wings flicked.

"She's here!" Raoul said excitedly. "Wake up!"

He flew over to the window and peeked out to see Giovonna. She wore her hair in a pink headband, a blue t-shirt, a black jacket, and had a full backpack slung over her shoulders. She waved with both hands.

"Can you open the door?" Giovonna asked, muffled by the glass between them.

Raoul shook his head. "It's too heavy!"

"Well wake one of them up. I feel weird standing out here like… a creeper…" Her eyes wandered behind her.

He flipped back the curtain to see Silas sitting up in bed. Once his grogginess passed, his tired eyes flew open, and he looked at the window to see a show in front of it. "It's Gia! Open the door!" said Raoul.

Silas rushed to the door. When he swung it open, Giovonna stood in the doorway with the biggest smile Raoul had ever seen. She went in for a hug with Silas, and he hugged her back, his arms not long enough to fit around her giant backpack.

"Hey!" Raoul greeted, waiting patiently behind Silas for his turn.

"Raoul!" she called out with arms open. Raoul grinned and flew right up to her chest, and she pressed him against her with a happy sigh. "Man, I missed you."

"Missed you too, Gia."

"You made it!" Devon shouted as he whipped the covers off him. He ran to her and jumped into her arms. Jet emerged from the covers to give her a sleepy smile followed by a yawn.

"Devon!" She held him tight. "You've grown since I last saw you, huh?" Giovonna smiled brightly and grabbed both his shoulders.

"I'm a Sparrow now!" Devon shouted, making Silas fully conscious.

"Whoa! Seriously? That's so awesome, dude! Gimme five!" Giovonna held her hand up and bit her lip with excitement.

Devon slapped it and giggled.

"Hey, Gia," Jet finally said.

"Hi, Jet!" She narrowed in for a hug from him too, even though he was more reluctant.

Silas shut the door and asked, "Everything went okay, I'm assuming?"

"Yeah, actually. It was so exhilarating! Flying all on my own. No parents, no rules, no one to shoot me down. I had a lot of time to reflect. But, uh, I do need to use the bathroom. So, if you'll excuse me…" Giovonna ran to the bathroom and slammed it shut.

"I'll go tell them she's here," said Silas. He threw on a pair of pants and shoes and left the room to go upstairs.

"Are we going to get Syd back now?" Devon looked up at Jet.

"Yep. Are you excited?"

"Uh-huh. I miss her. Do we get to fly again?"

Jet bounced on the bed as he took a seat. "No. No, not this time. Silas is still injured. But uh…" he sighed. "I need to talk to you about where we're going."

"What about it?" Devon asked and sat next to him.

"It's a dangerous place. There are very bad people there. They don't like people like us, who can fly. They will try to hurt us."

"Oh." Devon sulked. "Like Lacey?"

It took a second for Jet to respond. "Yeah, like Lacey…"

Raoul felt the mood change in the room. He could almost see the walls rising around Jet.

Devon furrowed his brows, looking over at Jet through his fingerprint smudged glasses. "But you're not hurting anyone. Why does he want to hurt you?"

Jet couldn't look at him so Raoul answered. "Some people are just bad. Can't help it. They're wired a different way than us."

Devon focused on Raoul. "Like the guy who killed my parents?"

Raoul saw Jet's face melt, but Jet quickly replied, "Uh… no, not like him."

"But he hurt my parents. When someone hurts someone, they deserve to be hurt too, right? That's what you said."

"It's complicated, man," Jet said irritably with a mumble. His fingers wiggled quickly against his knees while his leg shook.

Raoul felt bad for Jet. Before he could interject, the front door flew open, and Knox and the others came waltzing in.

"She here?!" Willow asked and threw her bag down.

Jet walked away from Devon, relieved by the sudden intrusion. He poured something into his coffee and took a long sip.

The bathroom door swung open, and Giovonna shrieked and giggled at the sight of Willow. Her friend laughed and held her arms open. When she jumped into her arms, Willow twirled her around in a circle.

Raoul grinned and watched the reunion from the dresser.

Knox stared at the girls. "Wow. Is she like Willow's long lost daughter or something?"

"You have no idea how much Willow talks about that girl," Harold said.

"I think it's muy precioso," Avani said while braiding her ebony hair.

Once Willow and Giovonna's reunion ended, they were finally good to leave. They took one last look around the room for supplies. Harold and Jet grabbed as much soap and other small things as they could shove in the packs. Once everyone was ready, they trampled down the stairs like a stampede.

Harold and Knox took the front seat of the vehicle, so Harold could help with directions the rest of the way to the headquarters. Raoul sat in the back with all of the luggage and a large window to look out of. A part of him wanted to sit up front with all the action, music, and talking, but most of him wanted to be alone. He wanted to get Sydona back, but then he remembered, she wasn't the only one who needed saving. His niece Jubilee was still in their custody. In all the recent chaos, Raoul almost forgot she was taken, too. He cringed at the idea of what the doctor or Natalia could be doing to her. If it was anything like what he did to the fairy in his office at Eagle Lake, she was in huge trouble.

Raoul shook his mind free of the dark thought and decided to make his way up to the front.

"Were you able to figure out the bracelets at all?" Silas asked, sitting across from Giovonna.

"I mean, it's only been a few days, but I did what I could. I just need to be able to test it."

"Kinda feel bad for the princess," Willow said. "I hate flyin', but I know how much she loved it."

"Me too," Knox added. "Can't imagine not flying."

"I wonder what he's gonna do when he finds out," said Avani, still braiding.

"Well he won't be happy, I can tell ya that much," Harold replied.

Jet joined in. "What do you think he'd do to her?"

Harold sighed heavily. "I honestly don't know."

The group sat quietly, lingering on uncertainty. Not even Harold could tell them what would happen, and he worked with the doctor for years. Raoul thought he could have more information but didn't want to set more of a depressing tone. He changed the subject to something more productive. "What are we going to do when we get there?"

Knox nodded his large, bald head. "You know the place, Harold. What are you thinking?"

Harold cleared his throat and took a chug of coffee. "Alright, so, John's sittin' on several acres of land with all of it protected with… us. There's a place to check into a mile before you even see his house. You need to be verified before gettin' past them."

"How you suppose we do that since you ain't a Vulture anymore?" Avani wondered.

"I still got my ID. I just hope they won't know I don't really do that anymore."

"You hope?" Jet scoffed. "Yeah, we're screwed."

"What's plan B?" Knox asked patiently.

"If that don't work, then we'll have to sneak in. Park somewhere far away and walk the rest of the way."

"You just said the place is surrounded by Vultures. That's an even worse idea than the first one!" Jet argued.

"Look, I told you where he was; it ain't my job to get you in, too," Harold said and slumped down in his seat.

Knox let out a heavy sigh.

"I'll do it," Devon said quietly from the back.

"What?" Jet asked.

"I'm small. I can sneak around them. And I'm not a flier, so they won't hurt me, right?"

Raoul grinned. Everyone else stayed silent with wide eyes and exchanged looks.

Jet spoke softly to the ten year old. "Devon, you don't have—"

"It's the only plan that might work. And I want to do it."

"Lacey would kill me if I let you go through with this, Dev," Jet warned.

"How else are we getting in if I don't go?" Devon argued.

Raoul saw his face harden.

Willow spoke up. "If we don't come up with anythin' else, son, we'll let ya know."

"What if I go with him?" Raoul proposed.

Giovonna glanced at him with hopeful eyes. "That could... actually work."

"Yeah!" Devon exclaimed.

"I can keep an eye out and tell him where he could go without being seen," said Raoul.

Silas agreed. "I like that plan. The best one I've heard so far."

"No, he's not going out there. I won't let him," Jet said.

"You can't do that! I'm a Sparrow just like you now. You can't tell me what to do!" Devon yelled.

"I'm in charge of you now, Devon, and I won't allow you to do this. Not by yourself!" Jet fired back.

It was a strange sight to see Jet trying to play the part of a parent. Maybe he thought he needed to replace Lacey or make up for something he did. Raoul would never fully understand him.

"You're not in charge of me! You're not my dad! I want to do this. I want to help," Devon cried with a cracking voice.

Jet soon wore a face of defeat. He wasn't Devon's father. And Jet knew that.

"You know what? Fine. Do it. But don't come crying to me if something happens."

"I won't because you ain't my dad!"

"You already said that!"

The car fell silent once again, and all that could be heard were Devon's sniffles.

A few hours passed by as they continued on their way to the house. Giovonna caught up on sleep while everyone else kept to themselves. Tensions remained high between Jet and Devon, and the entire energy of the group was unstable. Raoul couldn't wait to see his best friend again.

They drove until the stars came out, and the moon glinted over the mountains behind them. The glow from the dashboard shone on everyone's exhausted faces. Harold informed Knox when they were getting close. He took a dirt trail off the main road and parked way back into the woods. Everyone got out and stretched their legs.

"Alright, little man," Knox announced. "You still want to do this?"

"Yes, sir. Knox, sir." Devon saluted. He then glared at Jet who rolled his eyes.

With a grunt, Jet marched away from the van. The rest of the group scattered around the vehicle, waiting.

Devon stood at attention and pushed up his glasses. He was wide awake. "What do I need to do?"

Avani cleared her throat and grabbed Knox's arm. "Excuse us, niñito. I need to talk to my husband for just a second."

Raoul narrowed his eyes. She was going to try to talk him out of it. What other plan could work better than this one? Devon would be in and out so quickly, no one would even notice him. He could probably run faster than any of the adults, and he was harder to spot. If they did somehow try to shoot at him, he made a much smaller target than anyone else— other than himself. Raoul flew over to listen to the conversation.

"...think about what you're about to do here, Elias. He's just.. él es un niño," Avani whispered.

Knox sighed. "He wants to help, babe. It's the best idea we've got."

"What if he's delicado? Can you live with that? He's not *ours* to put in jeopardy. Not even Jet wants him to do this. *Jet!*"

"I'll be with him," Raoul said. "I'll make sure nothing happens."

Avani's eyes darted to him. "No offense, Raoul, but you're muy pequeño. Can't exactly protect him from a gun."

Raoul's face flushed and blood rushed to his head. "I can help in more ways than being a flying shield, Avani. Just ask Syd..."

Knox spoke. "Exactly. His size could benefit us more than we realize."

Avani crossed her arms and pursed her ruby lips.

"We have a radio to equip him with, so we can keep in contact with him that way, too. It will be fine, my darling." Knox reached out to uncross her arms, but she rejected it.

"Whateva. Consider me out of this mission, then. I don't want to be anywhere around this if it goes south." She stormed off and shut the van door behind her.

Raoul turned to Knox who was rubbing his bald head. "I will do anything to protect Devon, Knox. I promise."

"I know you will. You're a good man," Knox said, then inhaled through his large nose. "Let's get him suited up."

They returned to the car to get Devon in some darker clothing. Since he was so small, Knox found a black jacket for him to wear, but it came down to his knees. He said it could work in his favor to hide inside of it, in case anything happened. Devon stuck a tiny earpiece in his ear connected to a microphone with a wire. It worked both ways. Knox asked Devon to pick a codeword, and after deciding on one, he was finally ready. Raoul examined the bag Knox handed to him, and his heart sank. It was Sydona's. It smelled just the way it used to.

"All set?" asked Raoul, clearing his throat.

"Yes!" Devon said, and saluted him and Knox.

"Good. Just pay attention to me, and we'll be in and out quickly." Raoul heard the seriousness of his tone, and it filled him with pride. He was in charge. And he liked it.

Devon nodded his head. "Okay. What do we do when we find her?"

Raoul opened his mouth, but Harold cleared his throat and began spewing information. "So what you're gonna wanna do is find his gigantic white and clear house. It's big, you can't miss it. Even at night. Now, there's a garage to the right of it that's always open. Go in there and there's a door inside on your right-hand side. He's got a couple dozen cells down there full of fliers. She'll prolly be down there. Here's a key to get into the garage." Harold handed Devon the brass key, and he stuck it in the breast pocket.

"Won't there be guards?" Silas asked.

"I'll distract them," Raoul said.

"How?" asked Giovonna.

"I'll figure it out," Raoul replied shortly.

"What happens if you aren't able to and they catch him?" Jet asked as he marched up to the conversation.

"He's a kid and a human. They wouldn't hurt him," Raoul argued.

Avani angrily trudged behind him. "Just 'cause they won't hurt him, doesn't mean they won't capture him. What if they start to question why he's there?"

"I have this under control!" Raoul shouted but then paused to compose himself. "I'm taking this one step at a time. I need you all to trust me." His heart pounded in his ears.

"I'd trust you with my life, Raoul," Giovonna said honestly.

Raoul smiled at her. He always did like her. He then turned back to the boy. "I believe in you, Devon. You can do this."

Devon lifted his chin at this comment.

"I believe in you too, Dev," said Jet at the last second.

Devon heard but scoffed at him. Jet rolled his eyes and chugged the last of his coffee and hid in the van. Everyone made sure to give them a hug before they left the comfort of the group.

Raoul took a deep breath and glanced between everyone. "We'll keep in touch. Ready Devon?"

Devon nodded his head and adjusted his black-rimmed glasses.

Harold moved the walkie to his lips. "Testing, testing."

Raoul overheard him through the bud in Devon's ear. His voice was loud and clear, and the two headed off toward the doctor's lair.

Chapter Three

SYDONA

Darkness faded into a bright white light. This was heaven. She never really believed in anything. No single being or deity to rule the universe; it was much too vast. But the scene in front of her resembled something she assumed some people would associate with a heaven. Fog consumed what looked like her old living room, around a table full of food, family, and laughter. Giovonna, Willow, Silas, Raoul, and her parents crowded around a large wooden table in the center of the room. They laughed, drank, and ate together. Sydona was in a state of pure bliss. Everyone was back together, and she was weightless, like an angel, watching it from the end of the table. Silas sat next to her, his arm around her, and she melted into him. As Sydona reached out to kiss him, she somehow slipped further and further away. The front door flung open, she flew out of it backwards, and the fog disappeared. She yearned to hold the scene in front of her, but her lungs screamed at her to breathe.

Her eyes shot open as her body tried to inhale every ounce of oxygen in the room. Her head pounded intensely, followed by almost every other muscle in her body. Heaven was gone. And she wasn't dead. Tears rolled down her freshly scraped up face. It suddenly hit her that she was still alive, and she became deluged with emotion. Sydona took a few minutes to feel the soft covers on top of her, her limbs not broken, and her heart still in one piece. She wiped her face off on the pillow under her head.

With only a quick scan around the room, it was clear she was in a hospital. She struggled to lift her head. It was a large room, bigger than any hospital room she had been to before. She lay back down on a soft pillow and tried to straighten everything out in her head. How did she survive that fall? She felt the blow of the rocks; it was more than enough to kill her. There must have been others standing by when it happened. Did the doctor assume she would fall peacefully into the ocean if she couldn't fly? His confidence in her ability to fly far outweighed her potential lies.

She had little time to figure out what happened before Malik opened the door and marched straight over to her.

"You're awake…" he breathed, touching a strand of her hair as if he were comforting a child. Sydona jerked her head back from his touch and stared at him with pain and confusion. His hair was less greasy and the lines on his face showed worry. She swore she even saw a twinkle of a tear in his eye.

What the hell is going on... she thought to herself.

He cleared his throat and made himself comfortable in a chair next to her bed.

"I—" he cleared his throat deeper. "I can't believe I—" he shook his head, still in disbelief.

Sydona waited for him to finish his sentence. To admit what he'd done. "...can't believe you made me jump off a cliff? Took away my ability to fly? Kidnapped my father? Killed my mother? You only need to pick one, doctor."

"Yes, yes, yes. All of the above. I can't believe *I* was the one who ruined everything."

Sydona rolled her eyes and turned away from him.

"I'm... sorry, Miss Wilder."

She turned back to him. "Your apology doesn't mean shit to me."

Malik nodded and removed his spectacles. "You're right. I don't deserve forgiveness."

When Sydona didn't say anything, he continued, "I thought I had lost you. You were asleep for about twenty hours. Really didn't know if you were going to suffer a coma."

Sydona narrowed her eyes. "Don't act like you care that I lived. I'm just another guinea pig for you. And I can't fly so why save me, anyways?"

The doctor smirked. "You are not a guinea pig. You are special to me. You proved that even people who are half human can still fly. You are my only hope."

Sydona shook her head slightly. "Your *what*?"

"I—I just mean, my only hope is to finish what I started. What my father started…" He paused, and Sydona let him speak. What else was she supposed to do? "I've had others in the past, who were also partial but couldn't fly at all. But you *could*. You are— *were* the only one."

"Yeah, thanks to you," she said quietly.

Malik lifted his chin and looked at her with such determination. "But, I can fix you, Miss— Sydona. I *need* to fix you."

"I'm not some porcelain doll that shattered; I don't need fixed."

Malik narrowed his dark brown eyes. "Do you not ever want to fly again, Sydona?"

His words cut through her like glass. He knew exactly what she longed for. Worse, he might be the only one with the tools to help her. But this was doctor John Malik. The man she had been seeking vengeance on since the day she read his name in the paper. The man who sent hunters after her, killing anyone else who got in the way. The man who killed her own mother and countless other fliers because of his selfish need.

It then dawned on her. His need had become her need. Every ounce of her being loathed the dirty thought. Why did she *need* to fly so badly? Wasn't she the same person without it? The questions and doubt threatened to overwhelm her. Hours ago, she would never have considered helping him. The next word she spoke, she could barely get out, but it was almost like she had no choice.

"Yes." She closed her eyes as she heard her own voice saying it.

The doctor inhaled sharply. "Lovely." He patted his hands on her bed and used his cane to slowly stand up. "I'll get your room ready upstairs. But, you just rest here before then."

"My room?"

"Oh yes, we can't work together very well if I put you back in that cell. It's much too far away. Besides, it's been empty for a while. Might as well get some use out of it, yes?" he asked, but his thoughts seemed far away.

Sydona's eyes darted around the room, wondering if she may really be in a coma. When he didn't say anything else, she pressed her lips together and gave a small shrug.

He nodded and took steps toward the door.

Sydona then sat up quickly. "What about my dad? I think he's sick."

Malik stopped, lifted his head in response, and turned halfway around. "I think I can arrange something."

She was stunned at his spontaneous hospitality. "Okay."

He nodded, fully faced her, and pointed to her bedside table. "If you're in pain, I placed some pain-killers next to you. Don't go overboard though. They are strong."

She glanced at them, noticing a glass of water too. "Alright."

He tapped his finger on his cane a couple of times, then finally headed out of the room, shutting the door behind him.

Every bone in her body told her not to trust the pills. But those same bones were screaming. She downed two of them and chugged the entire glass of the best water she ever tasted. Her head hit the pillow, and she stared at the ceiling, still processing the conversation, including his subdued behavior. It was clear now that she was not in a hospital but still in the doctor's home. And the strangest thing was that he called her by her first name. Almost as if he was hoping to become friends with her, or at the very least, treat her as an equal.

With every bad thing he'd done in his life, he wasn't going to get off that easily. He was a bad person; he deserved to die. For treating thousands of her people like animals and lab rats. For killing them needlessly because he could. They obviously weren't helping him anyway; why did he need so many of them? No, he was going to pay for everything he'd done.

Her mind churned with thoughts of how she would work the situation to her advantage, but as the painkillers began to numb her body, she could not resist the heavy pull of sleep.

When the pills wore off, Sydona woke from what felt like the best sleep she had in years. As she sat up, she wondered how long she had been out. Her heart raced at the thought that she had slept well over twenty-four hours, but the doctor hadn't tricked her. She was safe and alone. She tried to relax. From the corner of her eye, she spotted a pile of clothes sitting on a chair near the door. A pair of black pants, a red t-shirt, and some socks and shoes. Oh, shoes. She never thought she'd be happy to see a crappy pair of shoes. They weren't exactly crappy. They were brand new tennis shoes, but they weren't her boots. Still, she could walk much more comfortably.

Then she thought: *shoes*? They would certainly make escape easier. It was almost as if they were handing her the keys to a car. Doctor Malik must have been confident that she wouldn't run.

He even left the door ajar. Her stomach twisted as she sat there in bed wondering about her next move. She was free to do as she pleased, and so her first thought was to find a weapon. Sliding her feet one by one off the edge of the bed, she kept the blanket wrapped tightly around her. The clothes she came in with were gone. A disturbing thought crossed her mind that the doctor saw her naked, and it made her shutter. She tiptoed to the door and clicked it shut. Unaware of the time or if anyone was around, she didn't want to alert them that she was awake. She silently dressed in the clothes, which weren't badly guessed in size. Though, it puzzled her how the doctor had women's clothing just laying around the house.

A large metal cabinet stood in the corner secured with a large padlock. There were machines and another cabinet on the opposite wall, but those were also locked and secured. He didn't trust her that much. If she wanted a weapon, she needed to venture out further.

The large kitchen she walked past earlier popped into her head. Would it be close by or on the other side of the house? A different building? Sydona grabbed the bottle of pills and shoved it into her pants pocket before exiting. The living room was only a few feet and several doors away. Like a stalking cat, she preyed past the rooms, using the bright moonlight shining through the towering living room windows.

Her heart raced as she snuck through the unfamiliar home surrounded by armed guards. Each sound that touched her ear, including the wind or even a drop of water from the sink, made her hair stick up. Hesitant, she made a B-line for the kitchen and searched quietly through the drawers.

Eventually she found one full of utensils and took a small paring knife, which would be easily concealable. It wasn't anything close to her dagger, but the feeling of holding a knife boosted her confidence and calmed her heart.

She found a sheath for it and paired it with the blade. She placed it in her back pocket so that her shirt would conceal it before opening other drawers in search of something better. A couple of drawers down, bright colors caught her eye. She pulled the drawer open further and squinted at an old sheet of paper. Written in blue, red, and yellow crayon was the name 'Pryah'. She flipped it over to reveal a heavy paper weighed down by stale macaroni. The noodles were glued into a heart shape with 'Daddy' written in purple in the center.

"He's... a father?" Sydona asked out loud.

Maybe he took it from another flier or Vulture. There were absolutely no pictures of this girl or of a family anywhere in sight. She couldn't make sense of it and gently placed the drawing back in the drawer.

As she turned around to figure out her next move, the back door caught her eye. Not a single Vulture seemed to be guarding the place. She could leave. Escape. But, she was in no shape to run. The painkillers were working great, but her muscles and bones were still sore. Not to mention her father was still there. She couldn't leave him. Her heart pounded in her chest.

One by one, her feet led her out of the kitchen and up the staircase. At the top were more doors and a much cozier, lower ceiling hallway. The walls were a dark red with a darker wood trim. Beautiful abstract paintings lined the wallpaper. All five doors were shut, except one. Assuming the one open was hers, she slipped inside..

A king sized bed sat in the middle with columns on each post and a drape covering it. A white door led to a private bathroom with a large tub and marble counters. One part of the room that immediately attracted her was a bay window with a bench lined in pillows. Rays from the moon shone brightly through the pink curtains, enough to read the books stacked on the window sill. The books mostly consisted of children's books and were impeccably organized.

"Did he have a daughter? What happened to her?" she asked herself out loud.

It was jarring to think of the doctor having a child of his own. After all he did to ruin the lives of innocent people, it was hard to imagine that same person raising a little girl. But where was she? The room that seemed to be hers at one point was well taken care of. Either she was gone temporarily or left a long time ago, and he was the one keeping the room clean.

As she pondered this new revelation, she sat on the bench next to the window and looked out toward the sea. Between the bench and window was a white ledge that she could easily picture Raoul's tiny bed sitting on, and her stomach suddenly ached. She grabbed a purple frilled pillow nearby and held it close to her chest. Ocean waves crashed in the distance while crickets filled the silences between. Her eyes searched the skies for any of her friends that may have gone looking for her. She missed them more than ever.

Chapter Four

RAOUL

Shadows from the forest disappeared behind them as Raoul took the lead. Devon whipped his head in every direction as he crept toward the large white mansion by the shore. Raoul radiated orange in the dark, so he tried to conceal himself in the bag wrapped around Devon until he was needed. Devon curled down inside of the oversized jacket anytime he heard something unfamiliar. His whispers were low and soft, but loud enough for Raoul to hear.

He hid behind large rocks and tree stumps, even though they still hadn't come across anyone. Raoul's gut twisted. Something didn't feel right. Where were all the guards Harold anticipated? He expected the place to be flocking with them.

A voice suddenly buzzed through the bud in Devon's ear.

"You doin' okay, kid?" asked Harold.

Devon pressed a button on the walkie and answered. "Yeah."

"No one seen you yet?"

"Not yet. Haven't seen anyone."

Soon, they approached a rocky road lined with small ground lights illuminating the path. Cricket sounds flooded Raoul's ears, matching the scene around him. He stuck his head above the bag and squinted his eyes to get a better look. It was eerily deserted. Only the waves a mile away made themselves known to the night. Devon crept to the other side of the road, which was lined with bushes. He used them for cover as they drew closer to the buildings ahead.

Once the road changed from rocks to a shiny blacktop, they spotted the enormous mansion standing proudly on a cliff that overlooked the Pacific. Raoul's jaw fell at the sight. Devon also couldn't peel his eyes from it and rose to his feet in awe. As Raoul admired the architecture, he spotted another building out of the corner of his eye. It was only a few yards away and resembled a garage. "There it is."

Devon called Harold on the radio. "I think we found it."

"Good, okay," Harold replied. *"Go around to the front. The door'll be locked, so use the key I gave ya to get in."*

Devon ran to the building, hunched and wide eyed. Raoul buzzed up the entrance first to familiarize himself. He took the key out and stuck it in the door, but it wouldn't turn. He tried a couple of times before giving up, afraid it would break.

"It's not working," Devon said.

"Dang. They probably changed the locks."

"Or he gave us the wrong key."

Raoul shrugged and searched for another way in. The moon illuminated one side of the building clearly, while the opposite side was pitch black. They both looked around the entire building for any possible way in. Raoul then spotted four tiny windows at the top of the garage in the back. He stood on the sliver of a window ledge and pressed his face against the glass. Three expensive looking cars were parked inside, and there was a door to the right of him. He guessed it was the same one Harold mentioned as it had a mechanism next to it with a red indicator light. He flicked his wings in excitement and tried pushing on the window. It didn't budge.

Raoul flew back to Devon who was trying the key again. "No way in."

Devon twisted his lips. "What do we do?"

Raoul shook his head and crossed his arms. "We just got here. We can't give up now. We know they're here."

"They? Who else besides Syd?"

"My little niece, Jubilee. She was taken, too." His hands curled into fists.

Devon pushed up his glasses and asked with a tilted head. "A baby fairy?"

Raoul smiled. "No, not a baby exactly, but she had just learned to fly." He quickly changed the subject before his emotions got the best of him. "Did you let them know our situation?"

"Yeah. Harold said bad words, but then said we should try to find another way in. But he didn't know of any other way… and cussed again." Devon shrugged.

Raoul let out a heavy sigh. "I hate to do it, but we may need to do this another time. Maybe during the day when it might be open or something. This isn't going to happen tonight."

"What if we check in the house?" Devon asked.

"Harold said this is where the doctor keeps fliers."

"Yeah, but, maybe they moved her because she's special."

Raoul rubbed his chin. "Maybe…" The thought of entering the house where the doctor lived brought back bad memories. Flashes of the office at Eagle Lake made him shutter.

"Should we try?"

"We need to be really careful. The doctor is unstable. If you sense any danger at all, tell the group immediately."

Devon called over the radio to report the new plan. Harold wasn't happy about it, but they kept moving.

As they approached the mansion, Raoul instructed Devon to hide in the shadows beneath a nearby shrub. He took it upon himself to check the rest of the windows and do a quick perimeter check. With the full-length windows, it was effortless to see inside. He watched for movements of any kind. Either from a person or possibly a guard dog. Raoul hated dogs; they always snapped at him like he was a bug. Cats were worse though. They had the hunting-small-things skill down really well. Luckily, no animals occupied the home, just bland, shiny furniture. After he made sure the first floor was clear and still saw no sign of Sydona, he checked the second floor windows.

Beyond one window was what appeared to be a bedroom. A man slept in the bed, but he didn't appear to be the doctor. His hair was white as snow. Who else lived here? Raoul noticed the window was slightly cracked and pushed it open just enough for himself to slip inside. It only took a second after the man rolled over to see it was Sydona's father.

"Ian?" Raoul asked. His heart pounded with confusion. The last he knew, he was living it up on the island. Why on earth was he sleeping on a bed in doctor Malik's mansion?

Ian slowly opened his eyes. "Raoul?"

Raoul flew to him with a smile. "It *is* you! What—why are you here?"

Ian sat up slightly in bed, leaning on his pillow. He kept his voice low. "Me? Why are you here?"

"To rescue Syd. Is that why you're here?" he asked. He knew it wasn't the right question, but maybe it would give him the right answers.

Ian chuckled. "Sydona is not a woman who needs saving. If she wanted to leave, she would have."

Raoul scratched his head. "What do you mean?"

"You know how stubborn she is. The doctor promised to help her fly again."

Raoul's jaw fell open, but then he narrowed his eyes.

Ian continued. "Natalia kidnapped her, but the doctor, well, he's the one who brought me here. I was told I was being used as leverage. They said if I didn't come with them, they'd do more than kill her."

"How'd they find you though? That island's not even on a map!" Raoul said angrily.

"I don't know. They wouldn't tell me. But my only concern was that my baby girl was alright. Nothing else mattered."

Raoul calmed. "Where is she now?"

"She's in the room beside me. She's probably still recovering though."

"Recovering?" Raoul paused. "What'd he do to her?"

Ian shook his head, and his face flushed. "I don't know."

Raoul let out a sigh. "How are you holding up?"

Ian swallowed and lifted his chin. "I've been worse." He chuckled, then coughed a bit. "Going from a cot for dozens of years, to another makeshift bed on the island, and now a king bed with feathers… I'm not one to complain."

Raoul smiled at his optimism. "So, he hasn't hurt you?"

Ian shook his head again. "No. The first few days I was brought here, they had me in a cell in the garage. But once Syd arrived, they put me up here—" a cough cut him off. Ian covered his mouth, but the coughing sounded terrible. His entire body shook, and he gasped for air before the fit finally stopped.

"Are you sure you're okay?" Raoul asked with a hand on Ian's shoulder.

Ian cleared his throat and swallowed a few times. "It's just a cold. It'll go away soon. I just need to rest." He turned and pulled the covers over him. Sniffles and quiet moans bled through, and it was too much for Raoul to take. Despite having more questions, he respected Ian's need to rest.

"Psst!" Devon called from the bushes. Raoul barely heard the kid through the crack in the window. He flew down with haste, letting the wind dry any tears that tried to fall.

Devon asked with furrowed brows, "Did you find her? What took you so long?"

"Sorry, Dev. Got caught up. I found her dad. But, I know where she is."

"Good. I'm going with you. Something in this bush keeps biting me."

Devon searched for an unlocked door, while Raoul flew up to the window he assumed was Sydona's.

His heart leaped at the sight of her blonde hair glowing in the moonlight. She sat in the window, looking out to the ocean. Sydona soon caught his eye, and she perked up. With a whoosh, she opened the window to let him buzz inside.

"Hey!" she exclaimed as he landed on her shoulder. "I didn't think I'd ever see you again!"

He hugged the side of her face. "Can't get rid of me that easily." He pulled back and winked. But as he looked her over, he noticed she was covered in bandages and bruises. Ian was right. Raoul wanted to ask what happened but remembered Devon.

"Hang on. I gotta figure out how to get Devon up here."

"Devon's here, too?" she asked with a twinge of excitement.

"Yep!" Raoul said and dove back down to the boy.

Devon looked straight up at him and pushed his glasses up. "That her?"

"Yeah. Did you find a door to get in?"

"Nah, everything is locked."

"Alright, I'll help you up. Ready?"

Devon nodded with a huge smile. Raoul began to circle around Devon, sharing his dust until he began to levitate. Devon bowed his arms out as his feet left the ground. He got past the first level windows when he slowed down. Sydona pushed the window open to see him floating just below her.

"You guys are going to get caught!" Sydona said. She threw half her body out of the window and extended her arms as far as she could reach. Even though Raoul buzzed around him trailing dust, it wasn't strong enough to levitate him that high. Devon timidly reached his hand up to Sydona, and she grabbed onto his tiny arm. Raoul noticed her face as she pulled him in, and it was clear she was still in pain.

Devon landed on the carpet and took a deep breath. "Can we *please* do that again?"

Raoul tended to Sydona and sprinkled her with just a little dust.

"Thanks Raoul."

Raoul nodded and sat next to her on the bench by the window. "You wanna tell me what happened?"

Devon could tell it wasn't time for fun and sat up and listened.

Sydona inhaled a sharp breath. "Not really."

Raoul crossed his arms. "Syd, why do you feel like you can't talk to me?"

"It's not that…"

"Does it have anything to do with the doctor promising to make you fly again?"

Sydona stayed silent for a moment, then looked at the ground. "My dad told you."

"You bet he did," Raoul said with disappointment.

"What else was I supposed to do? What if your dust was taken away, and he was the only one who knew how to get it back? Wouldn't you at least try? Try to see if whatever he has planned works?" Her voice was desperate.

"Syd!" Raoul shouted. "We are risking our lives to get you out. You're telling me that *now* you don't want to leave?"

"How can I? This might be the only chance I have to be normal again."

Raoul shook his head, "But—"

"You told Lacey you'd kill him," Devon said from a chair on the other side of the room. "You promised to her as she was dying that you'd kill that mother fucker."

"Devon!" Sydona spat.

"Sorry, but you promised her something, too. Does the doctor's promise mean more than your own friends?"

Raoul raised his brows, took a step back, and crossed his arms.

"That's—It's not that simple, guys." She stood up, paced around the room and waved her arms around. "I wouldn't be considering this if it meant harming anyone. I need to do this for myself. It's not right that he stole it from me. I'm going to make him make me fly again… then I'll kill him."

Raoul smirked. "You will?"

"Yes. Then everything will go back to normal. But I need to see if he can do it first."

"What happens if he can't?" Devon asked. "And he doesn't need you anymore?"

Sydona scrunched her hair into a ponytail. "He will. I know he can. And well, if he can't, I'll be ready. He ran the last time; he's a coward. He won't kill me."

Raoul shook his head and let out a sigh. "I'm glad you're so confident, Syd."

"Devon? Hello? You still out there?" The boy scrambled to grab the walkie and respond. "Yeah, I'm okay. I'm with Syd."

Sydona snatched the radio in excitement. "Silas?"

The radio crackled. *"Yes, it's me. How are you?"*

Sydona released a huge smile. "I'm good. Where are you?"

"Just inside the forest near the house. We sent Devon and Raoul to find you. Are you able to leave, or do we need to come get you?"

Her smile faded and her finger hovered over the call button as she went over how to answer. "I'm not sure how to say this, but I can't leave."

Raoul shook his head.

"Say no more, babe. We'll be there in two shakes."

"No! No, I mean I am choosing to stay here. Not being forced or anything," she said.

Raoul let out a sigh. Sydona bit her lip nervously. She wasn't as confident as she led on. Maybe she was just afraid of what everyone else would say. Afraid of what they would do to protect her.

"Syd, this is Gia."

Her eyes widened.

"I didn't come all this way for you to change your mind. I'm not really sure what's happened since the last time we spoke, but I think we need to talk in person. Where can we meet you?"

"The guys know your location. I'll follow them. Don't do anything else; I'm taking a huge risk here."

"Copy."

Sydona let out a huge breath and turned to face them. "When were you gonna tell me Gia came back?"

"It was gonna be a surprise!" Devon giggled.

She smiled at him and scrunched her nose. "Alright. Let's do this. Are you guys ready?" she asked.

Devon nodded, and Raoul flew to the bedroom door, waiting for it to be opened. He saw Sydona grab something under her pillow and conceal it in her clothes. Raoul was upset with her and didn't want to ask, but he assumed it was a weapon of some kind. His gut twisted as he struggled to understand her decision. Maybe he just needed time, but after everything, he never expected this from his best friend.

Chapter Five

SYDONA

With each step she took toward the forest, her heart pounded. Everything happened so suddenly, she wasn't sure if she had enough time to process all of it. Why was she so hesitant to see her friends? These were the same folks who risked their lives to rescue her. But she didn't need to be rescued. She needed to fly again, even if it meant staying with Dr. Malik was dangerous.

They made haste across the huge grassy yard, even though there were no threats of Vultures. Most of her was still excited to see everyone again. Her hand rested on the kitchen knife on her hip in case something went sideways. As they reached the edge of the forest, a vehicle and a small group of people came into view. Raoul buzzed over to them first. Devon ran up to Knox, and Knox bent down to examine him, making sure he was alright. He ran right past

Jet, completely ignoring him. Jet sipped from a paper cup and kicked some leaves on the ground.

She saw Silas, and her stomach instantly filled with butterflies. His smile made her smile. He barely gave her time to calm the butterflies before he kissed her. They wrapped each other up, and he held her tight, as if he were afraid she'd leave again. The thought made her pull away, but she let his taste linger on her lips.

From the corner of her eye, she saw Giovonna waiting for her turn.

"Gia, I can't believe you came back!" Sydona grinned and pulled her into an even tighter hug.

"Of course I did!" she said and wiped a tear off her cheek. "When I heard you were taken, I had to come back. You mean too much to me."

Sydona swallowed and held back her own tears. Sydona gently pulled Giovonna's head toward her and kissed her forehead. Knox, Avani, Jet, Willow, and Harold greeted her with open arms as well. It wasn't long before they got down to business.

"Are you wearing new clothes?" Avani asked with furrowed brows.

Sydona looked down at herself. "Yeah, uh, the doctor gave me these."

Willow exploded. "Wait— the doctor gave you clothes? Or ya took 'em?"

"No, he gave them to me. It's just clothes, what's the big deal?" she asked, even though she knew why Willow was shocked. Her heartbeat sped up.

Knox spoke with a calmer tone. "It's a big deal if you're somehow working with him." He raised a single eyebrow.

The group turned to her but with different, skeptical expressions. She clasped her hands together to stop them from shaking. "Things have... changed."

Avani stepped toward her and placed a hand on her shoulder. "You can talk to us, mija."

Sydona looked her in the eyes and saw genuine kindness. Her nerves calmed, and she took a deep breath. "He's promised to make me fly again. If there's anyone who can do it, it's him. But, in order to do that, I have to work with him. We can't... execute him. Not yet."

Silence ensued. Avani pulled her hand away and stepped back toward her husband.

"Someone please say something," she asked with a shaky voice.

"He's playin' you, girl," Harold said finally. "I don't know what his game is, but John is not a good man. I know. He acts like he's your best friend and talks to ya like you the only person that matters. But he's always plannin' something. Always."

"Harold's right," Knox said. "That man has a one track mind. If he doesn't get the results he's looking for, who knows what he'll do?"

"He sent out the announcements for more fliers when he wasn't getting results, remember?" Raoul asked. "What if it happens again?"

His words jabbed her in the stomach.

"Her father is here, too," Devon said.

"The one from the island?!" Avani said in shock.

Raoul answered, "The very same. He's okay with it all, too. Even joked about having an actual bed to sleep in. I just don't get it."

Sydona saw his face, and it twisted her gut. She feared no one would ever understand.

"How you think they found him, Syd?" Willow asked. "I ensured no one but the Sparrows knew where that island was. It musta slipped somehow."

"Maybe we got a rat," said Jet.

Sydona's throat dried up like a prune. She couldn't bear to tell the group that it was her screw up. "He's got eyes and ears everywhere. Could've been heard anywhere. The point is he's here now."

"So we'll get him out too," Jet added with a shrug.

"We still need to find Jubilee. She's in there somewhere. I know she is," Raoul said.

Sydona slid down the side of the car and sat on the ground. She pulled her legs up to press her head against her knees. She was at a loss.

"So it's a rescue mission now," Knox said. "There's enough of us. I think we can do it. And Devon, you said there's no security around?"

"Right," Devon said.

Willow spoke up. "Raoul, do you think you could find Jubilee while we get Ian?"

He nodded. "Yes, ma'am."

Sydona shook her head. "Stop. We can't. If I leave, everything will go back to the way it was."

The group stopped collaborating, and Giovonna spoke up. "You really want to stay?"

Sydona allowed her head to hit the side of the truck. "I don't know what other choice I have."

A soft laugh came from Knox and soon erupted into a heavy cackle. "With all due respect, Sydona, you don't call the shots here. We came here to rescue you and anyone else that needs our help, and that's precisely what we're going to do. I'd rather just squeeze the doctor's skinny neck between my fingers, but we can come back for that later."

She looked up at him and stood up straight. "He has the missing puzzle piece now. He won't hurt anyone else. It's over."

"It's not over until I say it is! It will never be over as long as he is still breathing the same air as us!" Knox yelled.

Avani grabbed his arm lovingly, showing Sydona she was on his side.

"Knox. I understand you're angry, but the threat is over. You can go home!"

"He has to pay," Jet slipped in, his eyes turning green. A few of them agreed with him, and it made Sydona feel extremely small.

"I don't want to fight with you all. I agree that he's a bad person and needs to answer for his actions, but I won't let you kill him! Not until he finishes what he started."

"You startin' to sound like him, princess," Willow said. Her eyes were sad and confused.

Sydona's nostrils flared and fists squeezed tight. "I do not… sound like him. I just… I don't know. All I know is I need to fly. I don't even feel like myself anymore without it."

Knox threw his hands up in frustration and marched away from the group to calm down. His behavior enraged her even more. After several minutes of silence, Harold cleared his throat. "What if he fails?"

Sydona released her tight fists. "What do you mean?"

Harold pushed his hands into his jean pockets. "I mean I been workin' with John for a long time. I uh—I don't know how to say this, but I don't think he's actually gonna be able to do it."

Silas spoke up, "Really? How come?"

"I 'unno. But everytime he thinks he's close to a breakthrough, something happens. It doesn't last.

Plus, he's a very stubborn man. One time, I suggested someone come an' help him, and he threatened to kill me. Says his father almost figured it out all on his own, no help, and that's how he wants to finish it."

Willow side-eyed him. "It's amazin' to me you worked next to that psychopath all these years. It really is." She pushed his head toward her and kissed his temple.

Harold could be right. And Sydona hated that the thought crossed her mind. What if he isn't really that close? What if the radio interview was just a ruse or PR to hype it up? Maybe it was just done in hopes that she would hear it and turn herself in. Maybe he was receiving donations by advertising as a public item. A pill that makes you fly. He could sell them for a million each. Even if it meant a one percent chance closer to curing herself, she had to take it.

"We'll find out, won't we?" Sydona said.

The group glanced at one another for assurance. No one wanted to talk, not even Knox. But Sydona felt a need to get back soon. She feared what might happen if he went to her room and found her missing.

"I need to get back," Sydona said while taking a step.

Raoul twitched his wings but flew alongside her. "I'm going with you."

"What are we supposed to do?" Silas asked. His guilty face made her stomach hurt.

She turned around. "I don't know. It's not good-bye, you know. We will figure it out." Then she kissed him as if she were never to see him again. His response was less than satisfying. He wasn't happy with her answer.

Giovonna stepped toward her. "Maybe I could help? I've been studying the bracelets for a while. I think he and I could probably do it."

"Gia, darlin'! You outta your damn mind?" Willow shouted.

"How would you even get in? He won't just allow anyone in his house, ya?" Jet asked.

"They have no one guarding the place right now, remember?" Sydona said.

Giovonna lifted a smile and Sydona returned it.

Knox spoke up, "Miss Wilder—"

"Don't fucking call me that."

Knox's cheeks puffed out, and he continued, "Sydona, you have exactly 24 hours to prove to me that Malik isn't just fucking with us. Until then, you will not be a part of the Sparrows."

"What?" Giovonna cried.

"Sir— You can't do that!" Willow said.

Knox's violet eyes pierced hers as she stared back.

"How am I supposed to do that, Knox?" Sydona argued.

Knox towered over her. "Figure it out."

Sydona wanted to walk away from him more than anything, but she came back to him, getting closer to his angry face. "After everything we've been through, I can't believe you won't trust me."

"I am not risking more lives because you *think* the doctor *might* help you," Knox said sternly. "You want to go rogue? Be my guest, but you won't be taking my people down with you."

Sydona turned away from him while laughing quietly to herself. She couldn't believe he was turning on her. Anger boiled up so much in her she wanted to scream. But knowing Knox, he wouldn't see reason until he saw proof. All she could do was accept his conditions.

After Knox knew he won the debate, he stepped away from her and headed back to the vehicle. "Avani, Willow, Jet, and Devon, you're coming with me."

Willow's mouth fell open. "But sir—"

"Sparrows who want to stay a Sparrow, step inside the van."

Knox sat inside the driver's seat and started it up. Avani, Jet, Devon, and Willow followed his instruction, even though it was a tad apprehensive. The doors shut and Knox spun out from the site, making dirt, rocks, and leaves fly through the air. She watched the red lights fade into the night. Giovonna lay her head against Sydona's shoulder, and it comforted her to know that she wasn't completely alone.

Silas looked at her and shrugged. "Now what?"

Chapter Six

KNOX

Knox wrapped his fingers tightly around the steering wheel as he drove out from the depths of the woods. His jaw clenched as he tried to forget the interaction he had with Sydona and the others.

"Elias, pull the car over right now!" Avani yelled from the passenger seat.

The group they left behind was just out of sight when he pulled to the side of the road. Dust and rocks flew from the back tires as they finally halted. Tension was high in the car. Knox laid his head back on the seat and stared up at the sagging cloth ceiling.

"I understand your anger, sweetheart. But what happens if she can't get the proof you want?"

"Then I'll take matters into my own hands," he groaned. His head began to ache, and he rubbed his temples.

"It's not like you. What's really going on?" Avani asked. Her voice was soft but concerned. He hated making her worry. He felt the eyes of Willow, Jet, and Devon from the back seat as he chose his words. Knox didn't want to lose his temper again. The situation was already tense.

"I didn't expect things to turn out this way," he said.

Willow spoke up from behind, "I don't think anyone did, sir."

"I expected Lacey and I to be holding hands in victory once it was all over," Jet said. "But—god damnit… I need a drink."

"And that, Jet, is exactly why I can't let this go," Knox said. He lifted his head and turned to look at them. Jet wiped his face and then turned away. Devon patted Jet on the leg in condolence.

"But what can we do, my dear?" Avani asked.

Knox gripped the steering wheel, grim determination overtaking his features. "I can't sit around and wait."

"Maybe we could help 'em," Willow said.

"How?" Devon asked.

"I dunno, but I agree we can't sit around twiddlin' our thumbs. It's not something we do as Sparrows," said Willow.

"We get ready," said Knox. He sat up in his seat. His heart pumped faster.

"Ready?" asked Avani.

"I'll gather up the remaining Sparrows, now that we know the location."

Willow cleared her throat. "That ain't exactly what I meant—"

Knox's eyes turned green as he glanced in the rearview mirror. "We need to be ready for anything."

Avani's slender, warm hand touched his bicep, and he turned to her.

"I want to start a family, Elias. And I know you do, too," Avani said softly. She kept her voice low so the others wouldn't overhear.

Knox sighed and caressed her rosey cheek. His eyes went back to lavender as he stared into his wife's wet gaze. She wanted it to end. So did he, but it would never truly be over until Malik was six feet under. The threat of him still being around without knowing if he was gone made his blood boil. Knox would die before he brought a baby into the world where fliers were threatened.

"It's just a precaution, Ava." His thumb wiped a tear away from her eye.

"I think I saw a liquor store on the way here," Jet said abruptly.

"It's two in the mornin', child. You'll be fine," Willow said.

Devon glared at him. "I thought you stopped doing that."

Jet didn't say anything and stared out the window. Knox noticed Jet holding his hands together to stop the shaking.

"I miss my mom and dad…" said Devon.

"I know, mijo," Avani said as she wiped her eyes and inhaled deeply. She reached around and grabbed his hand. "This will all be over before you know it. I promise."

Devon put his hand on top of hers. "What happens after it's all over? What happens to the Sparrows?"

Knox felt a lump in his throat. He watched Jet break his gaze away from the window and waited for Avani's answer.

"I wish I had all the answers, sweetheart. But no matter what happens, you are part of this family. We won't let anything happen to you, si?"

Devon nodded.

"Exactly," Jet said. "Just stick with me and everything will be fine." He grabbed Devon's shoulder until he looked him in the eye and nodded again.

Avani let go of the boy's hand and faced forward again. She shook her head with a quick eye roll and stared out the window.

Knox cleared his throat and gripped the wheel. "Let's get out of here. Maybe there's a breakfast place that's open." He ran his hands over his face and sniffed. He put the car back in gear, and they took off to find a place to get food. As he got back on the road, a pair of bright lights illuminated the rearview mirror. It was coming from the direction of the house.

Knox's massive boot pushed the pedal flat to the floor. With the headlights fast approaching, Knox yelled, "Everyone get down! Jet, hand me the gun in the red bag."

As Knox sped down the road at eighty-five miles an hour, the first gun shot hit the vehicle. Avani and Devon shrieked, and Knox swerved the car. "Jet! Now!"

"I got it, Knox," Willow said and rolled her window down.

A wave of cold air hit the back of his naked head. He glanced back and forth between the mirrors and the road ahead. A hidden road revealed itself, and he turned the car so fast, two tires left the ground. In that same moment, a popping sound rang out, and the car shook violently. They shot one of the tires. Knox felt whiplash from the car trying to steady itself.

"Can someone *please* give me a gun!?" Knox shouted.

"Here!" Jet placed a pistol in Knox's waiting hand.

Rolling his window down, he stuck half his body out and faced the back. He shot three times and one hit. The car behind them swerved, but then straightened out and sped up. Pop! Another tire shot out. Knox continued to accelerate as fast as possible, but it was no use. The van slowed to a stop, forcing the car behind to stop.

"Keep Devon safe," Knox said to Jet. He nodded and hovered over Devon in protection.

Knox reloaded his pistol while Willow did the same. Avani searched through the bags sitting next to her.

"What are you doing?" Knox asked her.

"Helping!" Avani said as she finally found another gun.

"That's my girl." He winked. Avani returned the wink and cocked the gun back.

The trees and shadows outside were silent. Knox bellowed out of his window, "Just step away and no one has to die!"

A crackling laugh echoed through the trees, and it sent a chill down his spine.

"Knoxy poo! I finally get to see you again! How the fuck ya been, cuñado?" Natalia asked as she approached the van. The headlights from behind turned her into a silhouette while dust swirled around her. She was barely clothed and using a fully-automatic machine gun to cover her naked stomach. She pointed her gun straight at him, gaining the upper hand. Her weapon put his tiny pistol to shame, but he still gripped it tightly. If he attempted to kill her, she'd kill him first. He had to keep a level head.

"What is with you guys and automatic guns?" Knox asked.

"Cause no one fucks with 'em," Natalia said and popped her chewing gum.

The three other Vultures with her laughed as they began to surround the vehicle.

Natalia continued. "Ain't you gonna come out and play?" Knox saw her pout her lips. He then glanced back at his group. His gaze stopped on Avani. She shook her head, and he took a deep breath. Removing one hand from the pistol, he slowly opened the door and pushed it out with his foot. Bearing his empty hand out in the open, he looked back at everyone else, hoping they'd do the same. Knox threw the gun to the grass a few feet ahead of him. Turning his body to let his feet touch the ground, he stood in front of Natalia with his hands up.

"No, no, no silly. How can we play without both of us having guns?" Natalia said. She motioned the tip of her gun to his on the ground.

"Not today…"

Natalia pouted her lips even more and tilted her head sideways at him. "You've changed."

Knox shrugged.

Natalia let out an aggravated, raspy noise and stomped her feet. "I wanted to have some fun, and dammit, I'm getting it! Get out! Everyone get the fuck out!"

"Nat, just let us go. No one needs to die," Knox pleaded. He hated to beg and regretted saying it immediately. But Avani's safety was all he could think of.

Natalia laughed wickedly. "No one said anything about dying." She lowered her voice and winked seductively at Knox. "Not today anyway."

"There's a child in here, Nat!" Avani shouted.

"I was wondering when you'd speak up, sis."

"Let us leave, Natalia. No one's been hurt. We can just walk away," said Knox in the calmest tone he could manage.

Natalia laughed again. "Well that's the problem isn't it?" She walked closer to the van and looked through all the windows. "Everyone looks peachy keen. Not a single bruise or missing limb in sight. We gotta change that."

Knox looked down at Natalia who stood only inches in front of him. She glanced over at Avani before she turned back to Knox and planted a hard kiss on his lips. Knox's eyes widened. He shoved her backwards, leaving Natalia with a huge smile.

She licked her lips and moaned. "I've been waiting *so long* to do that."

From the corner of his eye, he saw Avani leap over the car seat to attack her sister with nails out like a wildcat. "You bitch!"

The machine gun touched Avani's chest. She stopped with a huff and growl, sounding very Natalia-like. It made Knox feel odd. They had never behaved like each other, and Knox couldn't unsee their similarities.

"Alright, y'all. Let's not do nothin' crazy now," Willow said.

Natalia turned her attention to Willow in the back seat and flung her door open. "You calling me crazy?"

"Let's be honest, darlin', you ain't bodin' well in the normal category."

"Is that right?" Natalia answered with complete seriousness. "I don't like how you talk." Knox wished he could shut Willow's mouth, but it was too late. His stomach twisted.

Natalia flipped her gun around and smashed the butt into Willow's mouth. She screamed out in pain.

"What the hell is your problem, lady?" Willow yelled while holding her mouth.

"I don't have a problem, old timer. This is just a normal day for me."

Knox witnessed the boiling water pour over, and Willow lunged at Natalia. With all of Willow's weight and strength, Natalia couldn't do much. She was slammed against the ground with Willow wailing at her head. She attempted to pull Willow's red hair, but as she did, Willow bit her on the arm. At that point Natalia yelled at her men.

"What you fuckers just standing around for? Get this whale off of me!"

They did as they were told, and even with the help of two large guards, they struggled to pull Willow off. Each of them grabbed an arm, but Willow kept her chest out and wiggled as much as she could. As the men inched her further and further from Natalia, Willow spit on the ground next to her and spoke. "Better hope ya got guards around me day n' night, 'cause next time ya won't be so lucky. Skinny bitch." The last line she murmured under her breath, but Knox heard it clearly. With a quick chuckle, Natalia bared her bloody teeth and got herself off the ground. She used her hands to crack her neck and then wiped herself off.

"Okay, fun's over. Get everyone in the car. Bailey, search the van; make sure we didn't miss anything. Call me when you're done."

He nodded and climbed into the van.

Another Vulture spoke up. "Miss, I don't think we are going to be able to fit everyone inside."

Natalia looked straight at Willow, whose wild hair was even messier than normal. "This one looks like she could use the exercise. Stay with her. Make sure she doesn't try nothin'." Natalia stood nose to nose with Willow. "I'll be thinking of something creative for you on the ride back home." Knox could swear he saw steam billowing from her nose like an angry bull.

One of the Vultures put Willow in handcuffs and began to walk along the side of the road, back to the mansion. Knox was the last one shoved in the car. As the door slammed shut, he realized two very important things were missing from all the chaos. Jet and Devon were gone.

Chapter Seven

SYDONA

The five of them sat around for a minute, unable to comprehend Knox's decision. Giovonna checked on Silas's injury, while Harold made a nearby tree his punching bag and cursed Knox's name.

"This is so fucked," Silas grumbled. "How did we get to this point?"

Sydona hung her head low, and anxiously bounced on her feet. The longer she stayed away, the more the thought of the doctor finding her gone gnawed at her.

Raoul spoke up. "Harold, do you know where they might be keeping Jubilee?"

Harold gave one last kick to the tree and huffed. He took a few seconds to calm down. "Natalia either took her to John… or she kept her. Like a pet."

Giovonna narrowed her eyes. "Like a pet? That's really weird."

"Well, she don't exactly fit into the normal cate-gory, if ya catch my drift," Harold quipped.

Raoul balled up his tiny fists. "We gotta find her. Who knows what she's done to her…"

Sydona's heart sped up with every passing min-ute. Every possible scenario played out in her mind: Which one would get her ability back? Which one saved her father, or saved Jubilee? Which one would put an end to Natalia's madness? Were any possible? She had to focus on one at a time. Her father was still in the doctor's house, and she had been gone for at least an hour. It was well after midnight, but he could have someone checking up on her to make sure she didn't leave. Every second she wasn't in the bed-room or house, she thought about what personality he might morph into. She did not want to find out.

"I really want to help you, Raoul, but I need to get back. I wish I could help." She bit the insides of her cheeks while she waited for his reaction. The fact she was leaving him again tore her up, but she wor-ried more about her sick father.

"I understand, Syd. We'll come find you after," he said, his words rushed but casual.

Her jaw relaxed. "Wha — really?"

"You don't want to piss the doctor off more than he needs to be. You'll be okay without me?"

Sydona wanted to laugh. "Of course. I'll be fine. I'll look around to see if he hid Jubilee somewhere."

"Thank you." Raoul nodded. "Harold, think you can take me to Natalia's hideout? Or wherever she might be keeping my niece?"

Harold straightened up, almost taken aback by his proposal. "It would be my honor."

"I'll go with you, Syd," Giovonna said as the group began to break up. She tightened the straps of her backpack and waited for Sydona's command.

"Yeah, me too," Silas said, rubbing his leg.

With everything happening, Sydona had almost forgotten about Silas's injury. It was clearly still bothering him. She wondered how well he could walk, let alone run or fly, if anything happened. Her heart raced as she thought of what might happen if the doctor found her friends in the house.

She inhaled sharply. "It's too dangerous." She closed her eyes, preparing for backlash.

"What?" Giovonna said.

"I can't risk your lives. I'm already risking my father's. I just can't."

Silas grabbed her shoulders, and he shook her gently. "Syd. You are not risking anything. We're volunteering." He lifted her shaky chin, and she gazed into his soulful, violet eyes. "Like it or not, babe, you're stuck with us. We're a team."

Sydona melted into his encouraging words, but she still hesitated. "Silas, your leg."

"What about it?" He let go of her and looked down at his leg frantically. "Oh, you scared me for a second. Thought it was gone! I still got two, and it's feeling better every minute." He grinned and winked at her.

"Are you sure?" Sydona asked again.

"Syd, everything is going to be fine, okay?" Giovonna said. "Besides, we're prepared if crap hits the fan." She glanced down at her leg, where she had a small dagger strapped around her calf.

Sydona raised both brows in surprise. "Okay, okay. I can't talk you out of this. So, I'll just warn you. He's unpredictable, be on guard at all times."

Silas and Giovonna gave her a nod of agreement.

"Can you walk okay?" Sydona asked.

"I might need some help," Silas said, feigning the seriousness of his injury as an excuse to hold her closer. She grinned and put his arm around her shoulders. His closeness helped her calm down.

"Let's get you patched up," Sydona said. "I got some painkillers, too, if you need them."

"Oh, gimme!"

As Sydona poured some drugs out for Silas, Raoul buzzed over. "We'll meet up with you sometime tomorrow. Sound good?"

Sydona replied. "Yeah. Good luck, you guys. And please be careful." She raised her voice as Raoul flew away, making sure he heard her.

"I'm always careful. Except for, well, that one time…" Raoul's voice faded. Sydona knew exactly what he was talking about.

"Exactly," she warned. "And, Harold, if anything happens to him…"

Harold waved his arms around in offense. "Excuse me, miss thang. I know who I use ta be. You don't got nothin' to worry 'bout. And I don't know Raoul very well, but he seems like he can take pretty good care of himself."

Sydona furrowed her brows. "I know he can; that's not my point."

Harold shook his head and looked off into the trees. Raoul exchanged a glance at Sydona, easing her worries.

"This was temporary housin' by the way. He built these for us when he wanted us aroun' for a long time. I ain't been back since Eagle Lake." He flicked his eyes in her direction. Her nostrils flared.

The words hung in the air and no one said a thing.

After a minute, Harold cleared his throat. "We good to go, then?"

Everyone nodded. He took off with Raoul toward the houses in the distance. Sydona's assumption had been correct. The units *were* part of the doctor's property, and they likely housed Vultures. She wondered how someone could stand to live right next to where they worked.

Silas, Giovonna, and Sydona made their way back across the large grass lawn. They had to go slow since two of them were being used as crutches. There was still no one else around, but Sydona kept her guard up. She gripped the kitchen knife with her free hand.

"It's even bigger close up!" Giovonna shouted but was immediately shushed by the other two. She lowered her voice. "I'm sorry, but you get to live in a mansion, Syd. This is incredible!"

Sydona clicked the front door shut. "I'm not living here, Gia. Far from it. But you have to be quiet. I shouldn't have even brought you guys here."

Treading lightly, they entered her temporary bedroom and laid Silas down on the soft bed. Sydona caressed his face, which was covered with black stubble. "I'll try to find some supplies. I'll be right back. Don't open the door for anyone, okay?"

Silas saluted her while Giovonna scoffed. "Well, duh. But we should have a secret knock."

Sydona grinned. "How about just three knocks?"

"That'll work," Giovonna said with a shrug.

Sydona left the room and heard the lock click behind her. She headed down the long hallway and back toward the medical room. The painkillers were wearing off. Random spots on her body began to ache again, and she leaned on the wall with one arm outstretched to hold her up. She breathed through the pain until she could take the last few steps. She finally reached the medical room. It was just as she left it a few hours before.

As she glanced around the room, she remembered all the cabinets with anything of value were locked up. She took a quick trip back down to the kitchen for a small pick tool. Rummaging around in a drawer she found a slender metal tool with a small hook at the end. It wasn't something she'd worked with before, but she wasn't about to turn down a challenge. After she made her way back, she opened the first cabinet with ease. The amount of pills and medical supplies was a dream come true. Sydona shoved what she could into her pockets and cradled the rest in her arms.

She made her way back to the room without any issues. The lack of guards still baffled her. Despite her best efforts, she could not stop her pulse from drumming in her ears. Arms full, she knocked three times with her foot, and Giovonna opened the door slowly. She let Sydona in and checked the hallway again before shutting it.

"Wow, that's a lot of stuff. That all for me?" Silas asked from the bed.

"Most of it. I got some for me, too."

Silas removed his jeans to change the bandage on his upper thigh as Sydona got the wrap and antibiotics ready. "How are you feeling?" she asked.

Silas tilted his head from side to side. "I'll be better once we get out of this house."

"Agreed," said Giovonna, snooping through the closet.

Sydona sighed. "I know. Me too."

After she finished helping Silas with his leg, she removed her shirt to reveal a loose fitting bra and her torso covered in bruises and bandages.

"God damn, babe. What the hell happened to you?" Silas asked, gently touching her skin.

"Oh my god, Sydona," said Giovonna as she sat on the bed with them. "How are you able to move right now?"

She hadn't really seen her injuries yet, just felt them. She glanced in the vanity mirror across from the bed. If she were a fruit, not even Raoul would touch her.

"I'm fine." She winced as she removed a bandage covered in blood.

"I'm glad you're strong enough to admit you're fine, even though you're clearly not," said Silas. "But our question remains: how did this happen? And don't say you fell down the stairs."

There was no more room for lies. She had to be honest. "The doctor didn't believe me when I said I couldn't fly. So…" She inhaled sharply. "He forced me to jump off a cliff."

Giovonna gasped, and then her expression became unusually hard. "Syd! What the—"

"He threatened my father. Said he'd kill him if I didn't *prove* it to him. I didn't have a choice."

"You always have a choice," Silas said, voice heavy. The drugs must have kicked in.

"Not when his Vultures are holding guns to my head. And if I die, what's the point of keeping him alive? But… I didn't die. And now he knows my condition and seems to have turned a new leaf. He patched me up, put my father in a room with an actual mattress, and lets me come and go as I please. This is unusual for him. He really wants to help me and feels responsible for hindering my ability."

Giovonna shook her head. "I hope you know what you're doing."

"I do." She didn't, but what other option did she have?

They both helped her with her bandages in silence. The air in the room was heavy and tainted with unspoken worries. She knew her friends wanted to help her, but she hated the tension. All she wanted to do was ride on the medicine numbing her pain. The night was still young, with several hours remaining until morning. Giovonna grabbed a blanket from the closet and made herself comfortable at the foot of the large king bed. Sydona snuggled in close to Silas under the feather comforter and quickly fell asleep.

Chapter Eight

RAOUL

A waft of sour musk invaded Raoul's nose as he followed close behind Harold. Some could argue it was cologne, but whatever it was, it was no friend to fairies. Raoul held his breath and flew by Harold's side.

"Where are we going?"

Harold glanced sideways at him. "My old place."

"You don't think we'll get caught?" Raoul asked.

"I ain't really sure why there's no patrol goin' on tonight, but it may be to our advantage."

"What's at your house?"

"House," he chuckled. "That's a good one."

Raoul lifted an eyebrow. "Didn't you join because he was paying you a ton of money? Why don't you have a house or something?"

Harold's eyes narrowed but remained focused ahead of him. "It's just up here."

Several two story buildings stood in a large field to the south of the doctor's house. They exited the protection of the forest and stepped into a grassy lawn illuminated by the full moon. As they got closer, they passed over a hill, and Raoul was able to make out a black helicopter sitting on a helipad. Was it the same one Malik escaped in? Several dents and bullet holes caught the reflection of the moonlight, and it confirmed his speculation. The mere sight of it and what it represented made his stomach twist. Beyond the helipad was a cul-de-sac dotted with streetlights and lined by sidewalks. The windows of the apartments were black. Raoul still didn't know why they were going to Harold's place, but he followed cautiously. After all, Harold was sneaking around, just like him.

They soon arrived at the first brick building with roughly eight apartments occupying it. Harold flattened his back against the wall and began to scoot across it.

"Be my lookout, wouldja?" Harold whispered.

Raoul crossed his arms. "Me? What if they catch me?"

"Well, you're small. *You* can fly away!"

"And what if I'm caught? I'll be damned if I'm turned into someone's pet!" Raoul argued in the shadows of the building.

Exasperated, Harold rolled his eyes. "Natalia's the only one to do something like that, and she's already got one. And what do ya think they'd do to me if I'm caught? I'm the one who brought the lady who wants to kill the leader of the NFA! They won't be throwing me a parade."

Raoul stared at him. "What are we doing at your house anyway?"

He sighed. "I got some weapons stashed away. Ya know, for emergencies."

"What kind of weapons?"

"Guns an' stuff, you know."

Raoul flew backwards. "How do I know you won't use them on my friends?"

Harold scrunched his face in confusion. "What?" He flailed his arms. "Why would I do that?!"

"How do I know that wasn't the plan all along, Harold?" Raoul's heart pounded. "There's conveniently no security around, making it way too easy for us to just enter the doctor's house. And you have three fliers in there and a fairy next to you. What kind of reward is he giving you for that, huh?!" Raoul flew in his face.

"Have you lost your tiny little mind?" Harold yelled back. "I confessed everything to Sydona and your group. Willow and I… Well, it's all true. I'm a different man now. She's an amazin' woman." His brown eyes glazed over, and a silly grin grew on his face.

"You better be right. Or you can kiss your nipples goodbye," Raoul said with narrowed eyes. Using two fingers, he pointed at his own eyes, then at the man's chest. Harold's lovesick expression shifted to disgust. Raoul peeked around the corner and waved him ahead.

Harold took the lead once again and headed to a building across the empty road. He pulled out a key and unlocked the door. He let out a sound of surprise and happily pushed the door open. Raoul slipped in first. Flicking the light switch, Harold closed the door behind him and breathed in deeply. "Home sweet home."

Raoul didn't know what he expected of Harold, but it wasn't the small apartment before him. The space was fairly clean. Cleaner than Sydona's house had ever been. But then again, maybe it seemed clean because it was pretty empty. A dingy brown lounge chair sat in the corner with a metal tray leaning up against it. Next to the chair was a portable radio with a bent antenna and a floor light illuminating the blank white walls. The rest of the sad apartment was only populated by boxes and folded up clothes.

"You thirsty?" Harold asked as he walked five feet to the refrigerator. "Hmm, it still works."

Raoul landed on the tiny kitchen island counter-top. "Yes."

The fridge only had a few water bottles and cans of beer. Harold offered him a water bottle. As he held it up next to him, he shot Raoul a puzzled look. "Uh, how you s'pose to drink this?"

Raoul stood up on the counter and looked up at the bottle, which was a full inch taller than himself. "I normally just use a leaf, and Syd turns the water on for me."

Harold looked around his four-hundred square foot apartment. "Well, I ain't really got any leaves layin' around. Mind if I just pour some into the cap?"

"Sure," Raoul said.

Harold carefully added a few drops into the plastic cap with shaky hands. "How's that?" He stepped back, appearing satisfied with himself

Raoul held back a smile, "It's fine. Thank you, Harold." He held the cap like an oversized bowl and slurped carefully.

"Man. Look at us. A human and a fairy, just hangin' out. Like nothin' weird was going on."

Raoul wiped his mouth. "Yup."

Harold tapped the counter a couple times before walking out of the kitchen. Raoul looked after him with concern. As he drank more water, someone knocked on the front door. Both of them sprang up like prairie dogs. Raoul flew over to the only other door in the place and slid under the crack. Harold scrambled around for something under his bed while mumbling things under his breath. Raoul's heart raced as he stood on the doorknob of the bathroom. Raoul heard a sound resembling a gun being cocked back.

They knocked again. "Harold, it's just me. I saw your light on, man. Open up."

It must have been someone he knew because Harold instantly relaxed. He quickly opened the door to let them in and closed it behind him. The man shook Harold's hand and looked him over.

"Anyone see you?" Harold asked. He turned the light switch off, darkening the whole room, apart from the moon coming in through the only window.

"Nah, man. Everyone's sleeping. I knew you'd be back though. I just knew it!" he said.

"Quiet, Jones. We don't want everyone wakin' up." Harold flashed the gun in front of Jones.

"Whoa! What's with the gun?!" he shouted but was immediately shushed.

Harold pushed it into his pants. "Shut up, Jones. For the love of... It's just a precaution."

"You think Malik's out for you?"

"You thank bees sting just for the hell of it? Of course he's out for me!"

"Nah, man. He's good now. That Sydona girl showed up. He's got what he needs now."

Raoul's eyes widened. Jones turned his back to the kitchen to get a beer, and Raoul flew past him and landed on top of the fridge to get a better look and listen.

"What's his plan?" Harold asked, waving away the beer Jones offered.

"No idea. He's not telling anyone. Just told us to lay low for a while and treat Sydona and her dad like guests. Although, some of us aren't willing to sit back."

"Who would that be?" Harold pried.

"Nat. She's beyond upset to be kept in the dark. Said she's the one who brought her in; she should know the game plan. Malik shut her ass out." He burst out laughing.

As Jones tipped back the beer can, Harold noticed the bandage wrapped around his finger. "What's wrong with your finger?" he asked.

"That bitch, Sydona, fucking bit me! Can you believe that shit? I don't know what Malik's got planned, but whatever it is, she deserves it," Jones said and tilted his head up for another drink. While he was drinking, Raoul's anger boiled over. He imagined leaping from atop the fridge, flew up Jones's shirt, located a nipple, and bit down as hard as he could. A piece of flesh ripped off between Raoul's teeth. The taste of blood and skin was enough to make him vomit, but the reaction from Jones was worth it.

"Fuuuucccckkkk! What in the hell was that?!" he screamed and swatted at Raoul, trying to crush him against his body. But Raoul was already gone. The surprise attack left him coughing and choking on his beer.

But just then, Harold spoke up and interrupted Raoul's thoughts. "Hey, are you okay up there?"

Raoul shook his head. Jones caught his breath and turned to look up at him on top of the fridge. "Is that a fucking fairy?" Jones said and immediately grabbed Raoul. "I don't think you're supposed to be here, fella."

"Hey! I'm not a beer, dill hole! Put me down!" Raoul yelled and fluttered his wings as hard as he could. But Jones began to squeeze.

"Drop him," Harold said calmly.

All Raoul could see was the man's angry eyes, but they soon turned soft. He imagined Harold was putting his gun to use.

"Ha—rold…" Raoul wheezed.

"You're gonna shoot me over a fairy? Your best friend?" Jones said, loosening his grip.

"Best friend? Since when?"

Raoul coughed and gasped for breath. "Do you—really—need to do this—now?"

"Damnit, put him down right now!" Harold shouted.

Jones growled but dropped Raoul down on the counter. Raoul fought for air and crawled toward Harold. The two men stared at each other with intense focus while Raoul regained some strength.

"Sydona should have done more than just bite your finger," he spat.

Jones lunged to grab him again, but Raoul fluttered out of reach. Harold shoved the pistol into his face again and Jones backed away with his hands up in surrender. "You've changed, man."

"John has flown the coop, *man*. How can ya not see that?" Harold asked.

Jones stood back in silence. He had no way to answer him.

"Where's Natalia?" Raoul asked.

Jones's face hardened. "How do you know her?"

Harold wiggled the gun impatiently. "Just answer him."

"I don't know. No one knows where she goes anymore. Been off doing her own thing and doesn't tell anybody. Not even me."

"Oh, boo-hoo. The crazy chick keeps secrets from you. Are you really surprised?" Raoul mocked.

"Hey, what the—" Jones started but was cut off again by the fairy.

"Tell me where she lives so I can get Jubilee back!"

"Who?"

"Don't play games with me, Vulture!" Raoul balled up his fists.

Jones raised a single brow. "Vulture? And I'm *not*, fairy. I told you. She doesn't tell me anything. The last I saw her was the other night when Sydona was brought in. After we left her down there, we went our separate ways."

Harold put the gun down and chugged his friend's beer. He burped loudly. "I know where she lives. How 'bout we go pay a little visit?"

Jones replied, "Fine, but get that damn gun out of my face, Harold."

He obliged and shoved it into the back of his pants. Harold grabbed the rest of what he came to his apartment for, which turned out to be mostly guns and knives. He carefully concealed something in his back pocket, and Raoul watched with growing curiosity. He kept his mouth shut because Jones refused to take his eyes off Raoul while Harold gathered supplies. It rubbed him the wrong way.

Locking the door behind them, the three men headed for the sidewalk. Harold felt no need to hide any longer, but Raoul still felt uncomfortable being out in the open. He never thought of his slightly orange glow as a problem before tonight, but it really made him stick out. There was no tote or long hair to hide behind, so he had to fly from one object to another, staying invisible as much as possible. It made Raoul nervous to think there were others around like Jones, who would try to snatch him right out of the air. He wasn't as quick as he used to be.

The men looked as if they had already squashed their differences as they exchanged stories from their past. Jones was much more detailed and brutal, but Harold tried to change the subject when it got to be too much. It was obvious Harold missed his friend but didn't agree with everything he still continued to do.

Harold stopped at a door with the number 9 engraved in the middle. Within only a minute or so, Jones picked Natalia's lock and they were in. Still trying to be invisible, Raoul buzzed inside first, but then the light turned on. A device on the wall near the door began to beep. If Raoul hadn't been preoccupied with finding Jubilee, he might have tried to find out what it was, but his search had begun.

"An alarm system?" asked Harold. "Why the hell she got an alarm system in here? Did John approve this?"

"This is new. She musta just put this in. But why?" Jones said, just as confused.

Raoul knew they only had a limited time before the alarm sounded, and he wanted to at least see his niece. To make sure she was okay. The apartment was a mirror of Harold's, so he went for the door that probably led to the bedroom. It was locked.

"Hey! Help me open this door!" he yelled across the room.

"Raoul, we ain't got time!" Harold cautioned.

"I have to know if she's in there! Please!" Raoul cried. His hands jiggled the door handle. He felt tears surfacing while his heart thumped in his chest.

Harold saw his face and ran over to try and unlock the door.

"We gotta go!" Jones yelled as softly as he could.

At last, Harold opened the door and Raoul caught a glimpse of a yellow glow in the corner of the room.

"Jubilee!" he cried. But as soon as he yelled, the alarm sounded.

The fairy sat up inside the cage and rubbed her eyes. "Uncle?"

"Come on, Raoul! We have ta leave. Now!"

"No!" Raoul screamed and flew over to her. But before he got too far, Harold grabbed him in mid-air and held on. "Stop! Put me down!"

Harold slammed the door shut and ran out of the apartment. Jones was already gone. Raoul's relentless tears blurred the rest. He slammed his fists on Harold's hands, but it did nothing. He had been agonizing over the possibilities for days, but there were two things that were clear now: Jubilee was alive, and Natalia had her.

Chapter Nine

JET

As the taillights faded from sight, Devon stood up first from the bush and dusted himself off. Jet released the deep breath he was holding before stepping out of the brush. The cicadas began to sing again while they stood in the middle of the otherwise still forest. Once he knew they wouldn't be seen, Jet grabbed a flashlight from his backpack. He aimed the light around the woods, searching for signs of Vultures or anything out of place.

"That was a close one," Devon said.

"Tell me about it," Jet replied.

"What do you think is gonna happen to them?"

"I don't know."

"Are we going to help them?" Devon asked.

Jet zipped open the red bag from the van and searched inside for anything that could help. He remembered Knox saying something about maps or other groups of Sparrows.

"Earth to Jet," Devon said. "What are we gonna do?"

"Not right now, Devon. Here," he said, handing him a walkie talkie.

Devon took it and whined, "Jet, we can't let them get hurt."

"They're already hurt, Dev. Nothing we can do now."

"But I'm a Sparrow. And you're a Sparrow! We can't just give up!"

"Devon. Please. I'm trying to think," Jet snapped.

Devon stomped his foot and took his flashlight.

"Hey!" Jet yelled, but Devon walked too far away. He quickly searched for another flashlight and followed him. "Where are you going?"

"I'm saving our friends." His voice echoed through the trees.

Jet wrapped the large reg bag across his torso and grabbed Devon's shoulder. "Devon, stop. We don't have any weapons! They'll kill us as soon as they see us!"

"Well, what are we supposed to do out here in the middle of nowhere?"

"I don't know, but we need a plan first, okay?"

"Like what?"

Jet shook his head and searched through the pockets of the red bag. He located a small book of names and locations of Sparrows. He swallowed hard as he thought of what would happen if Natalia or the Vultures found that book. It had all the information they needed. The closest hideout to them was a winery in Santa Barbara. Jet wasn't entirely sure where they were in California but knew that he could probably fly there quickly. The leader's name attached to it was Tasha.

He looked for a map or something to help them know which way to go, but if Knox had brought one, it was still in the van. Still, they needed to find the other group; maybe they had people and weapons. It was the best option they had.

"Find anything?" Devon asked as he picked the bark off a stick.

"Looks like we're going to Santa Barbara."

"How far is that?"

"I'm not sure. We need a map."

Devon nodded. "So, we'll be going even farther away? What about Will—"

"Please, Devon. You have to trust me." His temper was shortening. His hands began to shake, and he suddenly felt parched.

"What's in Santa Barbara?"

"Help."

Devon perked up. "More Sparrows?"

"Yup," Jet said. *I hope so*, he thought. "We should get going. In case those Vultures come back. We'll stay in the woods but keep the road in sight. Maybe we'll find a gas station or convenience store."

Devon sighed loudly and walked with his hands shoved in his pockets. It was a silent stroll, and they traveled for what felt like miles. Then, a bright glowing light shone through the trunks, and Jet's heart leaped as they emerged from the dark forest. The lights came from a gas station. The look of it felt all too familiar. Glancing down at Devon who was glaring ahead, it seemed he had the same feeling. Devon didn't look at him but continued staring at the building. Jet's hands shook even more, but he kept walking.

"Don't sweat it, Dev. I'll be right here. Just pick whatever food you want, okay?"

He nodded his head hesitantly.

It was still dark out, and there was only one car parked nearby. The bell chimed above the door, and Devon slowly made his way toward the snack aisle. The man behind the counter greeted them. Jet gave him a silent nod of the head. While Devon was distracted with food, Jet went to the beverage aisle and grabbed a bottle of whiskey. In case he couldn't afford it, he twisted the cap off and began to chug.

The warm liquid made his knees weak, and he suddenly felt himself again. After waiting for the liquid to spread through him, he put the half-empty bottle in the back and grabbed a full one. He then searched the small store for maps. Flipping through the dozens of maps for different sections of California, he soon found one with a clear description of Santa Barbara. As he decided on the right one, pictures of other places caught his eye. Lots of ocean sunsets, beaches, cobblestone streets, antique buildings, people laughing, and dogs running. It hadn't hit him until that point that there was so much out there in the world he hadn't seen. He and Lacey used to talk about flying around the world one day. Of course, it was put on hold once Devon came into their lives. Jet grabbed a couple more brochures of appealing vacation spots. Maybe he would be able to go once everything settled down. He then wondered if Devon would want to go with him, too.

He found the kid still browsing the food aisle and concealed the bottle behind his back. He helped Devon pick a few sweet and salty snacks and headed up to the counter.

The gas station attendant side-eyed Jet, but continued to ring his items up. Jet cleared his throat and pulled his wallet out. He slapped the cash down while Devon stared at the bottle of amber liquid. They were just a few cents short, but the attendant grabbed a few pennies from the tray near the register. Once everything was run up, Devon grabbed his stuff, and Jet put the bottle in his bag. The bell chimed forcefully as Devon shoved the door open. Jet rushed after the kid as he stormed off.

"Hey, wait up," Jet said.

Devon stopped and turned around. "What?"

"I need to take a look at the map first," Jet said as he looked around for a bench or table. A metal picnic table, half covered in rust, sat on the side of the store. He made his way over, while Devon dragged his feet behind. The dim morning sun lit the sky, and they no longer needed the flashlight. Jet spread the map out and began to study it. Devon sat across from him, crunching his chips loudly with his mouth wide open. Jet glared at him from across the table, knowing he was doing it on purpose.

"Can you please stop?" Jet asked with a tight jaw.

Devon rolled his eyes and closed his mouth. Jet wasn't sure why he was suddenly upset, but once he took the whiskey out and transferred it to a flask, it became clear.

"Why do you drink so much?" Devon asked with a nasty look.

As he screwed the lid back on the bottle, Jet exhaled. "It makes me feel better."

"Really? That stuff doesn't seem to be working, then."

The words jabbed at Jet's heart. He hung his head and stared at the flask in his hand. Ever since the incident in the gas station, he had been drinking to muffle the truth about Devon's parents. The secret had gnawed at him for too long. He had to come clean.

"Dev, I don't exactly know how to say this…" he began, barely able to keep himself from taking another sip.

"Say what? That you're an alcoholic?" Devon snapped back with half-lid eyes. He sounded defeated and tired. Too much like an adult.

Jet furrowed his brows. "How do you know that word? But, no, not that…" The need to pour the whiskey down his throat made his legs shake along with his hands. He took a deep breath. "Remember…" he cleared his throat. "Remember the day we met?"

Devon's face immediately changed.

It made it even harder to say the next words. "The man who… killed your parents…" He exhaled and tried not to look away. "He was my friend."

"What?" Devon said in shock. His eyes were glued to Jet's, searching for answers. "What do you mean?"

"A couple days before that happened, he hit me up for money to help his wife in the hospital, but I turned him down. He was asking for a lot, and I just didn't have it. I didn't think it was that bad, but—" Jet stopped. His heart felt as if it was in his throat. He unscrewed the flask and took a long drink to push it back down. Too ashamed to look him in the face, Jet stared at a soda bottle cap laying on the concrete.

Devon was silent. The bag of chips sat open and forgotten in front of him.. "You—you've known this the whole time? That it was your friend? Why didn't you tell me?" His voice cracked.

"There was never a good time. I didn't know how to tell you. I didn't mean to keep it a secret."

"Lacey never would have kept that from me," Devon said under his breath.

Jet licked his lips. "She was the first person I told."

Devon made a scoffing noise.

Jet shook his head and threw it back with another gulp of the warming liquid. Devon went back to eating and chewing loudly. After several uncomfortable minutes, Jet finally got a lay of the land and knew which way to go. He folded the map violently and shoved it into the red bag. He hated that Devon was so angry with him.

As he was about to stand up and start walking, he paused, turned around to face the kid and extended his arm. Reaching his hand toward Devon, he opened his mouth to speak but nothing came out.

Devon caught his eye and scrunched his face. "What?"

Jet closed his mouth and retracted his hand. "Nothing. Let's go." He quickly got to his feet and rushed off.

"Where you goin'?" Devon asked with a squeak in his voice, still sitting at the table.

"Santa Barbara. Or did you forget already?" he shouted back.

"I'm not going anywhere with you. You're drunk!"

He stopped and hung his head. "I am not—" His fists curled but then relaxed. He decided to squeeze the strap on the bag instead.

"Yes you are. And why should I trust you? You killed my parents!"

"Devon!" He yelled louder than he intended. But he quickly changed his tone and took a deep breath. "Willow and everyone are in trouble. Do you want to save them or not?"

Devon held his chin up high, threw away his empty snack bags, and made his way over to Jet. "Yes, I do. But I am not talking to you anymore. From this point. Starting now." His attitude changed, and he stormed in front of him.

Jet rolled his eyes again. "Whatever. Let's just take off from here, man."

Devon groaned and turned back around to glare at Jet's extended hand. "You're drunk. What if we fall out of the sky?!"

"Oh my fucking god, Devon, just hold my hand so we can get out of here."

"It's not nice to say God's name in vain," Devon spat.

Jet had enough. He grabbed Devon's arm and began to run. Devon had no choice but to run with him. He struggled a bit and Jet spoke up. "If you let go, you *will* fall out of the sky! Now stop!"

At last, they took to the morning sky. He wished Raoul or a fairy was around to help. While normally holding one person in the air wasn't a big deal, the alcohol was already working its magic. Devon struggled at first, not at all happy about having to be close to his new least favorite person. But after a few minutes of being high above the trees, farms, and hills, he calmed down. Jet caught the flicker of a smile on the kid's face. At least flying made him happy.

They soared across forests, lakes, small cities, and neighborhoods until Jet spotted what he believed to be the location of the other Sparrows. Rows of dried up grape vines littered the rolling hills, and on the top of the hill stood a building covered in bricks and crawling vines.

They landed in a rocky parking lot with no cars in sight. The second they landed, Devon retracted his hand from Jet's grip. He jogged ahead of him to explore the area on his own. Jet groaned and rubbed his face, which felt tense from the cold air and frustration. Then, he took another long gulp of his whiskey and approached the old building.

It had a solid oak door, which turned out to be unlocked when he tested the handle. It creaked open, and he stepped inside. A long rustic bar ran along the right side of the room with stools lined up next to it. That was the only thing that resembled some kind of winery; everything else was barren aside from several bright yellow lockers.

"Hello?" Devon said, coming in right after Jet and practically ignoring his presence. Jet immediately shushed him, but Devon pushed past. "There're supposed to be Sparrows here, aren't there?"

Jet sighed heavily.

Devon walked off alone and casually checked out the building. Jet went straight behind the counter to see if any booze might have been left lying around. If they couldn't find help, they might as well take what they could. Jet heard Devon messing with the lockers and making a lot of noise.

"Dev, quit that."

"They're locked anyway," Devon spat and wandered even farther from Jet's sight.

Jet shook his head and let him do what he wanted. The shelves behind the counter were bare, but he didn't want to leave anything to chance. After a few minutes of searching every nook and cranny, he eventually gave up and took a drink from his flask. As he took a breath between sips, he glanced around the room again. Nothing in the place resembled a Sparrow hideout. No winged symbol, guns, clothing, communications, nothing. Maybe since the warehouse was Knox's territory, it was set up better. Since the war was over, maybe everyone just went home. But why would he dismiss everyone else and not the ones he was with?

Jet heard muffled speech from the direction Devon had headed. The other voice was indistinguishable, but it was low. The tones didn't indicate hostility, but Jet wandered back to him anyway, just in case. Turning the corner where massive metal vats once held wine, he found Devon speaking with a young woman.

"Whoa," she said, taking a step back. "Where'd you come from, mate?" Her smooth yet raspy voice carried a strong Australian accent.

"Uh, sorry. I was looking for this guy. Who are you?"

Devon answered for her. "This is Quinn. She's a Sparrow." He grinned up at the young woman, who returned a nervous smile.

"Hey, Quinn. I'm Jet, and you've already met Devon."

"Yeah, he's a cool kid," she said, pulling out a carton of cigarettes with a lighter hidden inside.

Jet curled a smirk at her habit and observed her while she lit up. Quinn couldn't be older than twenty-five. Her skin was tan as a typical Californian, and her mahogany colored hair was twisted up into a messy bun. A pair of old-fashioned leather and metal goggles also sat upon her head, making her look like a fighter pilot from the 20's. Her clothing consisted of a white tank top, jean capri pants with holes, and yellow flip flops. Her flimsy shoes made him wonder how she could run and fly without them slipping off. Her looks and personality contradicted each other, and a thousand more questions flooded Jet's head.

"What's with the goggles?" he asked with a small grin.

Quinn adjusted them on her head and shrugged. "Whaddya mean? You don't like 'em?"

"No, I do. I just—I haven't seen anyone wear them like a fashion statement before."

She laughed, and the sound made Jet's heart leap. "No, I use these all the time! I once had something fly into my eye, and it caused me to fall like a hundred feet. Almost pissed m'self. I ended up finding these at a yard sale, cleaned 'em up, and have been wearing them ever since. You should think about getting some. Lifesavers." She nodded and took a drag from her cigarette.

Jet nodded along with her, holding back a smile. "I'll consider it." The smoke wafted in his direction, and he embraced it with a deep breath. "So, where is everyone else?"

She grinned, then shrugged. "Dunno. Went home I guess."

"You're here alone?" Devon asked.

"No, I'm not alone. I got Dani with me, too."

"Who's Dani?" Jet and Devon asked together.

"A friend."

Jet paused, waiting for her to elaborate. "And where is she?"

"Dunno. Up on the roof maybe? She likes it up there." She took another drag, then laughed, puffing smoke out everywhere. "She likes to fight off big birds who try to eat her. Guess she didn't even see you guys comin'. Normally she tells me these things. Oh well. Good thing you're not a threat."

Jet scrunched his brow in both confusion and offense. He popped his chest out and lowered his voice. "Dani's a fairy?"

Quinn pointed her cigarette fingers at him. "You're quick."

"I love fairies! Can I see her?" Devon asked, bouncing on his feet.

"She'll come down when she's ready. Besides, I want to know more about you two. You haven't told me why you're here or how you even found me." She took one last long drag and squashed the butt into the ground.

"Knox," Jet stated, calming down a bit. "We found the leader of the NFA. But Knox and our group were taken. We came here to find help."

Quinn's lavender eyes grew large. "No way. What happened?"

"Natalia," Devon scowled.

Quinn raised a brow and sat cross legged on the bare concrete floor. "Who?"

Jet answered as he found a box to sit on. "I don't know a lot of the family drama, but I guess she's the sister of Knox's wife, Avani. She's always around a gang of big dudes, carrying big guns."

"Probably compensating for something, if you catch my drift," Quinn laughed but then got serious when Jet didn't react. "I mean, that sucks. What are you gonna do?"

"Take her down!" Devon pounded his tiny fist into his tiny hand.

"Dev, man. Chill out," Jet said.

"Jet wants you to cool your jets," Quinn said and side-eyed at Jet, pausing for a reaction. When none came, she laughed at her own joke. "Sorry, been waiting ta use that since you told me your name."

Jet breathed out a small chuckle, enough for Devon to turn to him with a raised brow. His cheeks grew pink. He hadn't realized how long it had been since he laughed.

Quinn messed with her hair and spoke. "Well, I'm sorry to hear that about Knox. I heard a lot about him; never met him m'self. But, I don't know what I can do to help. Me and Dani have really taken a likin' to this place. Plus, now that stuff has settled, it probably won't be used for a hideout anymore. I did always want to live in the country. It's so open. No noise. Except when Dani's fighting with a hawk."

Jet laughed again, this time catching Quinn's attention, and it made her smile. Jet noticed how beautiful her smile was with full, soft lips and perfect teeth. A flash of Lacey's face and smile went through his mind, and he paused. He came back to reality and shook his head. His smile dissipated. Pushing his hands into his knees, he stood up and took a drink of his flask.

"It was——-" Jet began.

"Oh, whatcha got there?" Quinn asked as she eyballed his flask. "Vodka, bourbon, little whiskey?"

Jet smirked, "Try it and find out." He began to unscrew the cap.

"Don't bother, mate," she said with a wave of her hand. "The only poison I like in my body is from these. That stuff..." she waved the cigarette box in front of him and pointed at his flask, "that stuff changes you."

Her words were soft yet strangely profound. Has it changed him? It was just alcohol. As he was about to give a rebuttal, Devon changed the subject.

"How come no one stayed behind with you?"

"Oh, uh, everyone had families, ya know? Dani is my family now. We just exist together."

"Like Syd and Raoul!"

"Uh, yeah, like them," Quinn said with unsure eyes. "Were they the ones who got taken away?"

Jet replied. "Syd is short for Sydona, which is the one the doctor was after. She actually chose to stay behind. Raoul is her fairy."

"She chose to stay? Why in the world would she do that?"

Devon spoke up. "Her dad's there. He's old, and she didn't want to leave him."

Quinn raised both brows. "Her dad, too? Shit, I feel like there's a whole lot that I'm missing."

Devon began to explain things, starting with the day his parents were killed. Unable to listen, Jet left them alone.

He walked out of earshot, which was difficult as every word that came out of Devon's mouth bounced off the walls. Quinn was polite, letting him get it all out without interrupting. He found a door in the very back of the place and opened it. It wasn't much bigger than a janitor's closet but resembeled a bedroom. A small cot layered in blankets and pillows hid in the very back. A sheet hung over part of it, held back with string to be swiftly let down for privacy. Closer to the door stood a dresser, littered with clothes, ammo, hair ties, and feathers of varying sizes. Above it, a corkboard held letters, photos, and postcards. One picture in particular caught his eye. In it was Quinn, a fairy, and another girl who looked similar to her. They were at a beach standing next to a big sand castle with big smiles and holding their arms out with pride. The fairy stood on top of it as if she were overseeing a queendom. Jet wondered who the girl was and why she wasn't with Quinn.

Just then a flying object flew into the side of his head hard enough to throw him slightly off balance.

"What in the—" a voice said from his right.

Jet whipped around to see a fairy with midnight blue wings, forest green hair, and golden eyes.

"Oh, you must be Dani. Sorry about—"

"Quinn? Quiiinn!" she bellowed as she flew out of the bedroom.

"Sorry about… that." Jet's voice faded because she was already gone. He left the room, shut the door and followed the yelling.

"Hey! It's about time you graced us with your presence, Dandelion!" Quinn said loudly.

"Why do you always need to say my full name in front of new people?" Dani growled. Her voice had more of an Irish sound and a slightly higher pitch.

"Because it's your name, Dandelion."

Dani threw her head back in frustration. "I will forever hate my parents for naming me that. And forever hate *you* for telling every person on the planet!"

"Oh, you love me," she said while kissing her index and middle finger and tapping them on the top of Dani's head.

Dani fluttered off from her with a scowl.

"I like your name," Devon said quietly and smiled at the uniquely colored fairy.

"Oh?" she asked.

"Yeah, dandelions are my favorite flower!"

Dani grinned. "No kidding! What's your name, then?"

"My name's Devon."

"Nice ta meet ya. What are you all doing here?"

Quinn spoke up. "Don't waste your breath, Dani. They were just leaving,"

"No, we're not leaving yet, are we?" Devon asked and glanced up at Jet, forgetting that he was mad at him. It only lasted a moment before he remembered and looked away..

Jet sighed and rubbed the back of his neck. "Yeah, I guess so. But since you won't help, got any weapons we can take back with us?" he asked the girls, but Quinn was busy whispering to Dani and redoing her hair.

"Hey," Jet repeated. "Any guns?"

Quinn perked up, and turned her full attention to him. "Oh, sure. Why not?" she said while tracing her index finger across Jet's jaw. Jet's head turned with her touch, as if she had flipped a switch. Quinn led him to the far end of the building, still walking beside the large metal cylinders. More lockers stood against the wall that she unlocked with ease. She handed him a pistol, a shotgun with a wrap, and ammo.

"Can the little one shoot a gun? And more importantly, do you want him to shoot something? And by shoot I mean kill," she said, holding up another handgun.

Jet held his hands out for the weapons, but her words made him think. Devon was still mad. Perhaps letting him have a gun wasn't the best idea. And as Quinn put it, could he allow a ten year old to kill a person? He suddenly realized how much Devon must be going through and that he was the main cause of it. The weight of the flask in his pocket got heavier. He needed to be there for him.

"Jet?" Quinn asked, pulling him back into the present.

"No, uh, nevermind. I'll just keep these for me." He nodded and swallowed hard.

She put the gun back and closed the locker with a sideways smirk on her face. They both looked over at Devon and Dani having a great time. Dani sprinkled her black and blue dust on Devon, making him float up a few inches. Jet glanced back at Quinn with a twist in his stomach. Rubbing his chin with his finger nervously, he reached into his oversized pocket and handed Quinn a map.

"This is where we're going. I know you can't help, but you'll know where to find someone. In case you get sick of this place."

She smiled politely and folded it back up. "Thanks, Jet. And I wish we could, ya know?"

"Yeah…" Jet said soberly. He took a deep breath and walked back to Devon and the fairy.

"Ready?"

Devon brushed off the dust, though it had mostly disappeared. "I guess," he said, barely moving his lips.

"Thanks, Quinn. Dani. Hope to see you soon," Jet said as the two boys stood in the doorway.

"Nice meeting you both," Dani said, waving.

Devon waved, then walked outside. Jet took one last look at Quinn's lavender eyes. She quickly flashed him a wink, then turned around to light up another cigarette. A smile curved across Jet's blushing face. He caught up with Devon and flew up high into the clouds.

Chapter Ten

RAOUL

Raoul flew ahead of Harold until the sound of the alarm dissolved into crickets. With each flutter of his wings taking him farther and farther away from Jubilee, his insides crumpled. Harold headed toward the ocean, where a large cliff looked out over the crashing waves.

"Where are you going?" Raoul asked. He almost couldn't form words. His mouth was as dry as the sand below.

"Found this little cavern down here 'few years ago. I wanna see if it's still intact."

Raoul followed Harold as he shimmied his way down the steep cliff about twenty feet. His boots hit the white sand and navigated several more feet until they reached a natural hole in the side. It was small, and Harold had to squeeze himself inside, but once he did, it opened up to a large room. He grabbed a matchbox from his jeans and struck a match to light an old-fashioned lantern. The flame revealed the ceiling being much higher up than he thought, and there was ample space, almost as large as Harold's actual apartment. For being so close to the ocean, the cave was surprisingly dry. Raoul could have mistaken this place for Harold's second home.

"Why is this here?" Raoul asked.

Harold sat on his bed, lined with several layers of blankets. "Oh, ya know. Gotta be prepared."

Raoul casually flew around the cave, trying to understand why so many things were down there.

"Is this like a bomb shelter?"

"Yeah, kinda like a bomb shelter. And I'd say the bomb's gone off, wouldn't you?"

Raoul sat on a stack of magazines with scantily dressed women. "What do you suppose she's done to her?"

Harold scratched the back of his neck. "I find it best to not think about things like that."

"You know what he did to the fairy at Eagle Lake, don't you?"

He looked away from him and only gave one tiny nod.

"I can't understand why Sydona would trust him now, even after I told her what he did. I trust *her*, but..." He faded off and held back tears.

Harold cleared his throat. "I had this friend, back in middle school, who used to take bullfrogs from the creek by our houses and put them in a little tank. He just loved 'em. He had up to ten of 'em at one point in this one little cage. I told him he needed to let them go, but ya know, keepin' one was fine. But he wanted all of them, even though they was walkin' on top of each other. His momma wouldn't buy another tank for him and wanted him to get rid of 'em too. Few days later, one died. I hated seein' those things locked up where they could barely walk. So I took it upon m'self to free them. Even if it meant he'd hate me for it. And he did. But I still felt it was the best thing for them. But he forgave me a few years later. He understood. It hurt at the time to have him hate me, but it had to be done."

Raoul crossed his arms and stood up. "So, are you saying, I need to do the right thing, even if it means Syd might hate me for it?"

Harold shrugged. "I been working with that man most of my adult life. After everything I have learned since then, I trust 'im as much as I hate you. In other words, I don't."

A quick smile curled on Raoul's face. "Thanks for trying to help, Harold. But Malik isn't a tank of frogs. He's a big guy with an entire fleet of armed men behind him. I can't exactly kill him on my own. I'd get squashed like a bug."

"What if I help?" Harold said. He stood up and pulled up his pants. "I can talk to folks. Maybe I can convince them to turn against 'im like I did. If we do that, he's lost."

"How are you going to do that? You can't just walk around handing out flyers to people."

Harold grinned. "Nah, it wouldn't be nothin' like that. I know pretty much everyone here. While some may not like me, they know how close I was with John, and that might be enough to convince 'em."

Raoul stroked his chin. "Maybe. But Syd still doesn't want us to do anything until he's able to make her fly."

Harold threw his hands up and smiled wider. "He ain't gonna do it, Raoul. He's never been able to do it. In the twenty-seven years I been here, he's never been able to crack it. Why don't none of y'all believe me?" He muttered the last sentence under his breath.

"He's never had Syd before though. She's a hybrid, or whatever. Isn't that all he needed?" Raoul asked.

"I'm tellin' ya. He's had fliers like her before. Where they got a human parent and a flier parent—"

"But she's the only one who's been able to actually fly—"

"Is that what he told you?" Harold laughed, and Raoul wanted to burst like a cherry bomb. He continued, "I don't mean to laugh, little man, but how could you really believe she's ever been the only one? It's rare, yes. He's only been able to find a handful in all his life. But not a single one of 'em helped."

Raoul felt his heart pounding in his throat. He didn't want to ask his next question, but another part of him needed to know. "What did he do with the others?"

Harold let out a sigh. "I think you know, bud."

Raoul smoothed his hair back and lifted his chin but trembled as he thought of the inevitable. Sydona wouldn't let that happen, right? She would see through him. It was one of her many talents.

"Well, where do we go from here, Harold?"

"I say we just wait it out 'til mornin'. 'Til things calm down." He flopped back down on his bed, pulled something out of his pocket, and twisted it around in his fingers.

Raoul tilted his head. "What's that?"

Harold side-eyed him and shrugged. "Oh, it's just a little rock I carry around with me."

"A rock?"

He smirked. "It's silly, but Willow actually threw this rock at me a long time ago. When we was in the Army and got a little drunk. I was teasin' her about somethin', and she threw the first thing she could find at me. It's got a couple sharp edges but then some smooth ones. Parts of it sparkle, and it's pink in some spots. I used to think her favorite color was pink, and she called me sexist. It's yella'. But, when she threw it, she had the biggest smile on her face… and I knew I was in love. She don't know I have it.

Prolly don't even remember that day. But I do; like it was yesterday…"

"Wow, Harold. I never pegged you for a romantic," said Raoul.

Harold nodded his head and smirked. "Guess I kinda am, huh?"

Raoul grinned and hearing his stories somehow made him more relaxed. Harold lay back on his cot and pulled out a magazine. After only a few minutes, though, images of Jubilee flashed in Raoul's head, and he became anxious again.

He paced around the cave, thinking of everything going on around him. Sydona could be in danger, Jubilee was a prisoner, and the rest of the Sparrows disappeared. It was time to take action. By himself he was nearly invisible. He could go back to Natalia's apartment, now that he knew where it was. He understood Harold's need to stay hidden, but Raoul needed to save them. He might be the only one willing to do so.

The first thing he needed to do was find the key to the cage holding Jubilee. He flew around to piles of things gathered around the cave and ended up finding a compact swiss army knife. It wasn't very heavy, so Raoul flew off with it. He heard Harold yell something as he left the cave, but he only beat his wings faster.

He quickly returned to the apartment building. The alarm had finally stopped, but a large crowd had gathered around it. Raoul froze in midair. He wanted to fly off, run away, and avoid being captured like Jubilee. His heart pounded hard in his chest. Finally, he lifted his chin, brushed his hair back, narrowed his eyes, and continued on his way to the apartment. He flew as fast as he possibly could to avoid being seen. He noticed a couple of heads turn while he flew past, but they couldn't spot him. He then arrived at a window attached to Natalia's apartment. Blinds fell over the window, but to his luck, an end piece was missing, and Raoul used the opening to look inside.

A soft yellow glow caught his eye first and there Jubilee was. He released a smile, but it faded as two very difficult obstacles became apparent. The window was completely closed with no clear entry nearby. And two Vultures stood in the room with her. Raoul panicked as he tried to think of how to get her to safety, but then, Jubilee stepped out of the cage and stretched her wings.

"What in the—" Raoul said to himself.

A man with blonde, shaggy hair then put the lock and key on the table next to the bolted down cage.

In his shock, Raoul didn't notice the other Vulture, with black rimmed glasses walking toward him to open the window.

Raoul jumped back and floated in the air a safe distance from the soldier.

"Uncle?!" Jubilee squealed.

A large smile swept across Raoul's face as Jubilee flew wobbly into him with extended arms. Squeezing her tightly, he closed his eyes, trying to slow the moment down as much as possible.

"I can't believe you're here, Uncle Raoul!" Jubilee said in a high pitched lilt.

"I could say the same about you." Noticing some rips and tears in her yellow wings, he suddenly felt a huge sense of responsibility. It was only a few months ago he was complaining to Sydona about how much she annoyed him, but it somehow felt like years.

"Why were you gone so long, uncle?"

Raoul brushed her long auburn hair out of her face. "I will explain everything later, but I promise, I'll never leave again." He took her hand and they landed on the window sill.

Jubilee hugged him again with that answer. Raoul continued to caress her head but then looked up at the Vultures.

"Why did you let her go?"

The man with glasses answered. "Just because Natalia does shit like this, doesn't mean we all do."

"The war is basically over," the blonde hair guy said. "Hell, we don't even know why we're still here."

"War?" Jubilee asked nervously. "What's going on?"

Raoul looked down at her and took a deep breath. "Syd's in a lot of danger. Do you wanna help her?"

"Yes, I want to help. It's *Syd*!" she said.

Raoul grinned and squeezed her hand. He glanced back up at the guards and crossed his arms, showing them he wasn't afraid.

"Are there a lot around like you? Who are just here for Malik and not because you hate us?"

"Yeah. Most of us, actually," the man with glasses whispered. "And we all think Natalia's fuckin' lost it."

Raoul laughed. "That's an understatement!" He waved them in closer and lowered his voice. "Think you can get a group together and meet us down on the beach tomorrow?"

The blonde haired Vulture spoke up, "Whoa, are we talking about taking out John? I don't think I can do that, fellas."

"Hey!" Jubilee shouted, startling Raoul. "Do you know who Sydona even is?!"

"Well, ain't she—"

"She is the bestest person in the entire world who cooked the best food and gave my entire family a home."

"Not only that," Raoul continued. "Malik messed me up real bad and even killed a fairy for information. He needs to be stopped." His fists curled tightly.

"Yeah, we heard," the man with glasses said. "Just tell us when and where."

Raoul relaxed. These two Vultures were nothing to fear any longer. "There's a cave down by the beach.

Tell as many people as you can, but make sure you can trust them first. Meet us tonight after the sun sets."

They nodded. When Raoul was confident they'd do as he said, he flew out the bedroom window with Jubilee. A surge of adrenaline and confidence pulsed through his body. He took Jubilee's hands and twirled her around in circles. An infectious laugh from the young fairy added an explosion of joy to his heart. He never felt more alive and free.

Chapter Eleven

SYDONA

The early morning California sun drifted through the window of the foreign bedroom. Giovonna was still curled into a ball at the foot of the bed, and Silas had his arm wrapped around Sydona. It still felt weird to be sleeping in the house of the man who killed her mother and dozens of other people. But thoughts of her father kept her from standing against him. Stranger things had happened, right? The pairing of Harold and Raoul came to mind, and she instantly wondered how Raoul was doing. They disappeared into the night and hadn't come back yet. She hoped he would be able to hold his own and that Harold wouldn't slip back into his old ways.

Silas woke up slowly, pulled her in with his arm, and gave her a kiss with his super fresh morning breath. She reciprocated, knowing hers wasn't any better. She turned around to face him, and they both stared at each other with half-lidded eyes.

"Morning," he whispered.

"Morning." She smiled back, nuzzled her head into him, and twisted her body to face the ceiling. Being in his presence made her feel incredibly safe. She wanted to stay in that moment forever.

He then yawned and asked softly. "So, what's the plan today?"

She let out a heavy sigh as she realized she would have to face the chaos around her, though she desperately wanted a moment to forget. "I'm going to talk to the doctor about Gia helping. Just saying it out loud makes me so nervous I could vomit."

Silas laughed. "I wish I could help. I feel so useless."

"You're not useless. But I really don't know what you could do…" Sydona said as she ran her fingers through his hair.

"Ooh, I know! I could kill him," he said with a casual shrug.

"Silas, stop."

"What? Was that not the plan all along?"

"Yes but, give him a chance to see if he can help me first."

"Yeah, yeah, but listen. After he gets you to fly and all that, I'll sneak up behind him and bam! We go home and make sweet, passionate love." His eyebrows wiggled along with a flirty lip bite.

"Ugg, you guys. I'm still here," Giovonna groaned.

"Good morning, Gia," Sydona said softly.

Giovonna turned away from them and pulled her blanket over her head.

Sydona took the opportunity to get up and out of bed.

"Hey, where you going?" asked Silas.

"To the bathroom. Is that okay?"

"Only if you promise to bring me a souvenir when you get back."

Sydona rolled her eyes playfully and shoved Silas. She let out a yawn as she headed for the en suite bathroom. The door clicked shut, and she smelled her own breath. Her nose scrunched as she looked for a toothbrush that was either sealed or looked untouched. She never considered herself someone who needed a lot, but hygiene was hard to escape. Since she couldn't find anything, she used her finger as a temporary substitute. She felt silly as she watched herself in the mirror. But her eyes soon caught her attention. She imagined what they would look like as their natural lavender color. A grin grew across her face as the feeling got stronger. She scrubbed her teeth as quickly and as hard as she could, then rinsed. Leaving the bathroom, she glanced over to Silas and Giovonna who had decided to sleep in a bit longer.

Somersaults rolled through her stomach as she crept down the hallway to see if the doctor was in his office. Her toes sank into the bleach white carpet, while her hands ran across the dark red wallpaper lining the hallway. Her ears soon caught whispers from the room at the end. She paused. One of the voices was obviously the doctor's and the other sounded like Avani's sister.

"Natalia, I am not going to say it again!" Malik said. His tone was deep and authoritative.

"We both know *I* am the reason she's here. Me alone. I'm entitled to all of it!" said Natalia.

"You needlessly killed six more of my soldiers just so you could roll in riches. What am I to tell their families when we need to bury all of them with none of the reward?"

"Oh please, you don't give a goddamn shit about any of those guys! You are going back on your promise, and that's fucked up. You can't do that!"

"I can do whatever I want. That's the beauty of being me," John said coolly.

Natalia paused for a moment. "I know what this is… you don't have it, do you?"

"Have what?" he replied lazily.

"The money, you pendejo…"

"Did you not hear me the first time, Ms. Flores? Your selfish behavior of putting good men in your path of destruction just to get money, it's despicable. You don't deserve a penny."

"Don't even go there, John! Don't preach to me about using people for selfish reasons."

Malik's voice grew louder than Sydona's ever heard. "Don't speak to me this way in my own office, in my own *house*! Leave! You're done here."

"Are you— what do you mean, done?!" Natalina squawked.

His voice lowered but remained stern. "You know what I mean."

"You can't… You can't fire me! I brought you the bitch! You'd still be looking for her if it wasn't for me!"

"Be fortunate I am just firing you and not having you killed, Ms. Flores," he threatened. "Leave, now."

The room was silent for a moment. "You gonna regret sayin' that, hombre. Better watch 'ya back."

Next thing Sydona knew, Natalia bumped into her in the hallway.

She stumbled into a freeze. Sydona's heart sank. Natalia gave her a look. A look so fierce, hateful, and intense that it was difficult to look away. Sydona stared back with the same intensity, and her hands shook with anticipation. Ready for anything. Natalia got even closer to her, and she quickly released a sharp smirk. And with a wink, she walked off.

Sydona glanced back at her, unsure of what the smile meant. Shaking it off, she continued to the doctor's office. She knocked, and he happily invited her inside.

"Sydona! How good to see you! Please, sit," he said, waving his hand over a chair on the opposite side of the desk.

Her feet moved closer to the chair, but she didn't know how she brought herself to move. Her legs were numb.

"How did you sleep, then?" he asked. His pleasantries still had a strange ring to them. Especially because this one in particular was the same question he asked at Eagle Lake. Flashes of the tents, the cots, and the battle made her heart race. All she wanted to do was finish the job she started.

"It was fine, thanks," she replied quickly.

"Wonderful. How did your friends sleep?"

Her eyes widened. "How—"

"—How did I know? Sydona, this is my home. I know everything." He smiled. His perfect, blinding white teeth sparkled, and she had a sudden urge to turn them red again. But his casual attitude hinted that he was okay with her friends being there.

"You won't hurt them, will you?" she asked timidly.

"As long as they don't hurt me, we'll be one big happy family."

Sydona swallowed. Her foot tapped the hardwood floor rapidly. "What else do you know?"

Doctor Malik relished in the baited question and slumped back in his shiny leather chair. "Well, I know that since you and I are finally together, I have dissolved the remaining labs. Your little rebellion group no longer has a purpose. Everyone is free to do as they please and can stop threatening me and my organization."

"You've killed a lot of people, doctor." Her words were tight and unapologetic.

"Oh, have I? You think you haven't? You think this has been a one way battle where I've only killed your people and mine are all scot-free? On the contrary, Miss Wilder. Before Eagle Lake, I had a staff of five-hundred and thirty-four, and now it's less than two-hundred. How many, Miss Wilder, have *you* lost?"

Her heart sped up and brows furrowed. "If it weren't for your fucking camps, none of this would have happened. You selfishly set your men up to protect you. And what did you do when things got too dangerous? You fucking ran away, like a cowardice piece of shit. I'm surprised they even still follow you after you led them to the slaughter. Not to mention, you even have a building full of children who can't even fly yet. The I.D.F… Institution for Developing Fliers. Fucking, *children,* John!"

"As I said, I have dissolved all of those places. Besides, the I.D.F didn't harm any of those kids. I'm not heartless. They needed to go some place while their parents were otherwise incompasitated. They would have ended up on the streets if—"

"Yeah because their parents were ripped away from them! How can you act so casually about this?!" Her blood boiled. His nonchalant behavior was enough to make her pull her hair out.

He paused and leaned forward in his chair, his hands folded over one another on the desk. "Look. We have both done questionable things. But, if it weren't for me telling the media about Eagle Lake, I never would have found you. And for that... I am undoubtedly and extremely grateful. If I hadn't escaped, you would probably have killed me, and then you wouldn't be able to ever fly again."

Sydona glared at him. "You're the one who took my ability away! Stop making yourself sound like a goddamn hero!"

He smirked, sat back again, and answered her with just a shrug. Her fists clenched. If this was what it was going to be like to work with him, it was going to be more difficult than she anticipated. She sat down in the chair and gripped the armrests tightly, her nails engraving the wood.

Malik finally spoke up. "So, where's your little fairy guy?" His hand waved in the air as if to symbolize wings.

"He's around," Sydona said with a clenched jaw. Malik was her answer to flying again, and he knew he was in control. It was almost as if he enjoyed irritating her.

"You don't know where he is?"

Sydona looked away from him. "He's somewhere plotting, probably."

"Plotting?" he said, amusement in his words. "Plotting what? My demise?"

She sighed. "Yep."

The doctor laughed hard and removed his glasses to wipe tears from his eyes.

Sydona snapped to her feet. "Can we get started now, or what?"

"Sure, sure we can. But you came in here for something else, didn't you?" he said, put his glasses back on, and stared intently at her.

She crossed her arms and exhaled from her nose. "I think Giovonna could help. She's incredibly smart when it comes to technology."

The man stared at her as if she would say more, then jerked his head back. "I don't think so," he said as he tapped a pile of papers on his desk and stood.

Sydona's brows furrowed. "Why not?"

"I do not need to answer questions in my own house!" he shouted. Then he instantly calmed and fixed his suit jacket. Clearing his throat, he walked over to the secret entrance and waited.

Sydona swallowed hard and kept to herself. The anger that raged inside her quickly dissolved. His shouting brought Knox's short temper and outbursts to mind. But Malik was different from Knox, more volatile and unpredictable. One wrong move, one wrong question could push him over the edge.

Her heart pounded as she followed him down the dark steps. She knew he wouldn't hurt her again, but that didn't mean he wouldn't go after her friends or her father. They walked past the first room where they first spoke.

He then led her to a larger room filled with monitors, wires, and devices completely foreign to her. It was definitely in Giovonna's wheelhouse. He opened a gray locker against the marble wall and grabbed a white lab coat. He put it on over his suit, went straight to a computer, and began typing. Sydona stood nearby, looking around and waiting until the silence became too much.

"What's the first thing we need to do?"

The bluish glow of the computer screen reflected off his bright white grin, and he said without looking up, "Someone's an eager beaver."

Sydona furrowed her brow. "I suppose." She looked to him for direction, but he kept typing and staring at the screen. "Do we need fairies for this to work?"

"No, no fairies. I just need to see how you fare with what I have so far. Here." He grabbed a bottle from his coat pocket and handed her a little round blue pill. Then, he continued typing.

"Do I get some water?"

He glanced up quickly then back to his glowing screen. "Just throw it way back; you don't need water."

Sydona averted her eyes in annoyance. The simple action of ingesting a strange pill made her hesitant. She stared at the blue pill, slowly dissolving from the sweat on her palm. It was the only thing standing between flying or walking. A flier or human. Still, could she bring herself to swallow something the infamous Dr. John Malik gave her? She toyed with the idea of wrapping one of the dozens of wires in the room around his throat instead. A dead doctor wouldn't do her any good though.

He glanced at her open hand. She turned away from him, threw the pill down her throat, and swallowed. After only a minute, the doctor led her down another set of steps. Sydona remembered Willow talking about locations with huge rooms for fliers to fly indoors without being seen by onlookers. It was a narrow space, about eight feet wide, but the ceiling was closer to thirty feet high, and the room stretched easily a hundred feet back. The doctor said nothing as he hooked her up to the same machine they used back at Eagle Lake. Sydona was already familiar with the set up and couldn't help but think of the first time she saw her parents again. A miniscule smile curled the edge of her lips.

"Ready?" he asked as he typed the last thing on the portable computer.

"Sure," Sydona said. Her pulse pounded in her ears. It could have been the drugs, but deep down, she was actually excited. She hoped it would work. But she feared it could turn out to be like the Vila Prah, and she would land flat on her face again. The ground was solid concrete, along with the walls. No soft, cushy grass landings here. If the pill failed, it would hurt more than just her pride.

"Can you feel it working yet?" he asked.

"What's it supposed to feel like?"

"Not entirely sure."

Great, she thought to herself.

"Alright, do I just go whenever?" she asked with a shrug.

"Be my guest." He waved his hand out in front of him and bowed slightly.

Sydona focused straight out in front of her. They were standing in nothing but a cold, concrete cage. She lifted her left foot first and took off into a sprint. Her body began to feel weightless, and her heart jumped with excitement. As both feet left the ground, she leaned her body forward and slightly up to elevate higher. Nothing happened. Her body stayed at the same level the entire time. If she leaned any further up, her toes would scrap the concrete. After only a minute, she forced her legs back down and jogged to a stop on the ground.

"Wh—what happened?" the doctor queried. His voice echoed from the other side.

She shook her head, shrugged, and slumped back to him.

"Why'd you stop?"

"I couldn't get higher. My hand could still touch the ground."

"Oh. Well how do you normally get higher?" he asked.

"Just have to lean forward a little. But not too much or you'll float back down to a landing position. It wasn't letting me get very high at all."

"Right. I see. It wouldn't do much good if we could only fly a few feet up."

Sydona finally made it back to the start. "Not really." Her excitement weighed down. The fact she could fly, even if only a little, made her trust the doctor much more. He was on to something.

Doctor Malik took his glasses off and used the edge of it to tap against his chin. "I wonder… What if I start you in a higher position?"

Sydona's stomach tightened as she relived the past. "You're not throwing me off a fucking cliff again."

"No!" he laughed. "No, no, not at all. I wouldn't dream of putting you through that again. I just mean, let's get a platform for you to run upon. Like wooden boards or something. Put it a couple feet high?"

Sydona relaxed. "Um, yeah. That might work."

"Excellent. I'll get Dwayne and Jake to set it up." He typed a couple of things on the computer and walked out of the room. Sydona followed him out as he picked up a corded phone on the wall. He ended the call and turned to her with a large smile. "This might take a while. Breakfast?"

Sydona looked back at him with wide, confused eyes. "Okay, sure."

Chapter Twelve

KNOX

Numbness faded from his body, and his eyes slowly opened to stare at the concrete floor, dotted with blood. A pounding in his head caused him to wake up. To his dismay, his hands and feet were bound to a metal chair bolted to the ground. Knox used all his strength to try freeing himself from the ropes, but they didn't budge. He glanced around the room to see nothing but dusty corners. The wounds on his body began to sear with pain. The blood on the ground was his. He had fought hard against the Vultures, leaving him with cuts on his arms when he almost got the upper hand and scratch marks on his face from Natalia's unnaturally pointed nails. What bothered him more than the pain: Avani was nowhere in sight.

He did his best to hear anything outside of the room he was in, which was protected with a clear wall. It was eerily silent. "Hey!" he shouted, then cleared his voice. "Hey!"

He stopped because it was so loud, hurting his own ears, but he hoped someone around heard him. He had no plan. He just wanted to get out and find his wife. Feeling completely useless, Knox tried to free himself. He swayed back and forth as hard as he could, but he was only able to make an inch of progress. Sweat covered his face, glistening off his bare head and dripping down to his chest. He roared out in frustration and a vein popped out from his temple.

Just then, a man casually walked in front of his area, holding his chin high and popping his knuckles. The smirk and low-set eyelids were enough to make Knox want to punch him in the face. As Knox attempted to free his hands again, the man saw the struggle and guffawed. He then turned his head and said something, but the words weren't clear.

The guard entered a code on the side of the wall and an opening appeared from nowhere. Sound poured into his cell. He heard screaming coming from down the hall, and it put a sharp pain in his chest. He recognized the cries as Willow's, but he could not help the small pang of relief he felt when he realized it was not Avani. Soon the screaming stopped, and a clacking from heels rushed toward him. Natalia then appeared in front of the entrance. She stopped and posed with her hips all the way to one side causing her chest to heave from the opposite. Her lips were bright red, and she bit them while gazing longingly into Knox's eyes.

"You might wanna leave, amigo. This shit gonna get nasty," she said to the guard with a permanent douchebag face.

"Don't have too much fun, man," he said to Knox and walked away.

Natalia laughed, then squealed in excitement. The way she sauntered to him reminded him of an alley cat. Her claws even matched this vision. Knox's heart sped up with each clack of her heels. She hardly had any clothing on, just enough to cover up. He was unsure if she was the one putting Willow in pain since she looked perfectly intact. Her makeup, hair, and clothes were perfectly placed. With how dolled-up Natalia looked, she reminded him of Avani. His blood began to boil thinking of her.

He looked her up and down. It was hard to resist. He never realized how alike they looked before. Knox had always been in a hurry and also wanting to murder her every time they met.

"Like what you see, Knoxy Poo?" she asked in a disturbing baby voice.

He tensed.

She finally reached him and one of her hands instantly caressed his manhood. Knox quivered and tried to get up, but the rope was sturdy as ever. He caught a whiff of her scent, and it made his nose hairs curl.

"Ooh, big boy. I've been waiting for this for a very long time," she said and began to undo his pants.

"What the hell are you doing?!" Knox shouted.

Natalia stopped as she crouched right in front of him. She looked up at him with sad eyes and slightly messy hair. "What's wrong, baby? Do you have a problem?"

"Where's my wife, Nat?"

"Don't you mean, where's my sister? And who cares? You have me now. We look a lot alike, don't you think?" She changed positions trying to look more like Avani.

Knox had to let out a laugh. "You're fucking crazy."

"Stop laughing! This is all hers! Don't you pay attention to anything? Dios mio. I'm your wife now, Elias." She bit her lip again and continued working on the pants.

"Wait, what? What do you mean?" His body shook with rage at what her words really meant.

"Come on, why are we still talking about her when I am standing—" she paused to stand slowly, pushing her body onto his, then sat on his leg. "—right in front of you."

Crossing her legs, she put an arm around Knox and kissed him passionately. Her tongue kept trying to make an entrance, but Knox refused to give in. He broke away from her and twisted his head away as fast as he could. She grabbed his face with her nails and forced him to face her. As she went in again, she paused as she heard a commotion down the hall.

Knox thought it sounded like a fight between two men and it kept Natalia's attention. She stood up straight and ran to the cell door, popping her head around to hear.

The commotion ended and it fell silent, with the sound of a door clicking.

Natalia called out, "Adam? Or... Aiden?" she scoffed. "Whatever. Is that you?"

A man's voice answered her, with a very southern twang. "Guess again, sweetheart."

Knox could feel her heart jump from across the room. Natalia pivoted back to Knox and cursed under her breath. "Shit."

She quickly put her clothes back on, not even paying attention if they were inside out and backwards. Knox smiled seeing her unequipped. The voice sounded like Harold which made him even happier, knowing their history. As she finished, she grabbed a tiny switch knife and swiftly cut all of Knox's ties apart.

"What are you doing?" Knox asked, confused on why she was letting him free.

"Shut the fuck up and don't make me slice your neck open," Natalia whispered in his ear.

Knox swallowed hard. She stood him up and kept her blade next to his neck, while she stood behind him and walked outside of the cell door. They turned to face Harold standing in the hallway and he pointed his pistol at them.

"Shoot me, he's dead," Natalia threatened.

"Do it, Harold," Knox said.

Harold paused for a moment while he tried deciding. "I can barely see her, Knox I'll hit you."

Knox didn't push it as her blade got extremely close to his neck. He could feel a small cut forming already. He put his hands up in surrender.

"Let me go, and he's yours."

"I ain't letting you go that easily," Harold said with bared teeth.

"Do as I say, Harold," Knox said sternly and winked.

Harold slowly lowered his gun at Knox's command. With Harolds guard down, Natalia slid past Harold, keeping her eyes directly on his, no words. As she backed toward the entrance of the cells, she pushed Knox away and ran out of the room.

Knox put his hand up to his nicked neck and wiped the blood away.

"Why did you let her escape?" Harold asked Knox.

"We'll find her, but first we need to find Willow."

"Yes, Willow!" Harold exclaimed and shook his head.

They headed back down the hallway and just past the cell Knox was in, they heard moaning from the cell next to it. Knox knew it was Willow, and before he reached it, he saw something small glimmer from in his cell. He stopped just past the entrance and turned back. As he reached for the shiny object, he already knew what it was. His palms began to sweat. It was Avani's wedding ring. Knox formed a fist around the ring and had immediate feelings of regret.

He wanted so much to go after Natalia at that second, but from the cries Harold was making in the cell next door, he suppressed the revenge and joined the other two.

Knox's jaw dropped when he saw Willow's condition: gashes on her arms, bruises on her face, and chest. Her clothes were ripped and teeth were red. Not to mention chunks of her hair missing, leaving behind raw patches from being pulled out. As she stood, tied against a pole in the middle of the room, she turned her head to the side and spit blood out onto the concrete floor.

"Willow..." Knox said. He immediately helped Harold untie her.

"Willow, darlin', it's us. It's Harold and Knox. We're gonna get you outa here, 'kay?"

Willow nodded. "Did we take care of her, then?" She started rubbing her wrists.

"Not yet," said Knox, his eyes turning bright green.

Harold shot him a look, "Yeah, she slipped right by us..."

"That slimy little..." Willow growled. "I can't wait to get my hands on 'er. Just you and me, Nat.

You might be crazy, but you haven't even seen my crazy side yet."

Harold nodded in agreement with her and helped fix her clothes and hair. "We need to get you patched up, baby doll."

"That would be nice, yeah," Willow gave a small laugh.

Knox tore off one of his sleeves and tied it around one of the large cuts on Willow's arm. "Any idea where Avani would be?" he asked Harold.

"Uh," Harold started and shook his head. "I got no clue. She could be held up anywhere."

"Well, better start lookin' now. Ain't got no time to waste," said Willow.

They patched up Willow the best they could and started heading out. While Knox and Harold helped her walk again, Willow spoke up. "Hey, sir, why ain't you all banged up like me?"

"Oh," he stammered and cleared his throat. "Uh, no reason, I guess?"

"Wha—she just tied you up and left you there? That don't seem like her."

"No, she tortured me, just… in a different sort of way."

"Really?" Willow chuckled. "What, did she dare you to crack a smile?"

Harold laughed and began to guess himself. "Or-or, make you eat vegetables?"

Knox gritted his teeth.

Willow put more of a pep in her step. "Oh, did she make fun of—"

"She dressed up as my wife and tried to seduce me!" he shouted.

"Oh," uttered Harold.

"That's— really messed up," Willow added.

Knox rolled his eyes. "Yep. Let's just focus on finding my wife, please."

The three stayed silent the rest of the way down the hall, to the stairway and out of the garage. Knox took a deep breath and let the fresh air fill his lungs. The air had a tinge of rain and noticed dark clouds blowing in from the sea. The contrast of the clouds with the brightly colored orange and yellow fairies floating toward him, made them easy to see. Once Raoul and Jubilee noticed who they were, they flew faster to them.

"Oh my gosh, Willow!" Raoul exclaimed before he'd even reached them. "What happened to you?"

Willow winced as she took a step toward him. "Take a wild guess, buddy."

Knox could see Raoul's face turning a dark shade of pink and his hands curl into fists. "Was she just here?"

"She was," said Harold. "She got away though."

"What!" Raoul shouted. "How did she just, get away?"

"Don't worry about it now," Knox interjected. "We have to find my wife."

"Avani!" Raoul said with raised brows. "Why isn't she with you guys?"

Harold spoke up. "Dunno, she took her some-place else."

Knox's heart pounded as they stood out in the open, unsure of where Natalia went after she escaped. He looked at his surroundings and tried to determine where Avani could be. Would Natalia go back to her? If they found Avani, maybe they would find her sister as well. Willow seemed to be in a lot of pain, but finding his wife was at the top of his list.

"Raoul, can you help Willow? With your, dust thing…" Knox cleared his throat.

Raoul raised a brow. "My dust thing?"

"Yeah," Knox sighed. "You know what I mean. Make her feel her wounds less?"

He nodded, gave him a salute and covered Willow with sparkling, orange dust.

As Raoul did this, a familiar face appeared from behind a hill in the distance. Devon saw them as well and his face lit up and began to run toward them. Jet followed soon after.

Chapter Thirteen

SYDONA

Malik's alligator boots clicked up the stairs in unison with his cane. She noticed he didn't always use his cane, but when he did, she thought back to that day. Pushing the memory down, she followed him down the hall and to the kitchen. The living room and kitchen lit up brilliantly as the sun shone through the giant windows. The white that decorated everything beamed even brighter, and it took her eyes a minute to adjust from the darkness of the basement.

Heading straight for the refrigerator, Malik began to grab items and spread them out on the counter. Sydona moved to sit down near him, though she felt weird sitting opposite of him. Malik hummed a melody as he cut up peppers and tomatoes, and she felt like she was dreaming again. To erase the feeling, she walked around the living room, looking at strange statues placed in random corners. Pictures littered the room of mostly scenery or abstract black and white photos; none of them were of people. She wondered again about the drawing she found in the kitchen drawer.

"Who's Priyah?" she asked casually.

The doctor paused his chopping. "It's rude to go around snooping in a house that isn't yours."

"Who is she though?" Sydona was on pins and needles as she observed the large knife in his hand.

"Why don't you invite your friends? I'm sure they're hungry, yes?" he asked and continued his chopping of mushrooms.

She glanced at him from across the room, and he stared blankly over his lenses at her and waited for an answer.

"Yeah, uh, sure. I'll go get them." Sydona sauntered across the living room and passed the kitchen.

"Oh, uh, you're not allergic to anything, are you?" he asked. "Onions or eggs or anything?"

Sydona stopped suddenly. She turned to him and shook her head.

"Excellent. I'm making my world famous omelet."

Sydona looked away wide eyed, but then turned back. "I don't eat meat, though…"

He smiled. "No bacon for me either, then."

Sydona smirked with confused brows but kept walking back to her room. She gave the secret knock, and Giovonna opened up.

"Hey," said Sydona.

"What's going on?" Giovonna asked.

"Nothing, yet. But, he invited all of us for breakfast."

"What? Seriously?" Silas asked from the bed.

Sydona wandered over and sat next to him, taking his hand. "Yeah. It's strange. He even asked if I was allergic to anything."

"That was nice of him," Giovonna said.

"Yeah, that's the strange part."

"Well none of this has been exactly normal, Syd. What's one more thing?" Silas said.

"I suppose."

Giovonna spoke up. "Is it okay though? If we go down there?"

"I think so. If he wanted to do anything, he would have done it by now, right?"

"That's not terrifying to think about at all," Silas said sarcastically.

Sydona chuckled. "It'll be fine. I'm going to tell my dad. I'll meet you down there." She helped Silas off the bed; his leg still caused him to limp. Giovonna led him down the hall while Sydona knocked on her father's bedroom door.

No answer. She turned the knob and it opened. "Dad?"

Ian was in bed but didn't move. Her heart leapt, and she rushed over.

"Dad!" she cried, shaking him.

"What?" Ian mumbled and rolled to face her. "Oh, Syd. You startled me."

Sydona examined his eyes and face, and he seemed much different than the other day. "Have you been in bed this whole time?"

Ian sat up slowly and flipped the comforter off him. He was still wearing the same clothes. "No, no. I've been up. I just... got tired again and laid back down. It's such a nice bed."

Sydona helped him stand up, but he wobbled. Putting his arm around her, she had to physically lift him up. His feet touched the floor, but once Sydona let him go, he flopped back down on the bed.

"Dad, are you okay?"

"I'm fine, darling. How've you been?" he asked, then coughed. He forced out a few more raspy coughs, cleared his throat, and then smiled at her. His smile mimicked his breaking heart, and it caused her to mourn internally. She sat next to him in bed and put her arm around him. It was then she noticed wet sheets and she swallowed.

"The doctor is making some breakfast. Do you want me to bring you some?" She could barely get the words out normally.

"No, I'll go down there. Just give me a couple minutes. Okay, sweetheart?" he said. His words were shaky and faint.

Sydona held back tears. "At least let me find some new sheets for you."

Ian turned his head to look back, as if he had just realized what he did. As he faced forward again, tears streamed down his wrinkled cheeks.

"Oh, Syd. I miss Evey so much..." he cried hysterically. "I can't do this without her. I just can't."

Sydona held him tightly, forcing herself not to cry. She had to stay strong for him. "I miss her too, daddy."

"I take it back... I take it all back to see her face again..."

She let go of him and asked, "Take what back?"

"I should have fought harder, baby. I should have known who those men in the coats were, and we should have flown. None of this would've happened. You'd still have a family; your mother would still be with us! I screwed it all up! I should have fought harder."

Sydona's heart tore into a million pieces. "Don't say that, dad! You did everything you could! They still would have found us. They were too powerful."

"I should have fought harder. I should have fought harder... I should have.. Fought... hard..." he coughed and coughed, more intensely than Sydona had ever heard. His body shook violently as he gasped for air in-between. Sydona held him and patted his damp back. She began to access his condition more closely and noticed his shirt was damp on his back. Using the back of her hand, she felt his fore-head. His skin seared against her hand.

"Dad, you are burning up! Just wait here," she said and ran out the door. Her heart pounded as she made her way back to the kitchen. Giovonna and Silas were just sitting down.

"Come quick. My dad's getting worse," she said to the doctor. Malik put the knife down, wiped his hands on a towel, and followed Sydona to the bedroom with haste. Giovonna and Silas followed close behind, too. Sounds of his coughing could be heard in the hallway, and the doctor rushed past her.

"Let's take him to the medical room down the hallway," Malik said, curling one of Ian's arms around his shoulder, while Sydona held the other one.

"What's wrong with him?" asked Giovonna, walking beside them in case they needed help.

"Not sure," said the doctor. "I'll run some tests."

"I'm fine, I swear," coughed Ian.

"Dad, you're not. Let Dr. Malik help you," Sydona uttered, shocked to hear the words coming from her own mouth.

As they reached the room, where Sydona stayed after the cliff incident, she helped him lay in the bed. The doctor began checking his vitals. After several painstaking minutes, Sydona, Silas, and Giovonna stood by his bed, waiting to hear results.

"Well?" Sydona asked once it looked like he was done examining Ian.

"I'm not a hundred percent sure, but I think he's got pneumonia."

Sydona's heart sank like an anchor.

"Is it serious?" asked Silas.

Malik nodded. "He's pretty dehydrated, too. He'll need to rest here for at least a few days, maybe more."

Sydona grabbed her father's hand, and he caressed her fingers with his. "I hope you start feeling better soon."

"Me too, darling," he said and kissed her hand.

The doctor finished hooking him up to machines, activated a humidifier, and gave him antibiotics.

"How does someone get pneumonia anyway?" Sydona asked curiously.

The doctor breathed in deeply. "Well, it usually affects kids or elderly more because of their immune system. It's either caused by a viral or bacterial infection, and if the immune system isn't strong enough, it can make the common cold or flu worse. We'll try antibiotics, and if he doesn't get better in a few days, I'll take a closer look."

Giovonna chimed in. "A weak immune system? So that wouldn't be caused by his living in a tent for decades at a time, but only because he's older?"

"Who's to say?" he said with a slight shrug.

"You're the doctor," Silas said sharply.

"It could be a combination of both."

No one spoke after that, but it got Sydona thinking. Her dad was roughly ninety years old and could certainly have several health problems because of that. But Giovonna's comment made her wonder whether things would have been different if her parents hadn't been in captivity for all those years. Ian did live on an island for a few months though, and maybe that affected him as well. She hated that the doctor was both the problem and the solution.

"I'll bring you some food, okay, dad? Need to build your strength back up," she said, smiling down at him.

Silas and Giovonna made their way back to the kitchen, where the smells of onion and fresh cut vegetables wafted into their room. "We'll just be down the hall if you need anything."

"Thank you, Sydona," Ian said and patted her arm with his soft hands.

Dr. Malik stayed behind to finish up while Sydona joined her friends. She took a stool next to Giovonna.

"Sorry about your dad, Syd. I wish I could help more," Giovonna said with a frown.

"Thanks. I just wonder how long it will be before he gets better. Don't really plan on staying here longer than we need to."

"Especially if the plan is to…" Silas said while making a throat cutting gesture with his finger. "…after we figure out the flying issue."

Sydona glared at him with angry eyes. "Silas—"

Just then the doctor came back in and continued his cooking, breaking eggs and heating up a stainless steel pan. A dry spot formed in her throat, and she chewed on her fingernails.

The doctor spoke up, "How many eggs does everyone want?"

"T-two please," said Giovonna, who sounded a mile away.

"Same," Silas said.

"None for me. I'm suddenly not very hungry..," Sydona said as she stared at the door separating her father from view.

"What?" the doctor said with a slight laugh. "You'll be needing your strength, miss. I'll give you two as well."

Sydona gazed out of the large windows, taking in the breathtaking ocean view. She knew he was still talking, but she couldn't be further from him. The line where sky and water met filled her with instant weightlessness. The vast unknown just waiting to be explored. Sydona imagined herself flying high above the water and fading into the sky, where freedom had no bounds. She had only been lost in her own head for a minute, but then Giovonna acted like they were talking for hours.

"...are you listening? Syd?" Giovonna said, clear as day. She gawked at her with a raised eyebrow.

"Am I listening to what?" she asked. She then noticed a plate of food in front of her, and everyone else's were already halfway eaten.

"Dr. Malik said he thinks I can help."

Sydona looked over at Silas, but he just shoveled food into his mouth.

"That's great, Gia. What would you do?"

She let out a long sigh, "Well, if you were listening, he thinks I can help the problem with what you had. Where you can't fly more than a few feet off the ground. I told him I almost reversed the effect the bracelets had."

"Yes!" the doctor interrupted. "We might have had the answer to everything right here. Maybe we don't need the pills at all. We could just reverse engineer the technology with the bracelets!"

Giovonna nodded excitedly. "Yeah! I like to change my radios into transmitters in my spare time and these work in basically the same way. The bracelets are frequency based and that's where I got the idea."

Sydona took a small bite of her omelet. "That's great Gia! But," she turned her attention to the doctor. "I thought you were insistent on no help. Why the sudden change?"

Doctor Malik sipped coffee from a tiny cup. "Well, Gia here can be very persuasive."

Giovonna flashed Sydona a huge, toothy smile.

Sydona raised a single eyebrow at her and held back a grin. "Apparently."

"Great!" Giovonna exclaimed. "Can't wait to get started!"

She caught Silas from the corner of her eye as Giovonna bent over the counter to eat faster. He shot her an unsure look, almost as if to say he still didn't trust the doctor at all. It made her insides squirm. But Sydona felt more confident now that Giovonna was on board and almost had the solution figured out.

It was now or never.

Chapter Fourteen

SYDONA

Wiping her mouth of coffee and egg residue, Sydona left the kitchen stool and stretched her muscles. It might have been the best meal she'd had since the cabin. The good smells, the full belly, and smiles, though some weren't as genuine, made her feel relaxed. Giovonna would be helping with the problem now, and Sydona was glad she wouldn't have to be alone with the doctor. Maybe Silas could join them. What else was he really supposed to do, especially with an injured leg?

"I'll be your moral support!" Silas announced, as if he read her mind. He limped off the chair and gently touched her back.

Sydona grinned at his enthusiasm. "You're too kind."

Giovonna followed the two out of the kitchen. The doctor left the room shortly before and told them all to meet downstairs when they were ready. Giovonna headed back to the room to grab equipment, while Sydona and Silas checked on Ian. As she twisted the knob, Sydona swallowed hard. But he was fast asleep with blankets pulled up over his nose.

"He looks so peaceful," she said to Silas.

"He does," he answered with a soft smile.

Sydona laid her head on his shoulder, and he kissed her forehead. "I hate that he's here. Hate that I can't do anything, you know."

"I know," he said. "It could be worse, though. Not to sound morbid, but there are way worse things that could've happened."

"Yeah. You're right. He's getting help now, and he'll be on his feet in no time, right?"

"Exactly. Just gotta stay positive. Everything will work out in the end," Silas said, a smile curling on his face.

Sydona couldn't help but absorb his positive energy and smiled back. She then turned to him and kissed him softly on the lips. Giovonna cleared her voice, stopping the intimate moment. They hadn't noticed her slip into the room.

"You guys ready?"

"Yeah," Sydona replied. She grazed her father's hand and left the room with Silas. They made their way down the long hallway and peered down the stairs hidden behind the bookshelf in his office.

"Well, this is kinda creepy," Giovonna said, holding Sydona's arm. "We really need to go down there?"

"Yes, it'll be fine," she said. Sydona wanted to help Silas down, but Giovonna insisted and wanted Sydona to be in front.

"Do you trust him?" Silas asked her, rubbing her arm.

"Of course I don't."

"You're still planning on killing him once we get the bracelets working?"

"Uh, yeah," Sydona stammered. The doctor approached them as they hit the last stair and flashed a big grin. She nodded nervously back at him as doubt bubbled up inside her.

"Have you given this a try yet?" the doctor asked her.

"No, not yet. Is there a place to do it down here?"

"Yes! Yes, come. Let's *do it*," he said like an excited schoolboy.

The large flying center had a platform of wood already built and her heart began to race. Especially when Giovonna snapped the reversed engineered bracelet back on her wrist with the permanent brown line. The bracelet that felt no different than the one she wore at Eagle Lake, and a shiver crawled up her spine. Images of white tents, her mother, and Raoul with tattered wings flickered through her mind. She forced her eyes shut to block it out. Sydona felt a hand on hers, and she opened her eyes again. Giovonna and Silas both smiled at her reassuringly. Eagle Lake was in the past.

She knew she needed to try, and she treaded forward.

With Giovonna and Silas watching from the sidelines, she began to sprint. Her feet moved as quickly as her heart beat, which felt as if it would burst from her chest. When she could run no faster, she kicked off and almost instantly, she felt gravity disappearing. She held her breath, anticipating that she would crumble back to earth. Yet, in only a few seconds, she was thirty feet into the air. She exhaled, leaving the largest grin plastered on her face as she watched Giovonna and Silas cheering from the other side of the room. An involuntary squeal escaped her lips, and her skin exploded with goosebumps.

It was a miracle. She didn't even need any of Raoul's dust to help her. But then, she thought more about him, and her smile faded slightly. Her best friend wasn't even there to witness her triumph.

"Sydona! You did it!" Doctor Malik cried out. His outburst was comical, even making Silas and Giovonna feel awkward as he tried to celebrate with them.

The scene relaxed her, and she came back down to embrace her friends. Silas squeezed her so tight she couldn't hold back the tears. Giovonna hugged her from the side, making the waterworks flow quicker.

"Now the real test," the doctor said from the corner, waiting for them to break apart.

He held out his soft, limp hand.

Sydona slowly let go of her family and stared doe-eyed at him.

"Oh. Wait. Let me remove my shoes. I'm afraid they weren't made for running," he chuckled as he pulled off his reptile skin boots, which were so pointy they could be a weapon of their own.

The three exchanged glances at his words and let out uncomfortable laughs. Giovonna met Sydona's eyes as she stepped toward her and removed the bracelet. As it clicked, it felt peculiar. Like shackles being released, but also her security blanket. Giovonna transferred the metal contraption to Malik, and it was as if he turned to butter. His eyes closed, and his entire body slumped with relaxation. He extended his arm in front of him to admire the piece, twisting it and examining all angles. Sydona swore she could see tears welling in the corners of his bronze eyes. Normally she would roll her eyes at this, but she understood completely. Giving someone the power of flight was almost the same as a god creating life. The feeling of being able to go anywhere at any time was something they had to just feel.

Malik took a long deep breath and stretched his legs and arms for a minute before he started running. The group stood aside to watch him in action. About twenty feet into his sprint he kicked off the ground and into the air he went. An explosion of laughter filled the room like a million rainbow balloons. He was a little shaky and wobbly, but he flew around the room with open arms, twists and turns, and smiled so bright it brought tears to Sydona's eyes. A feeling of relief hit her so strongly that she stopped crying, realizing what the feeling meant. Quickly wiping tears away, she hid her face from the others. But it seemed as though Silas and Giovonna were just as relieved to see the doctor fly.

After a minute or so, the doctor finally made a rough landing, and even though he fell, he laughed it off and stood back up on his own.

"Unbelievable! Sydona, did you see? Did you see me up there? I was like a falcon, soaring in the wind," he shouted, his voice bouncing off the walls and making her cringe a bit. His arms flailed around like a kid just learning to ride a bike. "Well, I guess there's no wind down here. I can't wait to go outside!"

Sydona snickered. His laugh and excitement was contagious. "Yeah, I saw—"

"Is that what it's always like?" Malik continued. "I mean, I couldn't even feel the pain in my leg. It's a miracle! I had no idea that it helps with that! We could market this to so many more businesses. Maybe even drug companies!"

"This isn't a drug," Silas interrupted.

The doctor stopped brainstorming with his large hand gestures and pivoted to Silas on a dime. It was as if he had forgotten they were still there. He glared at him while catching his breath with a heaving chest. "You're right. It's not a drug." He paused and released an even bigger grin than before. "It's better! It's… it's my invention. All me. I can't wait to show—"

"You wouldn't have been able to have a breakthrough at all if it weren't for me," snapped Giovonna. A sharp pain shot through Sydona's body as her eyes widened at her brave, young friend. She stood behind her and grabbed her arm subtly, afraid of any anger that might push through.

Malik ignored Silas and turned his attention to her. Sydona swallowed hard, but Giovonna lifted her chin. He stood close, his expression serious. "You're right! Thank you, Giovonna." His finger playfully bopped her nose, making her flinch, then turned back around, taking a springing pose. Back into the air he went.

High-pitched giggles filled the room again, and the three stared at each other. No one really knew what to do. They all waited as he attempted to do new tricks in the air. Sydona soon cleared her throat, "Do we need to be here to watch, or can we go?"

Malik let out one last burst of laughter. "You may go. I just wanted to enjoy this a little longer. We'll talk later."

Sydona nodded with a small grin. She wanted to be the one up there. But she let him have his moment. Once he came down from his high, she needed to take the bracelet back. Only one needed to work, and it needed to be on her own wrist. After that, they could finally be rid of Doctor John Malik.

As they all left the room and hiked up the stairs with worried faces, Sydona lingered in the doorway to watch. She didn't pay much attention to the fact he was flying, something he longed to do for most of his life, but to the pure joy plastered onto his face. Taking that expression away felt like taking milk from a baby. But then she thought back to Eagle Lake, her mother, her house, and Raoul. Fists formed at her sides. Visions of all the bad things that happened in her life were caused by this man. Sydona was almost sick of seeing so many dead people around her, the last being Lacey in the woods. But she knew killing Doctor Malik wouldn't bring her mother or Lacey or any of the hundreds of others who died back. Everything had come to an end. He had what he wanted. It was over.

The killing had to stop.

As she joined her friends, she was lost in thought, but then, she heard Silas and Giovonna panicking.

"...you sure you left it here?" Silas asked Giovonna as they searched all around the room with the computers and countertops with matching stools.

"Yes! I swear!" Giovonna said, voice shrill.

"What are you looking for?" Sydona asked.

"My backpack! With all the bracelets and things. It's gone." She ran around the room, looking under tables, and in any corners. The room was so bare with metal and white concrete, her bright colored backpack would have stuck out.

"Maybe someone stole it," Sydona wondered. And the very first face that popped up was Natalia's.

"Bet it was that *bitch*, Nat," Silas said.

Sydona gave him a nod that showed his answer was the obvious one.

"Gaahh!" Giovonna growled louder.

"I'll find her." Sydona narrowed her eyes.

"We'll go with," Giovonna said eagerly..

"No, stay here with Silas since he's well… sorry, babe…"

"No, no, it's fine. I'll keep an eye on you-know-who when he's done." Silas flopped down on a stool and rested his chin on his hand.

"Okay, great." Sydona blew him a kiss and took off running up the stairs to the office.

Adrenaline ran through her veins as she ran through each room. She soon arrived at the temporary hospital room. A gulp of air pushed down her throat as she caught Natalia standing next to her father. She was wearing Giovonna's backpack, along with an outfit she swore she saw Avani wearing before. Her eyes furrowed with confusion at the woman's clothes. She thought it was strange to be hung up on that right now, but Natalia didn't look like herself. Ian was still asleep, his head turned away from Natalia.

"Give me the backpack, Nat," Sydona said. Heat began to boil up inside of her.

Natalia absentmindedly latched onto the long straps hanging from the backpack. "What do I get if I give it to you?"

Sydona tightened her jaw, marched straight up to her and pulled at the pack.

But Natalia pivoted so quickly, Sydona lost her grip. Natalia shoved her backwards and grinned at how easily and far she pushed her.

"Oh, I'm sorry. I don't believe we've struck a deal yet. And it would be in your best interest if you don't fucking try to touch me again, bitch."

Sydona bit her lip in frustration and glared at her sideways. "I'll spare your life. Does that work for you?"

Natalia snickered. "You know, I don't like you, but I love your spirit. It's too bad you chose the wrong side. We could be great together." She began to walk slowly around Ian's bed, while Sydona took a second to process what Natalia said.

While Natalia's back was toward Sydona, she glanced over at her father, who moved slightly. She wondered if he was awake now.

"Just give me the damn backpack," Sydona said exhaustedly.

Natalia was on the other side of Ian's bed now and she sighed heavily. "Life is about give and take. If I give you this, what can I take?"

Sydona's hands curled into fists. "Stop playing games, Nat!"

"What can I take?" Natalia shouted.

"What do you want?" Sydona yelled back.

Natalia smirked. "Okay, now we're talking. What do *I* want, huh? Let me think…"

Sydona's nostrils flared and moved her hands to her face and rubbed the bridge of her nose. As Natalia thought about what she wanted and wasting valuable time, Sydona caught her father's eye. All he did was give her a wink, but this simple gesture made her stomach drop. The look in his eye, she's seen before. Back at Eagle Lake. Natalia's back was turned away from both of them, and Ian slowly peeled his covers off. His hand extended with a scalpel in grip, pointed right at Natalia. Sydona's eyes widened to twice the size, knowing what he planned to do. Sydona stood at the foot of the bed, stiff, but she was screaming inside.

As Ian managed to lift his arm up enough to reach Natalia's neck, she turned around at the last second and he sliced her right above her chest.

"What—what the fuck!" Natalia screamed.

And as if this infliction flipped a crazy switch, Natalia bared her teeth and grabbed Ian's hand with the scalpel, dripping with blood.

"Nat, stop!" Sydona yelled and lunged toward her.

With one quick motion, Natalia kicked Sydona back as hard as she could, while holding on to Ian's hand. From the floor, Sydona witnessed it all, and it happened so fast. Natalia turned the blade back on Ian and slowly inched it toward his neck.

"No, please!" Ian cried. His fragile arms were just as weak as his voice. "I'm sorry!"

"Too late for sorry, cabron." With that, she stuck the scalpel into Ian's neck.

"Dad!" Sydona screamed. She scrambled to her feet and lunged after Natalia again.

Sydona managed to tackle her so hard, she fell to her back, crushing the bracelets inside the backpack. Natalia swung her fists and kicked her legs, but Sydona only saw red. She sat on top of Natalia and punched her in the face over and over again.

Suddenly, she heard her name from behind.

"Syd!" Giovonna yelled and then gasped.

Sydona's heart jumped at the thought of Giovonna being near Natalia and whipped her head around at her voice. In those delicate few seconds, Natalia quickly reached for the bloody scalpel sitting next to Ian and pointed it at Sydona. As Sydona turned back around to face her, she put her hands up at the sight of the blade, covered in her fathers blood.

Sydona slowly got off of Natalia and backed away slowly from her. Giovonna and Silas stood by the doorway and kept their eyes glued to Natalia. She clumsily got back on her heels, with her weapon on the offense.

"And you all thought *I* was crazy," Natalia said as she quickly wiped her face, covered in blood. Then adjusted the backpack that rattled more than normal.

She walked briskly out of the room, leaving Sydona to deal with her father.

"Oh my God, Ian!" Silas said, his hands over his mouth.

Sydona turned to face her father, laying in a red stained bed.

Giovonna was faced the other way, looking only at Sydona. Her face was white. "How did this happen?"

Sydona couldn't take her eyes off of her father. She admired his bravery, but knew it would get him killed.

"It was my fault," she said quietly.

"Don't blame yourself, babe. Natalia is too unpredictable," Silas said while he covered Ian up.

"No, I mean, it's my fault he was here in the first place. If I just kept my mouth shut to Theo, my dad wouldn't be dead right now."

Giovonna hugged her tightly. Her warm and tight embrace was all Sydona needed to let the tears start flowing. And soon, her legs crumbled underneath her and they both dropped to the floor. Silas joined them and held Sydona from her other side. After a few silent moments, Silas started singing Amazing Grace for Ian and it made her cry harder.

The last of her parents were gone. And they did everything they could to protect her. She felt herself going down a dark path, and right at the cusp of a war. The timing couldn't be any worse.

Chapter Fifteen

JET

After soaring for a few hours, they finally reached some familiar land, and the doctor's house was easy to spot on the cliffside. Jet forced himself and Devon upward to make a landing just far enough up to stay out of sight. Messy onyx hair fell in front of his face, and he calmly brushed it out. Devon raced ahead, not waiting for Jet at all.

"Where are you going?" Jet asked.

Devon didn't answer and kept walking.

"Devon, wait," Jet shouted just loud enough for his voice to carry over the crashing waves..

"Walk faster," Devon called back.

Jet tightened his jaw and jogged up next to him. "What's your problem?"

"I don't have a problem. I just want to kill this guy so I can go home." He stared straight ahead, barely blinking.

Jet swallowed and furrowed his brows. "Dev… hang on, man. Hang on." He grabbed the boy's arm and crouched down.

"Let go!" he yelled.

"Devon, listen to me." His voice was masked with uncertainty. He wanted Malik dead, but to hear a child say it made him feel more sober than he'd felt in a long time. His death had been Lacey's dying wish. And as much as Jet wanted to fulfill that wish, he knew nothing they did would bring her back to him. To them. "No one wants to see that asshole burn as much as me, but you can't be the one who does this. I couldn't live with myself if you killed someone."

"He's not just 'someone'. And it's what Lacey wanted. She asked me to."

"I know bud, but you gotta know. Once you do something like that, you'll never be the same. And… I like who you are."

"Psh," said Devon, looking off to the side.

"Stop it. Listen to me… If all of our problems could be solved by eliminating the people we don't like, this would be a much happier world. But sadly, we can't. Nothing in this world is simple. Nothing. And that's why I drink…" he said, mumbling the last bit.

"Whatever. You're just scared." He wiggled, but Jet held him still.

"Devon, please," Jet said, stalling to find words to calm the kid down. Or at least get him to stop hating him. "Maybe I am scared, but being scared isn't a bad thing. Everyone gets scared sometimes."

"Not me! I'm a Sparrow, and we don't get scared!" Devon shouted. His face scrunched up, and his glasses slipped down to the tip of his tiny nose.

"I give up, man," Jet said and shoved him away.

"Yeah, go ahead. Quit!" Devon yelled while Jet rolled his eyes and began to walk past him. "You're good at quitting. 'Cept when you drink!"

A twig snapped, and Jet pivoted around to face him, yelling as loud as he could. "Why are you so angry? Why do you hate me?!"

"You never said you're sorry!" Devon screamed back, his words hitting him like a brick wall. Jet raised his brows with the worst realization.

"It's the *least* you could do, Jet, but you've never said it…" Devon sprinted past him, and all Jet could do was watch him run away.

"I'm sorry, Dev," he whispered to himself, but it was too late.

Devon was several feet in front of him now as he reached the top of a hill that overlooked the giant house. He saw him pause for a moment, then run down the other side, out of sight. Jet panicked and ran after him. The grassy hill was steep and he could run fast enough to fly. Soon, he reached the top and saw the reason he took off running; Willow, Harold,

Knox and Raoul and Jubilee were standing next to the stand-alone garage.

As he approached the group, they were greeting Devon with hugs and smiles. He gave one nod to Knox as he got closer and he just stared back.

"Where the hell did you two go?" Knox crossed his arms.

Jet looked over everyone and noticed the horrible condition Willow was in. "Away. And from the looks of it, I made the right decision." He held out a flask for Willow.

She side-eyed him but took his flask anyway. Willow took a sip, scrunched her face and gave it back to Jet. She coughed a few times and shook her head. "Thanks, but no thanks."

"Eh, more for me," Jet mumbled and took a sip or two for himself.

"No, but really," Harold said, while holding up Willow. "Did ya fly off somewhere?"

Jet sighed. "Yes, but it doesn't really matter now. What's been going on here?"

"Yeah, we met some people!" Devon chimed in.

Jet swallowed and stared off, away from the group.

"You did?" said Raoul, standing on Willow's shoulder, Jubilee on the other.

"Yes! We met another flier named Quinn and her fairy, Dandelion."

"Another fairy?" asked Jubilee, her face brightened up.

"Mm-hmm. She has a really funny accent and looks very different from you guys."

Jet grew impatient, listening to pointless conversation. "Where's Avani, Knox?"

Knox immediately turned his attention to him, almost relieved in the change of subject. "That's what we're trying to find out now."

Devon glared at Jet and pursed his lips.

"Any ideas of where she could be?" Jet continued.

Harold spoke up. "Only place that would make any sense, is down at the housin' units. But I ain't got a clue which one. Me and Raoul know she ain't at Nat's place."

Jet thought for a minute. "How many apartments are down there, Harold?"

Harold lifted his chin to think more clearly. "Uh, lets see…" he started counting on his boney, dried fingers. "Some of them got multiple people in, not sure how many but, I wanna say there's about forty or so different ones."

"You're telling me she could be in one of forty different places?" spat Knox.

"Just about," said Harold.

Raoul spoke up. "This is going to take all night."

With a heavy sigh from Knox, he then began barking out orders. "Harold, you said you know where Natalia's place is?"

Harold stood up at attention and nodded.

"Why don't you and Willow go there, even though she wasn't there earlier. It's a familiar place and may return. Jet and Devon, you're with me. We'll search the other buildings for any suspicious activity."

"We have radios, too," said Jet and handed one over to Harold.

"Great, yes, please let us know the moment you run into anything," said Knox.

"We need weapons," Willow added.

"Oh," Jet said and set his duffle bag on the ground. "I have plenty of those." He handed out pistols and a shotgun that Willow claimed instantly.

Harold chuckled. "Babe, you sure you can handle that right now?"

Willow glared at him. "Don't worry 'bout me. I will always have strength to shoot a sumbitch."

Everyone stared wide-eyed at each other.

"I'll go with Willow so I can dust her when she's in pain," said Raoul. "Jubilee, why don't you go with them so you can be their look out?"

Jubilee quivered. "No, uncle, I want to stay with you!"

"I know, but they need you to help them detect danger. You're the quickest fairy I know, you'll be a great asset to them."

Jubilee squeezed out a few tears and gave Raoul a hug. He said a few more things in her ear and she wiped her tears away. He lifted her chin up and she nodded confidently. After everyone got their weapons situated, Jet threw the much lighter bag over his back and they split up into the two groups.

Knox headed to the right of the garage, while the others took the left. Devon stayed closed behind Knox while Jet lagged behind, keeping watch in the back. He felt like Devon purposely stayed as far away from Jet as he possibly could. It was best he kept his distance while Devon processed everything going on. Knox snuck up the path of the garage and headed back into the darkness of the forest nearby. Jet thought they went way too far out of the way to go to the complex, but didn't question it. Jubilee did her best to be the light in the front of the group, waving them ahead when the coast was clear. Once they reached the forest, Knox had them regroup.

"Jet, let me see the radio."

Jet unclipped it from his jeans and handed it over.

"Harold, over," Knox said into the walkie-talkie.

After a few seconds, he answered. *"Harold here."*

"Location?"

"We just got to her place. She ain't here, but we're gonna talk to some of the men here and see what they know."

Jet narrowed his eyes, "Men? What men? The men who work for the doctor?"

Knox returned a look of confusion. "Harold, you can't trust those Vultures!" he said in a loud whisper.

"Yes we can," Jubilee spoke up with her high-pitched voice. "A couple of them help set me free."

"It's alright, sir. Me and Raoul have become acquainted with a few of 'em. We're gonna see if they've seen Avani anywhere or heard anything in the nearby apartments."

Knox shook his head and his forehead wrinkled. "Jubilee, what do you mean they set you free?"

She grinned and covered her mouth with her tiny hands. "Not all of them are bad people. That woman, she didn't treat me well but not all of them are like her."

"Why are they here then?" asked Jet.

"Exactly,' said Knox, his deep voice a steep contrast to hers. "They have to have something wrong with them if they are here in the first place."

Jet nodded. "I don't know how they can trust these people so easily. They do one good thing and we're supposed to forget all the bad?" He caught Devon's glance and saw him roll his eyes. Jet clenched his jaw. "What?"

Devon turned away from him with crossed arms.

Jet's heart began to pound from the tension between them. He wanted to pry more, but instead he reached for his flask to take the edge off.

The radio whirred before it reached his lips. *"They're sayin' they've heard some commotion coming from apartment 7C. But ain't sure if it's Avani in there or not."*

Knox answered. "It's worth checking out. We'll meet you over there."

"Over and out."

Knox handed the radio back to Jet. "Let's move."

They followed as Knox took the lead and headed to the apartment. The sky darkened with heavy clouds and the glow from Jubilee grew even brighter. She flew way far ahead of them to find the specific place. Coming from the forest, they were facing the back of the complex and Jet scanned the windows to see if he could see which one it was. Most of the windows were dark or covered up. They were either empty or used curtains to block out any on-lookers.

A rumble of thunder shook the ground as they finally reached one of the buildings. Jet noticed a few people standing around, talking in front of other apartments, some alone and smoking cigarettes. It was quiet, aside from the wind in the trees and occasional thunder. Soon, they rounded the corner to go to the other side and examine the numbers on the doors. It was then that Jet saw an orange ball of light heading toward them with Harold and Willow close behind. As they approached them, he noticed another man walking with them.

"Who's this?" Knox asked with his chest puffed out.

Willow answered. "Sir, this here is Benny. He's gonna help us."

Jet felt his heart race and sized the man up. He was slightly taller than Jet and had slicked back, black hair and a skinny mustache.

"Ben is fine," he said and stuck out his hand in front of Knox.

Knox didn't take his violet eyes off of him. "You're a Vulture?"

He darted his eyes over to Harold and Willow. "Uh, what's a Vul—"

"Why do you wanna help us now, Benny?" Knox interrupted.

Benny put his hand back in his pocket and shrugged. "You seem like decent people and they said your wife might be in trouble. I heard some commotion over here earlier and wondered if it might have been her."

Jet spoke up. "Why didn't you investigate it when you heard it?"

Benny smiled. "And possibly run into Nutty Natalia? Nah, no thanks, man. For all I knew, I could end up in there with her!"

"He thinks someone is guarding her though," said Harold. "We need to be prepared."

Jet saw a vein pop out of Knox's forehead but he didn't say another word.

Guided by pure rage, Knox used his massive size to kick the door down in one swift motion. The door flew off the hinges and shards of wood went flying through the air.

A burly, dark skinned woman turned around, bearing a machine gun. "I was wonderin' when you'd show up."

At first her face was hard and angry, but her expression changed in a blink once she recognized one of them. "Benny? Why are you here?"

"Regina, please let her go," he said calmly with hands in the air.

"What? Why?"

"Because he said *please*," said Knox, inching closer to the woman.

Just then, a muffled scream came from behind the door Regina was guarding. Knox snapped his head toward the sound and pulled his gun out. She refocused her barrel at Knox, then everyone else who had a weapon showed it.

Raoul instantly flew into the middle of Regina and Knox and floated between them. "Stop! We have got to stop this! What will be accomplished here if we all kill each other? It may not mean we stop the war, but if we're all dead, what's the point of anything? We need to come together, as a people. Not just humans, not just fliers. As people."

As everyone listened to Raoul's words, a yellow glowing caught Jet's eye just above Regina's head. Jubilee hovered a couple inches above, sprinkling a white powder onto the woman's head. Within seconds, her eyes rolled back, and she fell to the floor with a thud, gun and all. Jet's mouth fell open in shock. "Did… did you just kill her?"

Jubilee laughed so hard she held her stomach and waivered in the air. Her high pitched squealing bounced off the empty apartment walls. "Uncle Raoul, did you hear that? He thinks I just killed that woman! No, you silly goose! I just put her to sleep."

"Heavens be, child," Willow chimed in. "I didn't know fairies could do that."

Raoul glanced back to the group, with his eyes wide. "We don't… Jubilee, are you a pixie?"

Jubilee grinned. "I know I'm not supposed to use my powers, but I didn't want anyone to die..."

Raoul flew over to his niece and gave her a tight hug. "You are just full of surprises, young lady!"

The scream came once more, and the group had to refocus on the mission. Jet watched as Knox broke the cheap lock on the door and he swung it open violently.

Chapter Sixteen

KNOX

The scene before Knox's eyes would never be erased from his mind. Ropes hung from the ceiling, attached to a metal loop, and the other ends tied around each of Avani's wrists. Her arms spread out as far as they could go and the same went for her legs. Sweat beaded all over her body, and bruises and scratches peppered her skin. The clothes Natalia wore were undoubtedly from Avani as she had nothing on but a cloth that prevented her from speaking. Her eyes were red and black from smeared makeup. Knox froze in shock from the horrible state of his wife. Finally, he snapped out of it and ran up to her, shutting Jet and the group out. Shaking hands pulled off the gag. A strong odor of urine invaded his nostrils, and he knew instantly it was her.

He kissed her hard through her river of tears.

"Elias, get me out of here," Avani said with a cracked voice.

Knox didn't want to stop kissing her, afraid of never being able to again, but he couldn't leave her like this. He worked on untying the knots, but his fingers were too large to work it out. He ran to the door and cracked it open just enough to poke his head through.

"Any of you got a knife?"

"I got one," Benny replied. "Here." He walked up to Knox and handed the knife over. "Did you find your wife, how is—"

Knox grabbed the dagger and slammed the door shut. He sawed through the ropes, freeing her quickly. Avani instantly grabbed onto her husband and curled up as close as she could to him. She may have been covered in sweat, but she had goosebumps everywhere, too.

"I am so happy to see you, mi amor. Dios mio, I'm gonna kill her!" Avani said in a fit of sadness and rage.

"Now you see where I'm coming from," Knox said, holding her tightly, kissing every inch of her face and arms.

She looked him over as well, searching for injuries. "You look okay. Where've you been? Was Willow with you?"

"Yes, I'm fine, my love. Willow is… well, she's with us now. Nat did a number on her, too. She's got quite a list of folks wanting to put her six feet under."

Avani cradled his face and stared deeply into his eyes. He could stare into hers all day. Though they shifted from brown to green, they eventually landed on lavender, and he smiled. "Let's find you some clothes."

She kissed him deeply again and reverted back to her cradle position. "Hey. Hey!" He yelled to anyone in the other room.

The door cracked open. "Stop!" Knox shouted. "Don't open it any further." He waited for the person to listen and keep the door ajar. "Who am I talking to?"

"It's Harold."

"Harold, do you know where that woman lived? The one that passed out?"

"Regina? Uh, no. But maybe Benny knows."

"Ask him and see if he can grab some clothes for Avani."

"Oh, uh, what does she need?"

Knox hesitated. "Everything."

"You got it, boss."

Knox sat enjoying the warmth of his soul mate. He began to hum a song that she normally sang to him to calm him down. Avani rocked back and forth softly, taking comfort in the serenade.

Raoul soon interrupted the tender moment and spoke through the crack in the door. "Anything we can do?"

"Is there any water she can have?" Knox asked, and Avani nodded her head, nuzzling it against his chest.

"I'll check," Jet said.

Raoul hovered by the crack in the door. "We found Jubilee, Avani."

"You did? Muy bueno. She okay?"

"More than okay… She's a pixie!"

"Really?" Avani perked up, and stared at the door. "I thought they were just a myth."

"I've only heard the legends, too. I had no idea they were still around. And in my family no less!" Raoul said excitedly.

Knox heard Jubilee giggling again from behind the door. Just then, he heard rustling in the other room. Harold and Benny returned.

"Alrighty, so we got some pants here," Harold began, sticking random clothing items through the crack to show Knox and Avani. "I tried looking for the fanciest clothes she had, but truth be told, her wardrobe resembled shit I'd wear. So, these jeans might fit but they got a lot of holes in it."

"It's fine. Throw it here," Knox said. He caught the pants in mid-air and handed them to Avani.

"You didn't happen to find any... under garments, did you?" Avani asked shyly.

"Oh, right! Uh, yeah. I got this little diddy. It's not very big, but it's pink. Thought you might like it…" Knox could feel Harold's red face through the door.

Avani's eyes went big, and Knox tried not to laugh. "Was there anything not so stringy?"

"Sorry, Avani, we was in a rush."

Knox cleared his throat. "Harold, just throw it all in here; we'll sort through it. Thanks."

Harold did as instructed and dropped a pile of clothes near the entrance. Avani stood up and closed the door. She sorted through the clothes, judging each one and making comments about them.

"Dear, I know you went through some bad shit, but could you please pick something so we can get out of here?" Knox said as he leaned against the door.

"There's no bra?" she asked herself, then shouted. "Harold, you forgot a bra!"

"She, uh, didn't have any, ma'am."

"What self-respecting woman doesn't own a bra?!" Avani said to herself out loud, then continued to pick out items. After several moments of mumbling to herself in Spanish, she was finally dressed. Knox examined her completed outfit, and she was unrecognizable. Holey jeans with large boots, a puke colored green t-shirt, and a belt with metal studs. Her black hair was tangled and messy, not even braided or curled. Avani pulled up her pants and then posed for her husband with chin up and chest out. "Well?"

"You look gorgeous, sweetheart. Now can we please go?"

Avani rolled her eyes. "Only you could lie straight to my face, and I'd still walk by your side." She stood on her tiptoes to give him a peck. He slapped her on her behind, and she jumped. Avani swung the door open, and Knox watched the look on everyone's faces as they emerged. Each one of them gawked with wide eyes and gaped mouths.

"Wow," Jet said.

"Oh, be quiet!" Avani said, then rushed to Regina, still asleep on the floor. She grabbed her gun, strapped it over her shoulder and checked the ammunition. She then cocked it back like she was ready to go on a killing spree. The gun was about half her size, and Knox couldn't help but grin. The look of her carrying such a powerful weapon made him tingle.

"Here's some water for you," Jet said, holding a cup out.

Avani flung the gun around to her back and chugged it. "Gracias, Jet." Avani looked around the room and then back down at Regina. Bending down, she grabbed the woman's hair and slipped off her hair tie. Her head dropped back down with a thud, and Avani pulled her own hair back into a tight bun. "Alright. Now we can go."

Knox nodded. "First thing's first, is getting you and Willow some medical attention."

Knox held Avani up as she did her best to suppress the pain from bruises and scratches all over her skin. Knox could tell from how often she bared her teeth, she was still in pain. Raoul was tasked to cover not only Willow in dust, but Avani too.

"Harold, would you know where we can find something to tend to their injuries?" Knox asked as

the group walked along the sidewalk of the apartment complexes.

"John's got a room in his house that he uses for
patients. He prolly got things in there to patch them
up."

Knox felt a lump in his throat. "Inside his house?"

"Mm-hmm."

He felt a surge of anger bubbling to the surface,
knowing he would have to be in close proximity to
the doctor. His pace slowed down and Avani noticed.

"Elias, what's the hold up?"

"I don't know if I can go in there," he said, doing
his best to keep his temper in check.

"What, you scared?" said Jet with a chuckle.

Knox glared at Jet. "It's not that."

"Sir," Willow spoke up. "With all due respect, I
hate that man as much as you do. But if he got a hospital in that mansion, I am first in line. Who knows if
we'll even see him!"

Knox nodded as he looked her over as well as
Avani. He swallowed and took a deep breath. As the
group kept steady toward the house, they paused
once they reached the front door. Knox stared at the
double doors that stretched several feet higher than
a standard door. They were a frosted glass mate-
rial and the metal, vertical handles, stared back at
him. The house was much more intimidating than he
thought it would be and he slowly wrapped his hand
around the cylindrical handle. As he gripped it tight,

Sydona barged through from the other side and ran right past everyone.

She was covered in blood and had a shocked look on her face, she hadn't even detected the rest of the group was there. Knox and the others glanced at each other while they watched Sydona grab her knees and hurl over. A sinking feeling landed in Knox's stomach. Someone had died. As far as he knew, it was a crapshoot of who it could be. Raoul was the first to buzz to her aid. Jubilee followed him like a puppy, and their orange and yellow glows disappeared behind Sydona. Soon, the rest of the group, at least the ones close to her, joined as well.

They bombarded her with questions and made sure she was okay. From the distance that Knox kept, he overheard that it wasn't her blood, it was Ian's and Natalia was to blame. It was all Knox needed to hear to turn his eyes to a furious emerald.

Rampaging through the grand entrance of the mansion, he bellowed, "Natalia! Show yourself! Natalia!"

"Excuse me," a voice came from behind him. "May I help you?" It was so calm and sophisticated, it could be no one else but the person who owned the mansion.

Knox whiplashed around to face Doctor Malik. "You."

John Malik recognized Knox immediately and wore a large, toothy smile. "You must be the infamous Knox I hear so much about. Not as tall as I imagined though."

Knox snarled and puffed out his chest.

Malik backed up and put his hands up in surrender, but only for a second. He then held them at his torso and intertwined his fingers. "Relax, Knox. It was only a joke." Malik then walked back a few steps and grabbed a cane from another room. He rested his hand on it and shrugged his shoulders. "Natalia's not here. But she's destroying everything in her path. She always was a damn handful."

Another voice rang from the room Malik took his cane from. It was a young girl's voice. "Knox?" Giovonna said and emerged from the room with a dirty face full of tears and snot. "Knox!" She leaped at him, enveloping him in a bear hug.

He wanted to embrace her in return, but the fact that she ran right past the doctor without so much as a raised brow made him pause.

"Gia, what is going on here?!" he said and grabbed both her shoulders.

"Natalia… she—she killed Sydona's father," she cried. "It's so horrible…"

"No, I heard, but I mean, what are you doing with the doctor?"

"Oh, um," Giovonna began, but then Silas came out of the same room with a limp.

"He's not the problem now," Silas said. His face had more wrinkles than Knox last remembered.

"Excuse me?" Knox retorted, not happy with that answer. He pointed stiffly at Malik. "He's the reason we're all here!"

"You are correct, sir. But trust me when I say, if you don't stop that woman, she will continue on this killing streak."

Giovonna looked up at the doctor. "Can't you stop her? She works for you, right?"

Malik laughed slightly. "Actually, no. I had to let her go this morning. But I can't stop her anymore than a little fairy could."

"Where is she?" Knox asked.

"I'm not a gambling man," Malik said with a shrug.

Knox lifted one eyebrow high at Malik's nonchalant attitude. "Why are you so calm about all this, Malik? I feel like you haven't stopped grinning since I met you."

The doctor replied with another smile, then lifted his arm, showing off the metal bracelet on his dainty wrist. Knox cocked his head and tried to understand what the bracelet had to do with anything. He wasn't a flier.

"Am I missing something?"

"He can fly now," Silas muttered.

"What, seriously? The bracelet?" Knox asked, genuinely surprised.

Giovonna started to answer before the doctor interrupted. "Yes, the bracelet! Who would've thought? It's been under my nose the whole time. Can you believe it?"

"That's incredible. Does this mean Syd can fly again?" Knox asked.

"Yeah, it did," Sydona said as she walked slowly back through the front door. The rest of the party followed behind. "Until Natalia shattered all the rest of them into oblivion. You are the only one who has one now. Congratulations..."

Knox caught the doctor observing Sydona in a sad manner, as if he felt bad for her. No one else said a word. Ian's death hung heavy in the room. A dozen people or so scattered throughout the extended living room and kitchen. As Harold approached the doctor, the others edged away. The two of them stared at one another with squinted eyes.

"Nice cane, old man," Harold said.

The doctor grinned at his comment. "I guess the rumors were true. Braver than I thought to show your face around here again. Or daft. Yes, daft is much more logical."

"You lucky I turned a new leaf, John. Otherwise, I—"

"A new leaf, eh?" he asked, reexamining him again with his glasses adjusted. "Well, you do look cleaner than normal."

Harold's fist curled, but Willow held it by his side.

"I got a lot of words for you too, doctor," said Willow. "But I'ma save them 'cause Gia seems to trust ya. I ain't got a clue why, but consider this your lucky day."

Harold and John both kept their months shut and folded their arms in protest.

As much as Knox felt fired up about going after Natalia, they needed to get Avani and Willow medical attention first.

"Is there a place we can patch these ladies up?" Knox finally said in the tense silence.

John changed his hard expression to worry after he took a hard look at Willow and Avani. He stood up at attention, removed his glasses and raised his bushy eyebrows. "Did your sister do this?"

Avani tilted her head sideways at him. "Uh, yeah… How did you-"

"No matter, this way, dear," he said and gently guided her in the right direction by placing his hand on her shoulder.

Knox noticed this and his nostrils flared. Willow followed after with a slight limp.

He watched as the doctor led them into a room right off the kitchen, the same room Silas came out of. The doctor clicked the door shut and Knox felt useless. He took a seat on the couch in the living room and sat with his thoughts. He prayed that she would recover soon so they could find the woman responsible; and do what he does best. Giovonna sat closely next to him and rubbed his back gently. All he could do now was wait.

Chapter Seventeen

SYDONA

A whirlwind of emotions and fears spun around Sydona as she slumped in the corner of the dove white couch. The thought of Natalia lurking around, waiting to pounce and kill them all was at the forefront of her mind. Guilt followed closely behind as she tried to ignore the death of her last surviving family member. Her father still lay in the other room, soaked in his own blood. Each time she pictured the blade carving across his neck made her both enraged and nauseous. It paralyzed her in a much different way than the doctor's taser. She would have preferred the taser. Maybe it would take her mind off everything.

After Willow and Avani left the room, a mix of allied Vultures and Sparrows began to congregate and talk about everything going on. All she wanted was silence. She covered her ears with the pillows and sunk deeper into the couch cushions. Raoul flipped his head in her direction after a civil conversation with one of the Vultures. Sydona's stomach twisted as he flew over to her.

"Hey, you okay?" Raoul asked. He stood on the pillow she held against her stomach.

His simple question opened the floodgates. "No," she cracked. Paranoia surrounded her, a fear of everyone staring at her and watching what she would do next. Her emotions were controlling her far more than she could control them. She choked them back as best she could and wiped her face quickly.

"I'm so sorry about your dad, Syd," Raoul said. His eyes began to well up, too.

With a big gulp, Sydona stood, making Raoul fly off her pillow. She motioned her head to the back door of the house. He floated behind her, and they left the noise of the group. As the glass door clicked shut, she took another deep breath, gathering up her words.

"I… I can't keep doing this, Raoul." She sat on a concrete wall; her arms fell to her side.

"Do what, Syd?" Raoul asked.

"Pretending I'm okay. I am far from okay, and I'm tired of acting like I always am."

Raoul furrowed his brows. "Syd, it's okay to feel this way. A lot is going on right now…"

"Too much! And it's not even just what's going on right now. I haven't been okay since I saw that fucking article in the paper. I thought I could handle whatever it took to put this shit to an end, but… Not in my wildest dreams did I think it would be like this. I have no parents, Raoul. They were taken from me twice and then both killed in front of me. And now I can't even fly. I don't know who I am! Who am I, Raoul? I have nothing left." She looked to Raoul, who sat there speechless. Letting out a deep sigh and dropping her head, she continued, "They've won. What's even the point now? Everything is gone. Everything is so different now. She can just kill me; I don't even care anymore."

She sat up and looked to the sky. "You hear me, Natalia? I don't care! Put me out of my misery! I'm right fucking here!"

"Syd! Syd, calm down! Stop!" Raoul flew around her, covering her with dust.

"Stop with your dust, Raoul. It's not going to work!" Sydona shouted, backing away and forcing herself to stay grounded. "You just don't get it, do you? There's no way we can beat her. Just let her win. And make sure I'm dead before she takes over."

"No, *you* stop! Listen to me, Syd. I know you're emotional right now, but once we find her, we can finally go home. This will all be over soon."

"And when will that be, huh? Does anyone have any idea of where she is? No! She's like a goddamn ghost."

Raoul's face scrunched, and he crossed his arms. He didn't say a word but focused hard on her eyes.

Sydona raised a brow. "What?"

"Are you done making excuses yet?"

An exasperated puff fell from her mouth, and she shifted her weight.

"Good. Now that you got that all out, can we please try to get a plan ready?"

"I'm not letting it all out, Raoul… I'm just… I feel like I'm losing everyone. No matter what I do, I can't save everyone."

Raoul paused for a moment. "You know, you've really come a long way, since all of this."

Sydona sniffed. "What do you mean?"

"I mean, you used to not get attached to anyone, and now you are upset that you can't save everyone you love. You've changed."

Sydona swallowed and nodded with a small laugh. "You're right." But then her thoughts turned dark again. "This is why though. Getting attached hurts like fucking hell."

"I know, Syd," Raoul said. "And no amount of my dust can help you, but I thought you should know, that even though your father is no longer with us, you still have a family. And a family that would do anything for you."

A wave of tears flooded her eyes at his words and she buried her head into her hands. He was right. As much as it hurt that she no longer had parents, she still had a family, and a close one at that. She wouldn't be where she is now without them. And she knew they would go to the ends of the world for her.

"Thank you, Raoul. For everything."

Raoul flew up to her and playfully nudged her in the chin. "You ready to come back in?"

Sydona looked out at the vast ocean in front of her and turned to her. "I think I'm gonna hang out here a bit longer, if that's okay."

Raoul nodded with a smile. He flew over to the door and stopped when he had no way of opening it. "Oh, uh, can you let me in please?"

Sydona chuckled and opened the door a crack. He flew in and she returned to her seat on the concrete half-wall. She sat by herself for several minutes, soaking in the precious moments of quiet before what she could assume would be the last quiet time she would get for a while. In that time, she looked up to the sky, filled up with dark clouds, and imagined her father and mother reuniting in Heaven. It was the one positive thing she could think of in a time like this. She pictured her mother crying at the sight of her father and embracing each other. They looked in perfect health and couldn't stop smiling at each other. She welled up just thinking about them being together again. Sydona felt her cheeks warm up in the cool air. As she wiped away the last of her tears, she noticed the doctor walking toward the back and sliding open the door.

She turned back around to face the sea. The smell of his cologne found her first, and then, he took a seat next to her, careful to leave space between them.

They both sat and stared out, not speaking for a while. She caught a reflection of the bracelet on his wrist, and she gritted her teeth. The image of her happy parents dissipated.

"I, uh-" John said and then cleared his throat. "I took my daughter on a helicopter ride when she was just four years old." He paused to adjust himself for a long story. "I was nervous she wouldn't like it or throw up or something. My wife wasn't thrilled with the idea, but I convinced her somehow. You know how mothers can be." He chuckled. "So the day comes, and she's *so* excited, jumping up and down while I'm putting the helmet on and everything. We finally got up into the air, overlooking the city, and the look on her face…" He paused with a catch in his throat. "She saw the whole world in front of her, like it was magic. Like it was such a pure and raw emotion, that I had never seen before. She had never been someone to get overly excited about, anything really. I knew this experience was different, there was something about being above the world and seeing it below you. It was a feeling of invincibility and knowing you could do anything. At least, that's what I assumed she was feeling. It was then, at that exact moment, of seeing her face light up like that, I knew the world was what I wanted to give her. To see that look, all the time."

Sydona pretended to care and asked, "So, what happened?"

"I got caught up in perfecting it. I wanted to be the one to discover it. Be the one who could actually make her fly, without the help of a helicopter or airplanes. My father had tried back in the day but was never successful, obviously. I got so consumed by it and traveled *all* the time. I only came back home a few times a year. But, one day, I came back home after being gone for a few weeks, and my wife and daughter were nowhere to be seen. I found a note on the refrigerator door saying my wife took her and to not come looking for them. That was five years and forty-four days ago…" He paused and hung his head. "I can tell you loved your father dearly. My daughter would have never reacted that way if it were me instead."

An involuntary tear surfaced in her eye, and she had to swallow it down. "That painting was your daughter Priyah's. You did all of this for her?"

"Yes. It's silly, I know. My wife had a couple of miscarriages before. We prayed for Priyah every minute of every day that she wouldn't be the third. She was our angel. So I wanted to give her the entire world, and more."

"Why did you need to take us against our will and hold guns to our heads, though?" she asked, barely able to keep her voice calm.

He let out a half a chuckle. "A father cannot be held accountable for the things he does for his children. He just does them."

Sydona shook her head, "Yeah, but—"

"Are you saying you wouldn't go to the same lengths to make Giovonna happy?"

She started to shake her head but then stopped. "She's not my daughter."

"Not by blood. Your father was not your biological father either."

Sydona once again became speechless.

"That was quite an emotional reaction you had to someone who wasn't *really* your father." He paused and rubbed his palms on the head of his cane. "Natalia will be back. If you don't fight, who will protect that young girl in there? No one as fierce as you will do that. And I know," he said with a tap-tap of his cane and a soft chuckle.

Sydona grinned.

John continued. "If you want to give up, that's fine. But these people you brought, I can tell they admire you, look up to you. Even that big, angry fellow."

Suddenly, the massive weight on her shoulders evaporated into thin air. The doctor cupped her knee and then stood back up. He turned away from her to go back in, but before he walked away, he fiddled with something in his hands, then heard a faint clicking noise. "I think this belongs to you."

Sydona turned to him, and in his grasp was the silver bracelet. "This—is the only one that works though, isn't it?"

"It is."

"Why?" Sydona said. "After all that, you don't want it now?"

He smiled. "I thought being able to fly would fill me with more… lasting joy. But to tell you the truth, it was fun, yes. But it won't bring Priyah back to me." He let out a sigh, and Sydona took the bracelet from him. "More importantly, you've shown me how important family is. And once all this is over, I'm going to find her and my wife. I just hope it's not too late."

It was hard to respond to a man talking about his family when her own family was gone. If none of this happened though, she wouldn't have found Willow, Giovonna, or Silas. They were her family now, and they meant everything to her.

After a few moments of silence, he spoke again. "Oh, and I'm glad you didn't die. I've enjoyed having you around."

Sydona turned back to face him, but he had already shut the door. She fastened the bracelet on her wrist; it fit like a glove. She felt relieved she could fly again, but his words struck something inside her. She had been so focused on flying, she never realized how lucky she was to have found the people in her new family. They didn't care if she could fly or not. It didn't define her. Not anymore.

Squawks of sea birds sang with the rhythm of the waves in the distance. Normally she didn't like things about the ocean and preferred her tree birds, but something about the sounds soothed her. As if a new beginning was on the horizon. A beginning she wanted to be a part of and help create. His words about Giovonna touched Sydona, and just the thought of something happening to her caused heartache.

After several minutes of self reflection, she finally built up enough courage to go back inside. Her first action was to go to the bedroom with all of her belongings, including her dagger. Silas intercepted her in the kitchen.

"Wanna tell me what's going on?" Silas asked as he grabbed her wrist, breaking her train of thought.

She met his purple eyes, and she smiled. Overwhelmed with emotion, she planted her lips on his. Their eyes closed, and she melted into him. As good as it felt, she pulled away, suddenly realizing everyone was watching them.

"Come on." Sydona wrapped Silas's arm around the back of her neck.

"Where are we going?" he asked, not resisting in the slightest.

"You sure ask a lot of questions," she teased as she swiftly led him up the stairs.

"When I don't know what the hell is going on, yeah, I tend to do that sometimes."

They reached the bedroom, and she locked the door. "Take off your pants."

Silas flopped down on the bed with a face of excitement and confusion. "What?"

"Stop with the questions, babe. Just take them off."

Sydona began to strip the bloody clothes off herself as she felt adrenaline pump through her veins.

Silas let a nervous laugh escape. "I don't want to put a damper on this... very exciting thing that we might do for the first time. But, Syd, is this really the best time for that?"

Sydona took off her last piece of clothing, leaving just her undergarments on and bum rushed over to him on the bed. She reached for his zipper. "No time like the present, right?"

The sound of the zipper excited her but did the opposite for Silas. He did his best to scoot back from her and push her hand away. Then, he zipped up his pants. "Sydona, please. Your... your father just passed..."

Her hand retracted, and she nodded. A beige blanket laid nearby, and she wrapped it around her mostly nude body. The adrenaline fled, and she sat on the carpeted floor, feeling five inches tall.

"You're right. I don't know what I was thinking," she breathed. Her face was hot from embarrassment.

Silas joined her on the floor, his arms curling around her. "You have a lot going on right now. And as much as I would love to do... you... I just think we need to focus on finding Nat."

"It's a wonder how I haven't ravaged you earlier when you talk about doing me like that," she grinned.

"But, yes, we do need to find her. I want to shower and change first though. Can you please burn those clothes or something? I can't stand to look at them..."

Silas lifted her chin gently and made her look him in the eyes. "I love you, Sydona. We'll be downstairs when you're ready, okay?"

"Thank you," she said, and they kissed again. Her lips trembled, but Silas calmed them. Helping each other up, Silas limped his way out of the room, and Sydona stepped into the bathroom. After a long, steamy shower, Sydona found that her clothes were folded and sat in a neat pile on the counter. Not only were they her clothes from when she was taken by Natalia, but her dagger sat on top. Her boots and holster sat below them on the tiled floor. Her confidence shot off like a rocket, knowing she would be prepared for revenge.

Emerging from the shadows of the hallway and into the large, bright living area, she absorbed the conversations and the familiar togetherness. She hadn't realized how long it had been since everyone stood in the same room together. There were many unfamiliar faces as well, and she assumed they were Vultures who wanted to fight. It warmed her to know they might have a chance. Only one question still remained: where was Natalia?

Willow was the first to approach her as she made her way to the middle of the room. She looked better than before and had her scrapes and injuries bandaged up.

"How you holdin' up, Syd?" Willow asked.

"I'm better. But, Willow, how are *you*?"

"Oh, I'm—well, I'm hurtin', but it's nothin' I haven't dealt with before."

Sydona took a second to process what Willow must have gone through as she's been so consumed by her own problems. With barely a second to think about it, Sydona embraced Willow and squeezed her tightly. Willow was hesitant about her sudden friendliness but hugged her back. "You feelin' okay?"

Sydona smiled through tears and pulled away from her. She nodded and wiped more tears from her cheeks. "I'm just glad you're okay."

Willow furrowed her brows in confusion but brushed it off. "So, we got folks searching the grounds with heavy artillery. But they been under strict orders to not kill Nat. We'll leave that up to you, princess."

"Me?" Sydona sniffed and stopped in her tracks. "Why not just kill her?"

Willow crossed her meaty arms. "Don't ya wanna be the one who does it? After all she did to ya?"

"She caused Sparrows and Vultures to work together. I think she's affected everyone here in some way. I don't think it would be fair."

Raoul interrupted. "As long as she's not alive anymore, does it really matter?"

"It matters, buddy. Trust me," Harold said. Raoul gave him a nod of respect.

Sydona continued. "So we have Vultures searching the grounds, that's good. Why don't those of you who can fly search the skies?"

Knox replied, "That's what we were just about to do. The doctor here has also volunteered. He hasn't made us trust him enough for a gun even though he gave you the last bracelet."

"I completely understand," John said with his hands up in surrender. "And you may call me John, if you like. Oh, and I see you found your things," he directed at Sydona. "I trust it was all there?"

Sydona glanced down at her dagger and patted it.

He nodded back at her with satisfaction. He then cleared his throat, "I do have a sword hanging in my office that I could use. It's a funny story really… I—"

"Sydona," Knox cut him off with an eye roll. "What will you do?"

"I'll figure it out," Sydona said slyly.

"Just be careful," Avani noted.

"You too, Avani," Sydona replied.

Avani pulled her in for a quick hug. "Keep in touch, si? Let us know if you need help."

Sydona pulled away and nodded. "Will do."

"I'm going with you!" Giovonna exclaimed as she ran to Sydona's side and held her arm.

"Me too," Silas added. "Not much help running or flying around. But I'll do whatever you need me to do."

Raoul flew over to her shoulder and crossed his arms. Jubilee followed suit and landed on Giovonna's shoulder. Her smile matched Giovonna's wide grin.

"Aw, hell," spat Willow. "I can't let you guys go on your own. I'll come too." She kissed Harold good-bye and strutted over to the group. Knox and everyone else went their separate ways to look for Natalia.

Sydona flashed a quick look around, noticing the people surrounding her had been at her side since the beginning. She held back a large grin as butterflies tickled her stomach.

"Alright, let's go."

"Where to?" Raoul asked.

"Not sure, but we can go back to the apartments, see if she might be hiding somewhere over there."

It occurred to her that other Vultures and her group might have already searched there, but there was one person in particular she was hoping to find. A man with an injured finger. Raoul flew slightly ahead, Jubilee at his hip with every flit.

At last, they found three people behind one of the apartment buildings just talking. Sydona recognized one of them from her first encounter there, and as they approached them, he had a bandage wrapped around one of his fingers.

"Jones!" Sydona yelled.

Jones jumped and whipped his head toward them. His eyes grew big at the sight of her and took off running.

Giovonna took the initiative and ran after him. She ran fast enough to fly and caught up to him quickly. With a furious growl, she tackled him to the ground, face flat to the dirt. She sat on top of him as he flailed his arms, but she grabbed on to them and stiffened them at his sides. Sydona caught up, short of breath and kicked him hard in the side.

Sydona flipped her hair back. "Hello, Jones."

Giovonna pivoted her leg and got off the man. He turned around but still lay on the ground with his hands out and elbows down. "Fancy seeing you here."

"Enough with the small talk. Tell us where she is."

Jones cleared his throat. "Wh—ho? We have a lot of females here. Malik really felt like women needed—"

"You know who!" Silas interjected from behind her and slowly surrounded the man.

Soon, Willow, Silas and the fairies gathered around him. The men he was talking with right before didn't move a muscle, and he was on his own. Sydona pulled out a pistol and casually held it by her side.

"Oh, *her*. You know, I'm not really sure. She's a difficult one to keep track of these days."

"Don't make me ask you again, Jones," Sydona threatened.

"Ask John! He should know where his employees are!"

"We're asking you, Jones. I know you know."

Jones laughed. "You know nothing. But what I can tell you, is I wish I would have just five more minutes alone with you. Maybe then you wouldn't be so obsessed with finding a woman, if you know what I—"

Before he could finish, Silas grabbed Sydona's pistol, cocked the gun and shot Jones in the thigh without the slightest hesitation.

Jones screamed out. "Ahh! Fuck! Fuuuck you, fucking fuckers! Stop it with the biting and shooting! Goddamn!"

Sydona looked over at Silas who seemed satisfied with his shot. He then caught her gaze and winked at her. Sydona never felt so strongly about him before now. The quickness with which he defended her made him even more attractive to her. He then gently handed the gun back to her and she smirked.

Willow spoke up. "Then tell us, big shot. Or we'll shoot more than just your leg!" She aimed her trusty shotgun at his crotch.

"Okay, okay, fine!" he squealed, and his hands moved over to his precious jewels. "She's… she's probably at Daisy's…" The group stared at one another, trying to see if anyone knew who Daisy was. Shrugs all around.

"Who's Daisy?" asked Raoul.

Jones grinned. "Not who, what."

"Stop being cryptic. Where is Natalia?" Silas bellowed.

"Daisy's Pies. Now get that gun off my dick, bitch!"

Willow bared her teeth and readjusted her shotgun to the bottom of his chin. "This is clearly a bigger target anyway."

"Hang on," Raoul said, putting himself between the two. "I know you want to kill him. So do I. But, let Jubilee do her thing…"

Raoul looked at Jubilee, and she nodded.

Sydona spoke up. "What are you talking about, Raoul? She's just a youngling."

He put his index finger to his mouth while Jubilee floated above Jones's head. She released sparkling yellow dust mixed with a white powdery substance. Jones's eyes rolled backward, then closed and head fell to the side.

Sydona stared at the unconscious man and nudged him with the gun a few times. No movement. "How did she do that, Raoul?"

"I'm special. Right, Uncle?" Jubilee said gleefully.

"You are!"

"When did this happen?" Sydona asked, perplexed.

Willow answered, "She put the guard holding Avani hostage to sleep, too."

"Avani was held hostage?" Sydona said. "I've missed so much…"

"It's alright, Syd," said Giovoanna. "We'll fill you in on everything later. First, let's find out where Daisy's is."

They nodded. Willow instantly took her walkie talkie out and radioed Harold. "Willow here. Have I reached Harold?"

They waited for a minute. *"Harold here. How you doin', baby doll?"*

"We're fine, snookums. We're trying to find a place called Daisy's. You heard of it?"

"Oh yeah! It's got the best pies and shakes this side of the Rockies! Did ya get a lead?"

"Yep. You know the address?"

"'Course! It's just five miles south of here, off highway 45. Got a big red, white, and blue sign. Can't miss it!"

"Thanks, sugar plum. Willow over and out." She ended the transmission.

Silas rubbed the back of his neck and cleared his throat. "You guys are… uh…"

"The sweetest couple!" Giovonna said with big eyes.

Sydona jerked her head back. "The sweetest couple?" She exchanged glances with Silas, who looked just as offended.

Giovonna crossed her arms. "I haven't heard you guys call each other baby doll and sugar plum. That's the exact definition of 'sweet couple'."

"We—just aren't that kind of—nevermind! We have more important matters to focus on," Sydona said, putting her pistol back in the holster. "We need to find this pie place."

"What do we wanna do with him?" Raoul asked. Jones lay on the grass with drool leaking from his mouth.

"I can get him," Willow said and began to grab for his feet.

"No, no. We'll get…" Sydona began, then spied on a couple of Vultures who were fighting their own kind. "Hey, you two!" They looked at each other, finished punching out their opponents and hustled over to them.

"Can I trust you to take him back to the doctor's house and tie him up?"

They nodded and laughed when they saw Jones with a drool running down his chin.

Willow placed her hands on her hips. "Good. We don't know how long he'll be out for either, so be careful."

"We can handle Jones. Don't worry about that," one of the Vultures replied. They gladly took him by the feet and head and carried him off.

Sydona watched as they walked away and then gazed further out past the compound. "Everyone ready?" She took a sharp breath, like she was about to jump into the deep end of a pool. Raoul and Jubilee sprinkled the non-fliers with vibrant dust. Sprinting into flight, the group took to the sky and headed for Daisey's Pie shop.

Chapter Eighteen

SYDONA

The only sign for Daisy's sagged beside the highway, and the paint was curling off the wood. They buzzed past it. Landing on the outskirts of the rock-filled parking lot, Sydona observed the building with caution. It reminded her of the diner she first visited in Mayfield, a place she could easily see Harold visiting. Several pick-up trucks and cars covered in rusted edges were parked in front of the restaurant. As the thought of the diner in Mayfield left her mind, Giovonna spoke to Sydona. "This place reminds me of the one in Mayfield. The one where we first met."

The words she spoke were almost identical to her thoughts and Sydona couldn't help but smile. Giovonna grinned back, but the smile faded as they grew closer to the building. Sydona instantly put her arm around Giovonna's arm and squeezed it. A brief image of her sitting in the corner, reading books with her blue eyes was still so clear. Not knowing that she would end up changing so many things for her. In a matter of only a few months, she's adapted to a motherly role she never thought she had. Trying her best to focus on meeting Giovonna for the first time, Silas got her focused back on the task.

"Do you think it's a trap?" Silas asked.

"It could be… knowin' her," Willow said.

"If she comes here a lot though, someone may be able to tell us something," Giovonna said.

"You don't think she's here?" asked Raoul.

"There's only one way to know for sure," said Sydona. "Let's just be quick about it and get back as soon as we can."

She took the lead and confidently marched past the trucks. As she pushed through the dirty glass door, a waft of coffee and breakfast sausage filled her nose. "Keep this door open," she said casually over her shoulder. It was a small diner, and almost every seat filled. The rest of the group piled in and stood in the doorway, taking in the place all in one glance. It was lively with conversation and the smell of breakfast food filled the air. But as soon as their presence was known, the noise calmed and folks observed them one by one. Sydona adjusted her gun on her shoulder, keeping both hands securely on the strap. When she didn't notice Natalia, she cleared her throat.

"Looking for Natalia." She said it loud and clear.

The noise came to a complete stop and she felt every single eye on her. She swallowed and edged back to the comfort of the group.

A person at a table near the window stood up. He was dark and large and had a face that looked like he hadn't cracked a smile in his life. "Ain't no one here by that name, sweetheart."

Silas limped in front of Sydona and answered him. She blushed slightly at how quickly he stepped between her and the man. "We know she comes here. Anyone seen her in the last few hours?"

A voice rang from the opposite side of the diner as a woman with a mohawk the color of rotting leaves rose to her feet. "You really shouldn't have come here."

Willow took a turn and spoke up. "I will search every inch of this goddamn place unless you tell us where she is!"

She must have said the magic word.

Nearly every person in the diner pulled out a weapon of some kind and pointed it at the group. Sydona felt her heart jump and reversed the role. Her rifle along with Willow's shotgun, even Giovonna's crossbow.

As she glanced at Silas who was still out in front of the group, was standing with both arms outstretched on each side and both hands holding a submachine gun, borrowed from the Vultures trucks.

"The movies make this look way easier," he said as he tried to balance himself with one healthy leg.

"We got numbers but they got us outgunned," said one of the men, armed with nothing but a steak knife.

"Whoa, whoa, whoa!" Raoul interjected. He flew out into the middle of the diner with his hands outward, trying to make himself appear burlier. Jubilee, clinging to Giovonna's shoulder and could only watch from whatever safety she could perceive. "No need to get violent, we just want to find her. Not kill her!"

A different man from the counter pointed at Raoul uneasily. "Look a fairy! Kill 'em!"

"No!" Raoul shouted, but muzzled flashes of gunfire drowned out his voice. Sydona returned fire and hit a couple as she backed out of the diner and took cover behind the wall. Giovonna did the same but hid against the wall opposite of her. Willow, pumping and pulling as fast as she could, fired to the opposite side of the diner.

Silas, still with arms out, fired wildly in both directions as he stumbled backwards toward the door. The only response from the remaining Vultures was a handful of pistol fire, while several others took cover under tables and began crawling to their wounded. Either to assist them or take their weapons.

"Silas!" she shouted into the diner. "Get out of there!"

Willow responded as if she addressed her. "I'll join you in a bit, Syd!"

Silas stopped firing and fell to the side of his bed leg and hit the diner floor. She helped pull him behind a truck while still keeping an eye out for anyone trying to flank them. She shot out a few of the large windows and began looking for alternative cover. While she tried to process everything happening and made sure Silas didn't get himself killed, Giovonna was gone from her cover. Panic ensued. Each blast from Willow's shotgun made her heart beat even faster. She quickly wondered how Raoul and Jubilee were since they were caught right in the middle. Raoul was a quick fairy, so she took comfort in him finding a safe space in the chaos. While Silas situated himself to snipe from a truck bed, Sydona crawled around the cars, searching for Giovonna. At last, she located her, hiding behind a rusty, blue car with her head tucked between her legs. Sydona rushed to her side. "Gia!"

Giovonna lifted her head with the look of pure terror and streams of tears soaking her face. "It's gonna be alright," Sydona told her with a tight squeeze.

"I'm not a Sparrow, Syd! I can't do this! I don't want to die!"

"You won't die, baby girl," Sydona said and shot a man who got past Silas. "Wait, where's your crossbow?" The gun shot made Giovonna jump and cry more.

"I dropped it!" she cried. Her entire body shook. "I'm so sorry!"

"No, no! It's okay!" Sydona assured her. She held her even tighter. But the fear she was feeling needed to change to courage, and soon. The gunshots slowed way down and Willow's shotgun stopped as well. Both girls looked each other in the eye, thinking that was either a good thing or very bad.

"Jubilee is in there!" Giovonna said with wide eyes.

Sydona's heart leapt and she carefully peeked over the car.

A glimmer of sun caught a sparkling yellow puff of dust through the broken-out window. She smirked. "She's putting them to sleep."

Sydona reached down to her dagger and handed it to Giovonna. "Take this. Keep yourself armed. Don't let anyone kill you, okay?"

"Please don't leave me!" Giovonna whimpered and grabbed her shirt.

She caught the tears in her brown eyes and wanted so much to stay and protect her. What if she left and something happened? What if someone was hiding, waiting for them to let their guard down.

"You're a fighter, Gia. Just keep your eyes open and your chin up. I promise I'll be right back. I just want to check on the others."

Giovonna nodded her head. She wiped her tears, and Sydona kissed her forehead. "I'll be right back, alright?"

She let go of Sydona's shirt with another, more confident nod.

Sydona crept past the vehicles and when she heard nothing else inside, she stood up with her gun at the ready.

"I think this was a trap," Silas quipped as she approached him, still laying in the truck.

"Yeah, you think?" Sydona rolled her eyes at him.

Silas smiled. "You okay?"

Sydona nodded. "I'm good. You?"

"Right as rain."

"Can you go over to Gia, please? She's behind the blue sedan over there."

Silas instantly began to get up.

"You don't let anything happen to her, okay?" Sydona said with raised brows.

"Don't worry, babe," he said as he grabbed a pistol sitting next to him and loaded it. "I gotcha covered."

As Silas grunted his way out of the truck and headed across the parking lot to Giovonna, Willow called out. "Everyone okay?"

Sydona stood by the entrance, "Yeah, we're good."

Willow joined Sydona outside. "How 'bout Gia? Saw her shakin' like a leaf."

Sydona looked back over at the car she was behind. "She's shakin' alright. But Silas is with her now. You and I should check the back. Just in case there are stragglers."

Willow nodded and followed Sydona's lead. The diner was surrounded by a forest and fireflies glowed in the depths. Not a soul in sight and the quietness kept her on edge. It allowed her to hone in on any sudden noises.

Finally they reached a white, metal door at the back of the diner. Sydona reached for the door knob and turned it with ease, and clicked open. She caught Willow's eye at the unlocked door and she nodded. Sydona returned it and it filled her with hope that Willow had her back if anything happened inside. With her pistol held firmly in front of her, she edged her way in. It opened into the back kitchen and there wasn't anything inside to be heard. Jubilee must have put everyone completely asleep. So deep in sleep that not a single one of them snored. The silence was unbearing. Willow and her exchanged another glance, both confused on how loud it was only minutes ago, until now.

They both lightened their guard and searched the diner for Raoul and Jubilee. The restaurant was quiet but littered with bodies, sleeping in every direction. Not seeing any glowing fairies in the back of the diner, she pushed through the swinging door to the front of the house. Almost instantly, she spotted them at a table by the used-to-be front windows and

Jubilee lay on her back with her legs and arms spread out.

She rushed over to them. "Jubilee, are you okay?"

Raoul was right there with her. "No, she's exhausted."

"I'm—fine—uncle Raoul…" Jubilee managed to get out between breaths.

"No, you're not," he said sternly. Sydona raised her brows at his tone. She's never heard him use that voice before.

"She needs fruit, can you find something in the kitchen for her?" he asked.

Sydona nodded and headed back to the kitchen. Willow was still searching the diner for anyone left that wasn't unconscious. As Sydona was about to bring Jubilee apple slices, Willow signaled her and Sydona noticed her standing in front of a giant walk-in freezer. Sydona put the fruit down and got her pistol ready again. Willow nodded and used one hand to hold her shotgun and the other to open the freezer door. Both women stood firm and prepared themselves for anything.

The door swung open and a man stood in the freezer holding a pistol aimed right at Willow.

"Rot in hell!" the shivering man shouted.

Sydonas heart dropped as he held Willow at point blank. With almost zero time to decide, Sydona fired her gun and shot the man's hand. Within a split second, the blast from his pistol goes off, right after her shot hit and narrowly missed Willow. Right after the bullet whizzed by her, she pulled the trigger of her shotgun and the man flew backward, causing metal shelves to fall on top of him. Willow whipped her head around to Sydona with a nod. "Thanks, princess."

"Don't mention it," Sydona replied with a slight smile. "You owe me, though."

She walked toward Willow to retrieve the newly free gun.

"My gun was bigger than his so I woulda been fine without yer help," Willow mumbled.

"You already said thank you, nothing else you say counts," Sydona quipped back.

Willow smiled.

"Was that everyone then?" Sydona continued.

Willow put her shotgun over her shoulder and nodded. "Yup, that was it. Jubilee got all the rest o' them in dreamland. This guy... well, he ain't in no dreamland."

"Okay, good. We should probably get out of here then. Although we still have no idea where Natalia is." Sydona then picked the apple slices back up and headed straight over to the fairies.

Raoul was positioned in front of Jubilee with a puffed out chest and glowing a more vibrant orange than she's seen before. When he realized it was Sydona and Willow he dimmed down and flew over to them frantically.

"Are you guys okay? What happened back there?" he asked while he buzzed all around them, looking for injuries.

At that moment, Silas and Giovonna met them in the middle of the diner, too.

"Yeah, we're fine. Raoul… Why were you glowing so much right then?" Sydona asked.

"What, when?"

"Just now, before you saw who we were."

"I wasn't glowing, anymore than I usually do."

Willow chimed in. "Yeah, ya were. It was pretty obvious."

Raoul shrugged. "I don't know why. I was just making sure Jubilee would be safe if somehow it wasn't you guys that came from the back."

"Aw," Giovonna said with a pouty lip. "You really care about your niece, don't you, Raoul?"

"No!" Raoul said instantly but then stopped to rethink. He looked over at Jubilee eating cherries on a dirty plate on a different table. He couldn't help but smile. "I guess I do."

"If everyone is injury free, don't you think we should probably get going before everyone starts waking up?" Silas said. He then walked over to Sydona and embraced her from behind.

"I'm not sure how long they will stay asleep either," said Jubilee from across the room. Her mouth was covered in whipped cream and cherry juice.

"Enough reason for me," said Willow and was the first to head outside.

As the rest of them followed, Giovonna picked up her crossbow, laying on the rocky parking lot and cleans it off. As she secures it to her back, she hands Sydona back her dagger. The rest of them followed and congregated in the parking lot. The air smelled strongly of rain and Sydona looked up toward the sky. Darker clouds were blowing in and suddenly a crack of thunder made her jump.

Giovonna spoke up. "Where are we going now? We still have no idea of where she is."

No one responded for a minute as they were all unsure of the backup plan.

"I say we go back to the mansion an' just wait for her," Willow said at last.

"I agree with Will. She's gonna have to go back there at some point right?" said Silas.

"But why?" asked Raoul. "What's there for her?"

"The doctor," Sydona answered. "She wants revenge."

"Why?" Giovonna asked.

"'Cause he's stiffing her. Not giving her what she thinks she deserves for capturing me."

"That's disgusting," Silas said. "Like a trophy or something? Gross."

"What did he give her then?" Willow asked curiously.

Sydona smirked. "Nothing."

"Ooh," Raoul said with wide eyes. "No wonder she's so disgruntled."

"Yeah, seriously?" Silas chuckled. "She's the 'burn this effing place to the ground' type, too. Low blow, Malik. But, then again, fuck her."

"Now I'm wondering if we were purposely sent out here? She's planning something," Sydona said.

"I don't think this was a trap," Willow said. "I think it was just a distraction. That bastard knew exactly what kind of people come out here."

"Fuckin' Jones," Sydona gritted her teeth.

Raoul laughed. "He's the worst."

Sydona smiled with agreement but then took a couple minutes to decide their next plan of action. "Alright, let's go back. But we should grab as many weapons in these cars as we can before everyone wakes up." They all agreed to resupply and began looting the vehicles.

As Sydona worked on unlocking a car with an AR in the back seat, another crack of lightning made her jump and broke her concentration. She growled with frustration and glared up at the sky. The winds blew trees so hard the trunks became rubber, but just then, the winds blew in something peculiar. A silhouette of a flier soared a few hundred feet above them, with another flier by their side. She wondered who it could be and while she thought, one by one, dozens of smaller flying objects followed them. They all glowed different colors and the numbers continued into the hundreds.

Her heart pounded like a jackhammer. Rain drops began to fall and splash her in the face while she processed what this meant.

"Guys, look up at the sky!" She yelled with elation.

Each one of them stopped what they were doing and turned their noses to the clouds. They were only blurry silhouettes showing through the clouds, but the glowing rainbow of colors only meant one thing.

"Are those fairies?" Raoul exclaimed.

"Yes!" Giovonna hollered "Woo-hoo!"

"And they're going toward Maliks!" Willow shouted.

"Well, what are we still doing here?" Silas yelled over everyone. "Let's go!"

Chapter Nineteen

JET

Jet sat on the white couch across from Devon while everyone debated what to do next. The kid seemed focused on what Knox was yammering on about while he couldn't bring himself to do more than sulk. Anytime Jet glanced in Devon's direction, he would immediately avoid eye contact and turn his head back to the group. It ate him up inside how much Devon purposely avoided him, so he cleared his throat, thinking of something to break the tension.

He leaned over in his seat with his elbows on his knees and asked, "Do you want something to drink?"

Devon flicked his eyes over to him but then pretended not to hear.

Jet tried again. "Yo, Dev. I'm going to the kitchen anyway. Do you want something?"

To much of his surprise, Devon nodded his head ever so slightly. A spark of joy hit his heart, and he held back a grin. It was a small gesture, but at least Devon wasn't loathing him anymore. "I'll be right back," he said but once again received no response.

Jet stood up and made his way over to the kitchen, and he caught some of what Knox was discussing with the Vultures.

"...Not to mention, my wife was held hostage and tortured and you all just stood—" Knox started.

"Hey man, Natalia doesn't speak for all of us," a Hispanic man with a helmet argued. "I'm sorry about what happened to you and your wife, but that's why we're here. If you ain't gonna trust us, then…"

Knox sighed heavily, "It's not just that—" he stopped as he noticed Jet walking right past him.

"And where are you going?"

"Getting something to drink," Jet said with a lazy shrug.

Knox faced him fully. "I'm in the middle of discussing plans here."

"I can still hear you," he said and stole a glance at Devon. Knox didn't have a rebuttal but softly groaned as Jet continued to walk away.

His hand touched the cold marble counter in the kitchen and then the handle of the steel refrigerator. As Jet searched for a beverage, he noticed a bottle of wine on the bottom shelf. He stared at it while he let the coolness of the fridge hit his face. As he brushed his black silky hair out of the way, the weight of the flask in his pocket came into focus. He pulled it out, and a breeze from the kitchen window stirred the smell of cigarettes clinging to his clothes. Quinn's words about how alcohol changes a person gave him pause. From the corner of his eye, he caught an eye roll from Devon. His dismissive gesture made him think about how he was when he first met Devon, always giving him attitude and clung to Lacey. Jet knew he wasn't Devon's favorite person, but what could he do? He never drank as much as he did now. Maybe he had changed, but it wasn't too late to change back. A lump formed in his throat, and he knew what he had to do.

He shut the fridge door and twisted the cap off the flask. His heart pounded harder the closer he got to the porcelain sink. With a deep breath and shaky hands, he slowly tipped the flask sideways, and liquid began to circle the drain. Fearful of changing his mind, he tipped it completely over. The flask gasped for air. He had to shut his eyes, but he still heard the alcohol splash onto the sink and swirl into oblivion. After the last drop, he let out a sigh. Though he felt clarity, he didn't want to look at Devon. Not yet.

He placed the empty flask on the counter with a clink and left the cap next to it. Then, he filled up a glass of tap water. He chugged it as if he had never tasted water so fresh before. As the pure liquid quenched his unknowing thirst, he filled it up again. Once it was empty, he grabbed a second glass and brought that one to Devon.

Devon reluctantly took it, and while he was grabbing the glass, Jet bent over and whispered in his ear.

"I'm really sorry for everything. And please don't take this the wrong way, but I need to leave. But I'll be back."

Devon moved his head backwards in confusion, but his young, brown eyes met Jet's. "Quinn?"

Jet quickly smiled and nodded.

Devon nodded back, and Jet smiled wider. He squeezed the boy's shoulder and began to walk backwards. As he pivoted around to head to the back sliding door, Knox interrupted again.

"Jet! Where the hell are you going now?" His voice was on the verge of rage.

He turned back around to find everyone in the room staring at him. "Take care of Devon for me, okay?"

"Jet!" Knox bellowed again, but Jet was already outside.

Inhaling a deep breath of fresh, ocean air, he ran into a sprint and flew high into the sky. The entire trip, he could feel his body yearning for the flask. But every time it overwhelmed him, he would close his eyes and picture Quinn's face. The curve of her cheeks when she smiled, the silhouette of her with the goggles on her head, and her smooth accented voice helped calm him. He had only known her for a short time, but the impact was strong. He wasn't exactly sure what he was doing, but knew he had to make it up to Devon for everything he'd done. Jet was supposed to take care of him after Lacey's death, and he had never felt more like a failure. He flew faster than he ever thought he could, and the closer he got, the more excited he became.

Only a few hours later, the rustic winery at the top of the hill surrounded by dead grape vines came into view. He landed quietly and walked up to the door. He raised a fist to knock on the heavy, oak door, but wasn't sure why. He didn't knock before, so he pushed it open. Quinn stood behind the counter, cleaning guns.

Her purple eyes twinkled from the sunlight as Jet walked in. She held back a smile. "You again."

"You changed," he said, shutting the door behind him and looking over her new clothes. No more flip flops, but heavy, black boots. Her shirt seemed to have a vest underneath it as well. Quinn was prepared for a fight.

She looked down at herself and shrugged. "Yeah. That happens from time to time."

"Any particular reason why?"

Her smile grew. "No? Just felt like it. What's it to you?"

Jet shrugged. "You're cleaning guns, too. Interesting."

"I'm sorry, are you with the FBI or something?" She paused and focused all of her attention on him.

"I just thought it was interesting. Considering my last visit."

Quinn's fairy, Dani, flew into the room and landed on the counter, hands on hips. The stance reminded him of Raoul.

"Your last visit consisted of looking for any booze and trying to get me to leave this slice of paradise. I just like to clean this stuff," she said and went back to cleaning.

Dani spoke up, her Irish accent just as strong as before. "Where's the kid? He take off?"

"No, he's… I didn't bring him," Jet said, voice fading as he began to feel guilty for leaving Devon behind.

"Did ya just leave him in the middle of the woods?" she asked with a small chuckle.

"Of course not. He's back at the house."

"The doctor's house? Well that was kinda shitty of you," she said, staring down the barrel of a shotgun she was cleaning.

"I needed to see you…" he began, but as he heard his own words, his face grew hot. "I—uh, what I mean is… I stopped drinking."

Quinn raised both eyebrows in surprise. "Ya did? Why?"

Jet cleared his throat and grabbed one of his shaking hands. "Well, because you were right. It changed me. Devon saw right through me." He swallowed hard as he tried to search for the right words.

She released a smirk. "Oh." she paused and nodded. "I'm glad."

"Thanks."

Dani spoke up. "S'that all you came 'ere to tell us? That ya quit drinkin'? Reckon it wasn't a trip down the road, was it? Why you really here, mate?"

"Oh, uh," he cleared his throat. "I'm here because we all could really use your help."

Quinn shrugged, "Rosie toastie." She continued to wipe a gun down with a cloth.

Jet raised one brow, "Rosie toastie?"

She paused and let out a quick laugh. "Yeah…. uh, it's like 'okie pokie'." Her mind seemed to wander off somewhere far. Dani looked after her with concern.

"Oh," said Jet, not sure about the feeling in the room. "Okay—"

"My sister, little Gemma, could never say 'okie pokie' when she was little and she used to say something that sounded more like 'rosie toastie'. I made fun of her for it for years, and eventually Gemma embraced it and would say it on purpose anytime we saw each other. It would make us laugh every time. She was my best friend…"

Jet sank into her darkness and yearned to help. "What happened to her?"

"She disappeared one day and I… the first place I thought of was the fucking NFA, so I flew from my home in Sydney to the States. Took months to find her, and when I finally did, it was too late."

"I—I'm so sorry, Quinn." His hand gravitated toward her, but he stopped himself right before touching hers. "Were you there too?" he asked Dandelion.

Dani dropped her head. "She was mine. She was my flier. My soulmate."

"So, you two aren't…" Jet asked, pointing his finger at them both.

"No," Quinn replied with a quick sniff. "She's not mine. But being together and being able to talk to someone who knows your pain somehow makes shit a lot less shitty."

Jet nodded. He knew exactly what she felt and wondered if that was the issue with him and Devon. Tragedy loved company.

"It's good you have each other," he said, and dug out a pack of cigarettes. It was his last one, so he raised it as if raising a glass. "Cheers to you."

As he lit the end, Quinn wiped tears from her eyes. "Yeah, cheers. So, what do you need help with exactly?"

Jet took a drag and turned to Dani. "Are you a pixie?"

When Dani didn't answer right away, Quinn pressed. "Well, are you?"

"No, of course not," replied Dani. "You of all people would know that."

Jet exhaled smoke toward the ceiling. "Figured…"

"Why?" asked Dani, who crossed her arms and gave Jet her full attention. The mention of pixies seemed to always give people pause.

"We found out a fairy of ours is one and can put people to sleep almost instantly. Just thought that maybe if you could do that too, we could have a very good chance of surviving this."

Dani laughed. "Trust me, if I had powers like that, I wouldn't be hanging out with this loser." She pointed her thumb at Quinn.

"Excuse me," said Quinn. "If you were a pixie, I woulda sold your ass a long time ago."

Jet watched as they bickered playfully at each other. Even if some of their words felt truthful. "Well, anyways," he interrupted, feeling awkward. "I guess I'll just go then…"

As Jet turned his back and headed for the door, Quinn said something in the sweetest, quietest voice. "Hang on, Jet… Dani…" she said. Jet stopped and turned back around with a sigh.

The girls wandered to the far side of the bar and Jet sat on a bar stool, resting his arms on the wooden countertop as they talked. It felt like they were talking for a long time, so he took his time dragging in what was left of his last cigarette. He also had time to admire her. She was just about the same height and size as Lacey. It pained him to think of being interested in another girl so quickly after her death. His violet eyes quickly took to the wood rafters in the ceiling, counting each one.

Finally, they turned around to face him, and Quinn was the first to say something. "I think we can help."

Jet sucked in a long drag of his cigarette and asked as he exhaled. "How?"

"The last I heard from my friend Virgil was he was staying somewhere near Las Vegas. He's, uh, kind of like a protector of pixies."

He squinted his eyes at her through the cloud of smoke, unsure of what she meant. His expression must have warranted enough confusion that Dani continued speaking.

"Probably shouldn't be telling you this, but he's also part pixie. Meaning, he's a flier, but harnesses abilities that are the same as pixies. The highest order of shamans have granted him the position, and now, he looks after other pixies."

"Wait, wait, wait," Jet said, letting go of his last puff and squishing the butt out on the counter. "Now that has to be bullshit. Fliers can't do that stuff. It's unheard of. Where did you even find this guy? He's probably full of it."

"It's not shit," Quinn said quickly with a hard-ened face. "I met him in passing when I found my sister."

"In passing? He was probably trying to get your— I'm— Not that I care about that…"

"Okay, it was more than passing. I saved him from a camp, and he told me where to find him if I ever needed him. This was only six months ago."

"But why? Why would he tell you all this? You just met," Jet said, getting slightly angry.

"I don't know! He asked my name; I told him and he just told me all that. He also said I would meet someone unexpected with a three-lettered name. He said the prophecy was a little blurry."

Jet shook his head and stepped off the bar stool, unable to comprehend what he was being fed.

Dani spoke up in the long stretch of silence. "Virgil also said dragons exist. Indefinitely."

"Yeah, but the ones who can turn into dragons *are* a myth, Dani. No one has actually seen it," said Quinn.

"Is that what Virgil can do?" asked Jet.

"No, not at all. Well, actually, I'm not exactly sure of his ability. But he is a pixie."

"What do they call people like him?" asked Jet.

Dani replied. "Don't think they have a name. Mine and Quinn's family have never heard of or been taught about pixies. Maybe they just never existed where we were."

"Not just you," Jet spoke. "Never talked about them in my family or told stories from the past." He thought about all of the possibilities the pixies had and was anxious to find them. "Should we go see him then? Do you think he'd help?"

Quinn raised her brows. "Couldn't hurt to try! If the prophecy was real, that means we met by fate."

Jet blushed and turned quickly away. He tried not to dwell on the moment and helped them bag up their supplies. A large duffle bag full of guns straddled Quinn's body. Jet took a few of his own to help carry the load.

"I reckon it will take about an hour to fly there," said Quinn as she secured her bag.

Jet nodded. "Well, it's unclear what Natalia is planning, but I think we should try to get back as soon as we possibly can."

"I can help with making you go faster," said Dani. "Don't you worry, mate."

Jet noticed how hefty the bag was, now that it was bursting with fire power. "Damn, these things get real heavy, don't they?"

"Too heavy for you?" Quinn teased.

"Oh, don't worry. I'm fine. But you got more than me. You want me to take some more?"

"Not a chance," Quinn said, while Dani's dust went to work on the heaviness.

Jet shook his head and held back a smile.

Quinn led the way, with Dani following close beside her. Jet met her gaze when she glanced back. She gave him a large grin and a wink. It was difficult for him not to smile back.

Desert lands spread for miles, with some mountains and hills nearby. He'd never been in the desert but could certainly feel the heat from the setting sun. Cacti, tall and short, populated the terrain as if making up for the lack of trees and grass. The different shapes they took on were interesting to look at. Swirls of desert dust reminded him of the fairies and gave him hope. A larger cloud of dust swept toward them, and they had to detour around it.

The trip also helped sober him up, but he could already feel the pain of absence. His hands began to quiver. But soon the landscape shifted, and the excitement of flying through rocky canyons pushed the need of alcohol to the back of his mind. Jet searched the ground for a house or tent or tree or something that would tell them they were in the right place. He followed Quinn to the bottom of the canyon, and they landed in what felt like nowhere. A large cave gaped in the rocky wall ahead, and Jet assumed it was where they were headed. Dani and Quinn walked around a bit, admiring the breathtaking canyon, but Jet was confused. He took it upon himself to examine the cave, but as he got swallowed into the depths, the feeling of an inevitable unknown overwhelmed him. It felt almost clarifying, as if his mind went black and reset. His heart began to pound with each step and he wasn't exactly sure why. And as his hands started shaking, he paused, held his arms down at his side. "It's just withdrawal," he assured himself. When the strange sensations didn't stop, he quickly headed back out of the cave.

As he stepped back into the dying sunlight, his words echoed through the canyon to the girls. "Did we take a wrong turn?"

"No, I'm sure it's here…" Quinn said.

"Virgil!" Dani shouted, her voice surprisingly loud.

Jet laughed. "I don't think he's here, guys. I can fly around to see if I see something that…"

His voice faded as a house appeared out of thin air, ten feet in front of him. His heart pounded quickly. He was just happy that it didn't crush him. The way the house sat in the ground, it was as if it had been there for years, but why had he only just now noticed it?

"I knew it!" Quinn exclaimed and jumped up. "His ability is creating mirages. I knew, I knew it! He uses it to hide the pixies."

"Quinn, dear! How are you?" a small, stubby man yelled out from the front door and held his arms out for a hug. Quinn bent down, and he wrapped his arms around her. "Is that little Dandelion, too? Get in here!"

Dani grinned and hugged him in return. The girls went inside the house, slipping in behind Virgil, but Jet stood waiting on the welcome mat. A frown replaced the man's smile. Jet looked down at him, and even though he was more than a foot shorter, the gaze from Virgil's dark purple eyes made him feel small.

"What's your name, son?" asked Virgil sternly. A small pair of glasses sat on the edge of his large nose, and he managed to glare down at Jet even though he was looking up. "J—" he cleared his throat as his voice caught. "Jet, sir." He heard Quinn snigger. Her arms were crossed, as Dani stood on top of them.

"That's a peculiar name. I'm assuming 'sir' is not your last name, is it?"

"Jet Shi… sir."

Virgil turned to Quinn. "Polite one, isn't he?" Quinn nodded. Jet finally met his eyes, and Virgil winked playfully. He continued, "You're a flier, I see. Are you in affiliation with anyone?"

"I'm a Sparrow," he answered confidently.

"Like Quinn and Dani here," he confirmed out loud to himself. Virgil narrowed his eyes at him as if he knew something but wasn't saying. "Well, you three must be exhausted. Please come in. I'll put some tea on." He held his small arm out signaling for him to come inside. Jet nodded respectively and stepped in, past Quinn, catching her smile at him.

The home was cozy, filled with several rugs in all designs, covering a dark wooden floor. Every inch of the walls were covered with either art work, or other rugs. Each window was dressed with curtains, and there were enough chairs in the living room to sit about a dozen people. A small television sat in the corner and a thick layer of dust sat on top, along with the remote.

"Please make yourselves comfortable," Virgil said from the kitchen window. As everyone got settled, Virgil kept speaking from the other room. "Quinny, how long has it been?"

Quinn sat on the couch and turned her head to answer. "About six months."

"Is that all?! Man, I feel like it's been much longer..." he said with a chuckle.

"Yep," she cleared her throat. "Still feels like yesterday to me."

"Oh, dear," he said and poked his head out from around the corner. "I'm sorry to bring your sister up again. My deepest condolences."

Quinn shook her head with a smile. "No apology needed, Virgil. It is really good to see you."

Virgil entered the room carrying a tray of tea cups and tea bags already seeping into the steamy water. "Good to see you too, deary. And, I think I know why you're here."

"You do?" Jet asked as he leaned against the brick fireplace.

"Yes." He took a small sip of tea and held onto it, staring at the floating leaves. He took a deep breath before speaking again. "You may not know Mr. Shi, but I am in close relationships with the shamans. As you saw, I have unique powers that only pixies possess. As rare as pixies are, fliers with abilities, other than flying, is even more uncommon. They took me under their wings, so to speak, and helped me harness it. Once I mastered the ability, I've been tasked with hiding pixies from the rest of the world. But being so close to the shamans, they have warned me of a threat that could change everything for us." He took another sip of tea.

Jet hung on to his every word, waiting patiently for him to continue the story. Quinn and Dani sat next to him, eyes unrelenting.

"Have you heard of the name 'Natalia'?"

As the name slipped so casually from Virgil's lips, Jet felt his heart jump from his chest.

"How did— She— Yes. I know her well," he replied, but his mouth felt absent of moisture.

Virgil hyper focused onto Jet, setting his tea down and moving to the edge of his seat. "What do you know?"

"Oh, uh, well I know she has a sister who's a flier, but she's not."

"How do you mean, exactly?"

"Well, she doesn't have our eyes and she can't fly. She's also a Vulture."

Quinn interrupted. "How did her name come up with the shamans?"

Virgil replied. "Last I heard she was hunting them down. And if their prophecy of her is accurate, we're in a lot of trouble. She is… like me."

Dani spoke up. "As in, she can cast mirages?"

Virgil shook his head and his eyes faded to brown. "Not exactly."

The three of them had their eyes glued to him as he stood up and walked to the window. The silence was killing Jet.

"They think she has the ability to become... a dragon." He then gave a quick glance at Jet and locked onto his eyes. Jet felt his entire body shutter and furrowed his brows at Virgil.

"What?!" Dani shouted "Bulox!"

"Virgil..." Quinn spoke. "You believe them?" Her words quivered.

"Hang on, hang on," said Dani, flying into the middle of the room waving her arms. "Are we talking about a dragon the size of a person, or like a fully full-grown, burn cities down type of dragon?"

Virgil replied. "It's unclear. But from their predictions, I assume the latter."

"Does it matter?" Quinn said, her eyes turning into emeralds. "A dragon is a dragon. If that prophecy is even half correct, we need to find her, like yesterday."

"This can't be possible..." Jet uttered. He sat down as his legs suddenly turned to jelly.

Virgil turned his body to face them again. "I wish that were true, lad..." After a few minutes of quiet as everyone let the earth-shattering news sink in, he spoke again. "Come. I have something to show you."

Virgil led them out of his back door and onto the rocky, dirt ground. The sun had almost completely set now, making the pitch black cave ahead ominous. The three didn't question him as he waddled down a slope, delving deeper inside. Jet wondered what was actually in there as he checked only moments before and it was void. Except for his heart that began to pound hard again. Maybe it wasn't just withdrawal. For only a couple of seconds it was so dark, he couldn't see his own hand in front of his face. But soon, a small glow bounced off a rock bending just around the corner. Once light came, with each step closer it became increasingly brighter. All at once he took the scene in. It was as if the sun had a second home. Glowing from hundreds of pixies lit up the cave, revealing a massive city within. Pinks, yellows and blues bounced brilliantly off Jet's porcelain, smiling cheeks. He hadn't seen or experienced many things that made him want to cry, but this one did. He squashed them as soon as they tried to surface, and spoke aloud.

"This is fucking incredible."

"Wow, Virgil. I agree with Jet. This is what you've been hiding?" Quinn said.

"It is," Virgil replied. "And so far it's worked out. Only the Shamans and you three know of its whereabouts."

"Do they live here?" asked Dani, flicking her blue wings.

"Most of them do now. But mainly it's a place to practice their abilities."

"Do they know of the prophecy?" Quinn asked.

Virgil closed his eyes and nodded. "They do. They've been preparing, in fact." He began walking further into the glowing city.

The group followed him slowly into the rocks. Jet noticed several holes in the cavern's walls and each one filled with a pixie or furniture. Stalagmites jetted out from the cave floor, providing even more homes. Flat surfaces had structures built on top like tiny buildings for other pixies. All around him, they were practicing, almost like they were preparing for a war. Not a single one was sitting down or relaxing. Although the colors made it feel fantastical and magical, the seriousness on faces changed the tone. Virgil called out a pixies name as he stood in the middle of the cave. He leaned against a stalagmite that stood a foot taller than himself.

Soon a glowing red pixie with black hair and black and red wings buzzed up to the group. He smiled brightly and greeted Virgil like an old friend.

"Everyone, this is Kieran," Virgil introduced happily.

"Hey!" he said. But Jet noticed he lingered on Dani a bit longer than everyone else.

"Hey," Dani replied with blushing cheeks. "What's your ability, Kieran?"

Quinn looked at her sideways with confused brows.

Virgil spoke. "Do you want to show them what you can do?"

Keiran nodded and backed away from them a bit. He closed his rust colored eyes and pushed his hands together. Within seconds, a cloud of red dust formed around him and with a slick hand trick, each speck of dust transformed into flames. Soon, the little pixie was consumed by a ball of fire, which he quickly tamed into a controlled flame with only his hand. Jet's eyes grew wide at the rare magic. Glancing to his left, Quinn and Dani felt the same. Their jaws opened wide and stared at him with awe and excitement.

Keiran paused to let the scene soak in, as if he'd done it a hundred times before. Then, he shifted the position of his hand, moving the flame back into a fireball, then pushing outwards and throwing it into the abyss. The three watched it until it disappeared and Keiran took a bow. Quinn and Dani applauded him generously as Jet gave him an impressive nod.

"That was amazing, Keiran!" Quinn said. "And you're not even burnt!"

"Nope! Fire doesn't bother me," he said proudly.

"Not even your wings are singed!" Dani flew up to him and yanked on one of them, forcing Keiran off balance. "Sorry!" she giggled.

"It's fine," he grinned and twitched his wings.

Virgil joined in. "Kieran is a very special pixie," he said with a grin at him. "He's the only one among us so far that not only can create and control fire, but can also become a dragon, too."

Quinn had to shake her head to understand. "Beg pardon?"

Kieran exchanged a worried look with Virgil. Virgil replied. "You heard right. But the shamans believe once a pixie becomes this form, there's no turning back."

Jet furrowed his brows. "You mean, we may actually have a chance?"

Dani flew into Jet's face. "What? You think just because he 'as an ability you like you can just use him as a prop in your war?"

"No, that's not what I meant, I'm just saying… If Nat can really turn into one, too, what better way to fight a dragon than with another dragon? What better plan have we got than that?"

Quinn glanced at him with arms crossed, "Jet, it's suicide."

As Jet was about to retort, Virgil took the floor again. "Kieran is well aware of what it means. Everyone knows what it means." He paused, and as Jet looked around the cave, the pixies stopped what they were doing and all looked upon the group. "But there is just… one more thing. Jet." He turned to look up at him with a smile. "It's not a coincidence that you're here, son."

Jet furrowed his brows and looked to Quinn and Dani for clarity, but they were just as confused. "I don't follow."

"You, my good man, are like me," Virgil grinned.

Jet shook his head and narrowed his eyes.

"Actually, you're more like Kieran!"

Quinn laughed. "He can control fire?!"

Virgil bellowed. "No! Not exactly, dear. He can transform into a dragon!"

A huge lump formed in Jet's dry throat. Not able to find anything to say to this, Jet just laughed, progressively getting louder. Eventually, he shook his head and crossed his arms. "There's no way that's true, man."

Virgil stepped closer to him. "I know it's a lot to process."

Jet burst out laughing again. He turned away from him and began pacing the cave floor.

"This is a joke, right Virgil?" Quinn asked. Her question comforted Jet slightly. He wasn't the only one who was in disbelief.

All Virgil did was interlock his hands together and shook his head with seriousness.

"Hang on," Dani chimed in. "If it's true he's a dragon, and he actually does it, don't that mean he'll… not be able to turn back?"

Virgil dropped his head, closed his eyes and nodded. Jet's stomach felt as if an anchor had just dropped into it. He reached for his flask, but then remembered he left it at the house.

"Perfect," he uttered.

Quinn turned to him, sensing the sarcasm in his voice and she touched his arm. The light from the pixies reflected in Quinn's wet eyes. Virgil, Dani and the rest of the pixies stared at him, waiting to hear what he'd say next. When he didn't speak for a minute, trying to understand, Kieran flew over to him and landed on a stalagmite nearby. He spoke softly so the others wouldn't overhear.

"Tell me something. When you entered this cave, you had an — overwhelming feeling rush over you. A feeling that couldn't really be explained, rationally."

Jet narrowed his eyes. "Yes, actually."

Kieren gave him a sideways smirk. "I don't know exactly what brought you here, but, for me? I wasn't doing anyone any favors and when Virgil came to me, I thought he was insane. I didn't even know I could cast fire before I met him! But, anyways," he paused. "Whatever life you had before this, whatever bad things you did in the past… this can be your way out. By protecting *him*."

Jet stared at the fairy with confusion. He somehow knew that Kieran knew who Devon was, with how powerful Virgil and the shamans were. They knew what he was before he did. He had to put himself in a new mindset, and actually start believing that dragons were real.

"I'm gonna need a minute," he said and made his way out of the cave.

He never felt his heart beat so fast in his life. Once he reached the mouth of the cave and Virgil's house appeared, he ran. His fists curled tightly, his feet slammed on the rocky canyon ground and once he knew he was far away from everyone, he yelled as loud as he possibly could. His voice echoed through the canyon, intensifying it so much it made his ears ring, but he didn't care. He yelled until his face turned red and his voice began to crack. With shaky hands, he threw them over his face and sat abruptly on the ground. Tears began to pour out. If there was ever a time for alcohol, this would have been it.

His mind ran at a million miles a minute. Should he or shouldn't he? On one hand, having that ability could put an end to Natalia. But if he did, he'd still die. If he didn't do it, they might still have a chance to win with all the pixies he found. But if they lost, he would never be able to forgive himself. Just more things he could add to his list of regrets. He had to make things right with Devon before he made any decisions. Maybe being a dragon would be enough to have Devon forgive him. But if it didn't, he would die for nothing.

"Hey you okay?" Quinn asked from behind him.

Jet quickly wiped his eyes of tears.

She sat down next to him. "Of course you're not. What a stupid question…"

He shook his head. "It's fine."

"No, it's not. It's a lot to spring on a person like that. What an impossible thing to decide."

Jet gave a small chuckle. "Yeah, tell me about it."

Quinn put her hand on top of his. "No one will blame you if you don't do it, Jet."

Jet swallowed hard. He put his other hand on top of hers and squeezed. "Thank you, Quinn."

They sat together in silence for a few more minutes, with Quinn resting her head on Jet's shoulder. Jet tried to take in every little thing about this moment as it may be the last calm and relaxing thing he'd ever do.

"Guess we should get back," Jet said as he stood up. Quinn got up too, and as they began to walk back to the cave, he stuck his hand out. Quinn grabbed it and interlocked her fingers with his.

Darkness of the cave soon grew brighter as they reached the secret city and Virgil ended a conversation he was having with some of the pixies. Dani was talking to Keiran as they arrived and promptly flew up to them.

"Well?" she asked Jet. The entire cave went silent as they waited for his decision.

Jet let go of Quinn's hand and he crossed his arms to prevent his hands from shaking. "So, how does this work exactly?" he asked with a deep inhale, quickly glancing at Kieran.

He noticed Quinn turned away from him and hid her face. His heart ached.

Virgil clapped his hands together. "Marvelous!" He then patted his back and walked slowly around the cave with him.

"Kieran will be your mentor, but there will be a few shamans that will help you reveal your hidden identity. Kieran will be there to help you learn how to control it."

"But he's never been a dragon before. How would he help with that, exactly?"

Kieran flew up to them and answered. "I may not have transformed before, but I do possess fire abilities. As long as you know the basics of harnessing magical abilities, you'll be able to know the feeling. The shamans will help with the transformation."

"Will you be transforming with me?" Jet asked nervously.

"You betcha! Been waiting a long time for this," he said confidently. "It's our destiny."

Jet smirked. Maybe it was his destiny, too. As nerve-racked as he was, he was somewhat looking forward to becoming such a rare, all powerful creature. He could be the one to stop the war and senseless killings. "So, what can all the other pixies do?"

Virgil took a deep breath and looked to the ceiling while he counted on his fingers. "There's... Ginger who can make others harm themselves instead of hurting her. Nelly produces a very powerful sleeping dust, to the point of putting them into a coma. Sandrine can speak fluently to any animal she wishes and convince them to do what she wants. Rosey can make you think you're drowning, even though you're not around any water. And Orion confuses them to the point where they are brain dead for a few hours. These of course are just a few. The possibilities are endless."

Dani laughed, but with excitement. "They can do all of that?! That's insane! I can't even get Quinn to pick up all of her hair-ties!"

Quinn laughed back and pushed the fairy hovering next to her. "Whatever!"

Jet chuckled to himself at the girl's antics. "Well," he said with a deep breath and a spark of determination that he thought faded long ago, "What are we waiting for?"

Chapter Twenty

SYDONA

A chill ran down Sydona's spine as they came upon the mansion on the hillside. Flashbacks of Eagle Lake kept appearing in her mind. The echoes from gunshots, screaming and overall chaos and noise from killings made her weary. Her first thought was to see the progress made with Natalia. She had to be back there. There was nowhere else she could be.

She pulled out her gun as her left foot hit the ground and shot and killed a Vulture running at them. Giovonna stayed close behind and screamed as Sydona took the shot at another one.

Silas and Willow took care of themselves and fought off a couple guys coming at them from behind. Sydona made a break for the house as most of the chaos took place outside. As she ran, she noticed some peculiar things happening. It was obvious more fairies were there than usual, but also that the humans attacking them were either turning around to kill their allies or they took their own gun and shot themselves.

"What the f…" she said, but then saw another Vulture collapse to the ground and they began to have seizures. She quickly glanced behind her for Giovonna, who stared at the woman on the ground, shaking violently. Giovonna widened her eyes and went back and forth between her and Sydona. She was just as confused, but at the same time happy to see her enemies falling like flies. Sydona grabbed Giovonna's hand and led her inside the house. Knox was set up on the island in the kitchen like a sniper, pointing his weapon at anyone brave enough to come in the front door. Avani was stationed behind the couch watching the back door, waiting for anyone to walk through.

"They're back!" Avani yelled.

Silas soon came too, along with Raoul, Jubilee and Willow.

"Have you found her yet?" Sydona asked first.

"Not yet," shouted Knox and pulled the trigger on an intruder. "But looks like she sent reinforcements."

"What the hell is she doing?" asked Silas.

"Who knows," Avani said with a shaking head.

"Where's Devon?" Giovonna asked.

"He's in one of the bedrooms," Knox said. "I didn't want him to get mixed up in this kind of battle."

"No, sweetheart," Avani commented. "You said 'He's a Sparrow now, he needs to fight like a Sparrow' but I said, "No! He's just a little kid!"

"Well, whatever. He's up there," Knox said. Avani raised her brows and put her tongue in her cheek. But she quickly let it go and went back to manning her position.

Giovonna took off running to the bedroom to find Devon. Willow grabbed an automatic gun laying next to a Vulture in the living room and took cover behind one of the couches.

"Where did all the fairies come from?" Raoul asked.

"Actually… they're pixies," Knox said, shooting another Vulture. "Jet brought them."

"You're kidding!" Silas laughed. "Our Jet? The one who can't breathe without whiskey?"

"Yeah, I was surprised, too."

"How in the hell did he find so many?" Raoul asked.

"Uh, well, it's a long story, but a man named Virgil was protecting them. Preparing them…" said Knox with a sense of pride.

Sydona put all of it together, remembering legends of pixies long ago and it filled her with joy.

"Natalia talked to me about pixies like this when she had me in the cage," said Jubilee. Her voice barely held over the sounds of battle.

"What do you mean?" Sydona asked as got closer to hear her better.

Both Avani and Willow shot their guns at more intruders, making Jubilee flinch.

Raoul spoke up. "Let's go find Gia and Devon in the bedroom where it's safe."

"Good idea, Raoul," shouted Knox. "We'll hold the fort down here."

The group of them rushed to the bedroom and Sydona knocked on the door. "It's just us."

After several clicks of locks being unlocked from behind the door, Giovonna swung it open. Sydona pushed through and looked for Devon. He jumped off the bed and gave her a hug around the waist.

"Hey kiddo. You okay up here?"

Devon nodded. "Where did Jet go?"

"He's out there; protecting you," she said with a gentle and sincere tone.

He wiped his nose and grabbed her hand. Silas locked the door behind them and made his way over to the window, covered with a curtain. He peeked out every so often.

Raoul began the conversation again. "So, what did Natalia tell you?"

Jubilee flicked her yellow wings and stood in the middle of the bed with the rest of them surrounding her. "Well, she said that I was rare. That I had an ability that most fairies don't have."

"How did she know that?" asked Giovonna.

"I don't know…" she said. She stayed close to Raoul, standing on the bed next to her. "She kept asking me about our shaman. But I told her that he died a year ago. I didn't know what she wanted with him."

"That was clever," said Raoul with a grin.

Jubilee blushed. "It was?"

"Yes," he laughed. "What did she say next?"

"She got really angry when I told her that. And when she went to take me out of the cage, I got scared and told her I heard of another place. I just made it up, but I hoped it would make her leave me alone. You came and rescued me, Uncle Raoul, before she came back."

"Where did you send her?" Sydona asked.

"A place I've only heard of once before. Called Florida. I don't know where that is exactly, but she seemed upset. I guess it was far."

Raoul asked, "Did Shaman Faro ever talk to you about your ability?"

"Yeah. He told me that we have a different aura that surrounds us. Unless the fairy… or pixie discovers it on their own, Shamans are the only ones who can sense it."

"I don't understand," Giovonna spoke up. "I've read everything I could about fliers and fairies. I've never once remembered reading about pixies."

"Shaman Faro said it would be too dangerous to expose us to the world. That if the humans found out, it could be fatal."

"Did he say why fliers don't possess powers like that?" asked Sydona.

"Um, actually, he said that some fliers can. But the chances are almost a zillion to one. He said it would be even more dangerous if fliers knew. Because anyone who found out would come after the pixies next. It could wipe us out completely."

Sydona's heart sped up. She wondered if she could be one of them.

Then Devon spoke. "Natalia is human, isn't she? Why would she need a shaman fairy?"

The group sat and thought about his question. Then it hit Sydona like a bag of bricks. "She's a flier. Remember? She's a blood relative to Avani, she just couldn't fly. What if she's the one in a million flier with a pixie ability?"

"But she can't even fly," said Silas from the window. "She's broken. The gene never passed down to her."

Giovonna perked up and put her index finger up straight. "What if it's just hidden? A recessive gene. Meaning, she could still have other types of abilities. That's why she's looking for a shaman. They can tell. And even possibly teach her to use it."

"Why would they teach her, Gia?" asked Raoul.

"I don't know! Maybe she's threatened to kill them or expose them to the world. Either way, teaching her would give her what she wants."

"But the big question is, *what* exactly is her ability?" Sydona pressed. She and the others looked at Jubilee who stuck her hands up.

"I wish I knew. She never told me. But I'm not even sure she knows."

Sydona pushed her fingers through her short blonde hair in frustration. "We need to find her…"

"No one knows where she is though," said Silas.

Raoul then spoke up. "There's a place Harold took me earlier. It's a cave on a cliffside by the ocean. I have no idea if she knows it's there, but it's worth a try. Maybe she knows of it too and took a shaman there to practice."

"Really? Harold took you there?" asked Sydona.

"Yeah. It was where he would hide out sometimes. Maybe another Vulture found it and told her."

Sydona glanced around the room. "Let's give it a shot. You want to come with us, Dev?"

Devon slinked down in a pile of pillows. "I—I don't know…"

"I'll stay with him, Syd," said Silas. "My leg still isn't a hundred percent." He turned to the 10-year old. "You want to hang out with me, bud?"

Devon nodded with a slight smile. "Can we find Jet, too?"

"Of course, man. We'll see where he's at," Silas walked over to his side and sat down. "I'll teach you how to use this too, okay?" He put the pistol on safety and handed it to him. Devon's brown eyes widened and turned the gun over a few times. "Okay."

"You're a Sparrow, remember?" Silas playfully bumped his shoulder.

Devon nodded and timidly held it out in front of him and aimed at something across the room.

Sydona smiled at Silas, and he returned a wink. "Let's get going, then." Giovonna, Raoul and Jubilee made their way to the door. Giovonna hoisted her crossbow over her shoulder and Sydona grabbed the arrows to hand to her.

She then turned to Silas, not wanting to leave him. Especially without a proper good-bye. Walking to the other side of the bed, she wrapped her arms around him and squeezed tight. It took a second for Silas to hold her back, but when he did, he held her just as tightly. Before any tears slipped out, she pulled away and kissed him square on his unassuming lips. Silas kissed even more aggressively, holding her while doing so.

He pulled away and gazed into her wet eyes. "Please be careful."

Sydona sniffed and nodded. "You too."

Before her emotions took over much more, she let him go and unlocked the door. She and Giovonna kept their guard up, while Raoul and Jubilee took the lead as their lookout. As they made their way through the house and out the back door, Giovonna spoke up. "I wonder where the doctor went?"

"He's not really a fighter, so my guess is he is hiding somewhere. Before shit really hits the fan…" said Sydona.

Raoul yelled from the front. "We should fly there. I watched Harold climb down the cliff; it's pretty steep."

"I'll get you, Syd," said Giovonna with a grin and held her hand out.

"Thanks but uh, I'm covered," Sydona said and pulled the bracelet out from her pocket.

"How did you—" Raoul started, confused.

"John gave it to me…" she answered as it clicked onto her wrist.

"What, from the kindness of his cold heart?" Raoul said sarcastically.

Sydona rolled her eyes playfully. "Let's just go."

Thunder cracked in the distance as they took their descent onto the rocky beach. The sun had gone down fully and the moon hid behind large gray clouds. The scent of rain was at the cusp and ready to fall at any moment. Goosebumps appeared on Sydona's milky skin as the breeze off the rapid ocean waves washed over her. It may have just been the storm, but she felt another storm of sorts was on its way. The need to find Natalia was at an all time high.

A large hole carved into the cliffside was finally shown in the flashes of distant lightning. Raoul buzzed straight to it, with Sydona and Giovonna not far behind. They landed next to it and squeezed themselves inside. Giovonna made a sound and it echoed slightly. It wasn't a large cave, but still big enough for a few people to hide inside.

"Show yourself, Natalia!" Sydona yelled.

"Miss Wilder?" said a familiar voice. The doctor turned on his flashlight and pointed it directly at them.

"What are you doing here, Dr. Malik?" asked Giovonna.

Sydona stared at him. He stood in a crevice with a gun and a tiny flashlight. His hair was completely unkempt and his suit was dirty and ripped.

"I was waiting for Natalia… thought she may have come here."

"How do *you* know about this place?" asked Raoul.

"Doesn't everybody?" John shrugged.

Raoul gawked at Sydona. "Harold told me it was a secret!"

"Shh!" Giovonna said, quieting the room. She stood still, listening intently to something outside.

Sydona heard something, too. She and Giovonna headed to the entrance, where rain had started to pour, but a voice carried on the wind. Sydona fled from the cave and ran out into the rain. Shuffling across jagged rocks, she followed the voice and she noticed movement on a sandy peninsula ahead. In the thick rain, it was hard to tell what exactly was going on. Sydona squinted her eyes and walked a little further. Once she saw a glowing blue light, followed by several others, the voice screamed at her. It was Natalia. Her hands and body shook and every ounce of her wanted to explode.

"Natalia!" she roared as loud as she possibly could. So much so, it hurt her throat.

She must have heard, because the dancing and moving around from the glowing lights stopped, for just a second. It seemed as if Natalia looked right at her, but she couldn't tell. But then the glowing lights began to move around again, almost faster than before.

Sydona gasped, knowing exactly what she was attempting to do. Sydona pivoted back to the cave to warn Giovonna and the others.

"Raoul—" she spoke, but then tripped on a rock. "Raoul! She's here!"

Giovonna ran outside to meet her. "Where?"

"There," she pointed in her direction. "We need to stop whatever she's doing."

The bank was so jagged and sharp with rocks, it was difficult to walk on, let alone run fast enough to fly. The group made their way slowly over to her, doing their best to not twist an ankle. As they got closer, Natalia came into view better and the glowing lights surrounding her were fairies.

"Oh no!" Jubilee shrieked. Sydona felt the scream shiver down her spine. But not because of the high pitch, but because of what was happening to Natalia.

"Natalia! Stop!" Sydona screamed.

Natalia whipped her head around to face them and she yelled back. "Why?! You jealous of what I can do?"

Wind and water swirled around her as the storm intensified. As the thunder got closer, her adrenaline rose and her hands curled into fists. "What are you even talking about?!"

"You'll see!" Natalia replied, her voice drifting off in the storm. She yelled louder. "You will regret everything. You *all* will!"

The group finally made it to a patch of sand, close enough to see clearly, but far enough away to stay safe. Before they were able to make another move, she was already transforming from a human into a twenty-foot, black, spiney, fire-breathing dragon.

"She's… a *dragon*?!" Raoul horrifically shouted.

The dragon let out an ear-shattering roar that could be heard further than the thunder surrounding them. Sydona backed away slowly with her blue eyes glued to it. Nothing in the entire universe could have prepared her for something of this magnitude.

"How is that possible?" John asked, stiffened with shock.

Sydona lost the ability to move and almost forgot how to speak. The dragon's claws dug deep into the sand as it regained focus and aimed at them. Sydona quickly learned how to move again.

"Ruunn!!"

"I think you mean fly!" Raoul yelled.

Giovonna grabbed the doctor's hand since he no longer had the bracelet, and they ran along the small sand shore to fly up into the sky. Sydona's adrenaline pumped through her so fast, she almost couldn't contain it. She heard John yell out while they flew back to the house. "Why are you helping me, Gia?!"

"Why? Well, I don't know if you noticed, doctor, but a person just turned into a dragon. Is that a good enough reason for you?"

John paused but then answered. "Yup, that's good!"

Raoul and Jubilee covered the two with dust so it wouldn't burden Giovonna even more. The dragon wailed again and Sydona felt almost as if it cracked her in half. The sound of the wing flaps made her want to fly even faster. Sydona led the group but didn't want to go back to the house quite yet as it would lead the dragon to everyone else.

"We need a plan!"

"Okay," Raoul said. "How exactly do we kill a dragon?"

The dragon screeched as it gained on the group's heels. It blew a stream of fire at them and they dodged just out of the way. Sydona felt the intense heat of it and it terrified her to her core. The question posed an unsolvable problem. The Sparrows never taught her how to deal with something like slaying dragons.

The doctor's mansion stood at the top of the cliff, looking worse for wear. Flames engulfed bushes and other areas of the property, including the garage where Sydona was first held hostage. Quickly glancing down at the battle below, she noticed everyone stop and look toward them. Pixies quickly turned their attention to the dragon behind and bravely flew toward it. Not to mention the dozens of birds there on command, tearing at her and aiming for her eyes. The dragon stopped chasing them and worked on fighting off the tiny fighters.

Now was their chance. They swung back around to make their landing on solid ground.

Sydona asked John as soon as their feet touched down. "Can we use your basement?"

"Yes! It's very secure down there, everyone should be able to fit! I'll work on opening it."

"Good, I'll grab everyone and tell them where to go," Sydona said and was already spreading the word to anyone she saw, Vulture or not. Everyone in their group, including a brunette woman with a fairy and stubby older man quickly joined them downstairs. John and Sydona stood on the stairs while John locked it securely and Sydona counted the tops of heads. She couldn't think of anyone who was missing and walked down the rest of the way to join her group.

"Where did the dragon come from?!" Devon asked, his voice shaky and cracking.

"It's Natalia!" said Giovonna. "We saw her turn into one."

"Well I'll be damned," said Harold. "I knew there was always somethin' weird about her. This form definitely suits her better..."

Willow laughed out loud and threw her head back. She then held her side and moaned.

The older, bald man spoke up. "This is no laughing matter..."

Willow looked down and frowned at him. "Just tryin' to lighten the mood."

"While we appreciate the thought... we been waiting for this."

"And might I ask who the hell you are, pops?" Willow demanded with crossed arms.

The man straightened up, adding another half inch to his height. "My name is Virgil. I am a flier with pixie abilities, personally selected by the most elite shamans in existence. They foretold a prophecy that would change the world. We're here to make sure it doesn't happen."

"What did the prophecy say, exactly?" asked Giovonna.

"It said a dragon would rise up in the time of betrayal. And a man who was bound to the skies is the only one to match the strength. When I heard through the grapevine that a human woman was asking around for fairy shamans, I knew it was getting close. And then, Quinn and Dani found me in Nevada with none other than this man." Virgil patted Jet on the shoulder. Jet seemed to look much paler than normal.

Silas spoke up. "So, hang on. Are you saying *Jet* is the only one to go up against Natalia? Our Jet?"

"What's that supposed to mean?" Jet spat and started coming at Silas. Silas backed up and Sydona stopped him with her hand.

"Sorry, man. Just not my first pick."

"Fuck you, Silas. You have no idea what I'm going through right now." Jet walked away and his eyes turned auburn. Sydona narrowed her eyes.

"Both of you, stop," said Sydona. She thought about the prophecy and said something out loud she never thought she would say. "It means Jet is a dragon, too. Right?"

"What?" Devon exclaimed in shock. "That's not it, right Jet?"

Jet didn't even look Devon in the eyes.

Jet's friend Quinn spoke in an elegant Australian accent. "That's what Virgil is trying to say. But, once he transforms into one, he uh… he can't turn back."

Sydona asked, "What do you mean?"

Virgil answered for her. "The transformation can only transpire once. If he tries to turn back, he'll die."

Giovonna inquired. "What if he doesn't try to turn back? How long can he be a dragon for?"

"Not long. It's more of a defensive thing, it can only last a few days at the most. After that…"

"So…" Willow spoke up softly and carefully. "You gonna sacrifice yourself, for us?"

Jet turned away from the group. Sydona could tell how hard this was for him. It was impossible. But the news made her a little happy as well. It meant Natalia would suffer the same fate. "I'm sorry about everything Jet. I really wish there was another way to do this… But maybe the fact that Natalia is already a dragon and turning back into a human would ultimately destroy her, we should think of how we can convince her to be a human again."

The group stared at each other. A few scared faces, but mostly confused. "No offense, Syd," said Raoul. "But how do you expect us to talk, let alone reason, with a dragon who wants us for dinner?"

"Well… she's got a thing for Knox, right? What if we lure him into the open? Where she could clearly see him."

"Um, that's cute," Dani said. "But we're not entirely sure if she is the same person inside. She could have been replaced by this ginormous reptile and is no longer Natalia. Knox could be killed for nothing."

"Wait, what?" Avani said as she made her way to the smaller groups conversation. Her husband's name must have been spoken too many times to ignore. "What do you want with him?"

Sydona swallowed at Avani's bubbling anger and soon spoke up. "I don't know why but your sister seems to really like Knox. So we thought maybe if we put him out there and she sees him, she'll want to turn human again. And when she does, she'll… go on her own…"

Avani shot daggers at Sydona. "Lemme get this straight. You wanna sacrifice my husband to a dragon in hopes that it will kill my sister?! Is that what you're trying to tell me right now?"

"Well when you put it that w—" Sydona said sheepishly.

"No way in hell, amiga. You gonna have to think of something else. Either way, I am losin' someone I love. Don't make me choose on top of that!" Avani said and began to cry. Knox was right behind her and Avani cried into his chest. He just shook his head and the couple walked to the other side of the basement and sat down together.

Raoul landed on Sydona's shoulder. "Okay, well, what's plan B?"

"I'll take care of her," Jet spoke up clearly.

Sydona's heart pounded. Jet walked through the crowd of humans, fliers and pixies with his head held high. "Jet… you don't have to do this, you know. We all know what it will do to y—"

"Just trust me."

Harold laughed loudly. "You?! What are you going to do? Drown her in bourbon?"

"Joke all you want," Jet spat, his fists clenched. "I know I haven't been… helpful or whatever." He then spotted Devon and put his full attention to him. "I'm really sorry Devon, for everything I put you through. You deserve better. Better than me. I hope you know how much I care about you and I'm… sorry I let you down. I let all of you down." He turned back to Sydona and looked up to the door. "I just hope you can remember me for what I'm about to do, and not for what I've done in the past."

Giovonna placed herself in front of him. "Don't worry Jet. We can totally think of something. You have… so much more life to live!" She grinned, but then lowered her voice to a whisper. "Devon needs you, Jet. Don't leave him, not here."

All Jet did was grab Giovonna's shoulders and move her to the side.

His tone made Sydona fear the worst though. As if he were going down in a blaze of glory. A pixie with red and black wings, as well as three fairies who resembled shamans followed him up the set of stairs.

Devon ran up to him just as he touched the door knob. "Jet, stop! What are you doing?!"

Jet just smiled. "I'm ending this."

Devon cried, ran up the stairs and wrapped his small arms around Jet.

"Don't go!" the boy cried.

"It's my destiny, Dev. Avani and Knox will take good care of you, okay?" Jet said calmly.

"No! I want to stay with you!"

Sydona noticed the sounds above getting louder and everyone felt the tension growing. She gently grabbed his waist so Jet could leave.

"No!" he cried again. "I forgive you! I forgive you for my parents!"

Jet grinned wider and tears started falling from his auburn eyes. "Thank you Dev." He sniffed. "That means... so much."

"So you'll stay?!" Devon asked with a cracking voice.

Sydona felt her heart breaking for them, but she kept a firm grasp on the boy.

"I'm sorry, little man."

Sydona brought Devon back downstairs and he immediately ran away from them all. Soon, Quinn ran up the stairs and grabbed his hand.

"Jet, I—just wanted to say how glad I am to have met you. Whether it was because of a prophecy or whatever, I'll never forget you. I want you to know that..."

Jet didn't say anything in response and pulled her in close to him. He put both hands on her ears, tilted her head down slightly and kissed her forehead. Streams of tears fell down Quinn's cheeks. Jet took a deep breath, turned to the door and opened it. As the door swung open, a magical sphere engulfed Jet and the pixies inside. For just a brief moment, Sydona could see glass shattering from the window and the sphere made it disappear. Roars from the dragon screeched again. A shiver crept down Sydona's back. She slammed the door shut and locked it up again.

"Alright, everyone. We need to help them while they fight her off. Any ideas?" Sydona asked everyone in general.

Virgil was the first to speak up. "I can create an illusion around the house. Make it look invisible."

"Oh, yeah!" Dani exclaimed. "We had a hell of a time findin' him when he did this to his own place."

Sydona nodded. "But she already knows where we are. How long do you think it will fool her?"

"Unless you can figure out how to maybe just move the house, make her think it's a few dozen feet to the right?" asked Silas.

Virgil chuckled. "It doesn't quite work that way, but good thinking. It's hard to know if she is still herself in that form or just a dragon. We can only hope she has a small brain and forgets."

"Smaller than what she already has?!" Harold spat, holding back a laugh.

"I heard that, muchacho…" Avani said from the other side of the room.

Sydona examined the room, looking for weapons or tools they could use, just in case she was still in there. "John, do you have anything useful in here we can use? Maybe ropes or something to tie her down?"

John nodded. "I'm not sure, I can have Corry or Ben look for some." He looked around the crowd of people and saw the two men he mentioned stare straight back at them. After an awkward silence, he spoke again. "Or, I can look for them, too."

The men smirked and mumbled to each other as John wandered around, trying to think where to find anything. Sydona stepped down to help John look for supplies. Silas approached her soon after.

"Hey you," he said softly. He grabbed her hand and kissed her lips.

Sydona smiled. "What was that for?"

"Just 'cause," he shrugged. "This might be it for us, so I want to get my lovin' in before, you know…"

"Don't say that Silas. But, I won't say stop," she teased and kissed him again.

A brash clearing of Willow's throat interrupted the tender moment. "Sorry to interrupt, y'all but, I think you may wanna give a little pep talk to everyone. If we gonna win, we need to raise some spirits."

Sydona glanced around the room and it was quiet, despite the amount of people. "What am I supposed to say?"

"Whatever you can, princess. My sergeant always gave one to us before going into battle. It really helps build confidence."

"But why me?" she asked, a little nervous of the proposition.

"'Cause you the reason we all here. People look up to you. I—I look up to you…" Willow faded off shyly.

Sydona smiled. "Willow… you look—"

"Oh don't go making a big deal out of it. Just get the hell up there and speak from the heart, will ya?!"

She felt her heart leap with happiness. As she thought of what to say, Silas gave her one last kiss on her cheek and went back into the crowd. Sydona made her way up a couple of steps so everyone could see her.

"Listen up, everyone!" She spoke loudly and grabbed the attention of most people. "I know you have been through a lot, but we still have a long way to go. Hopefully Jet and uh, Kieran can finish the job, but if not, we need to be prepared! I'm sure you know how insane Natalia can be, so we must prepare for anything. If we can find rope or anything to tie her down and prevent her from flying, that will be the first step. If not, Willow, I am putting you in charge of gathering up weapons, and distributing as needed. All of the newcomer pixies are doing a fantastic job, keep it up! As for anyone suffering from injuries, if there are pixies with healing abilities, please do your best to assist them."

Three pixies made themselves known and flew around the room and started going to work.

Sydona continued. "I realize there is a mix of people here. Humans, fliers, Vultures, Sparrows, pixies and fairies. But now is not the time to fight amongst yourselves. Now is the time to come together to survive, whatever may happen. We've all come so far and hope is on the horizon to stop all the senseless fighting and killing. If all of this madness has taught me anything… it's that people can change." She glanced over at Harold, then at John. "The only thing we can do now is move forward. Everything you do tonight will undoubtedly make history. Your sacrifice will not be in vain! If there is one thing you should keep in mind out there, it's to fight and love without fear!"

Willow cheered loudly and whistled, causing everyone else to roar with applause. The sound made her feel like her speech did something and maybe they will actually win. She walked back down the steps, Raoul landed on her shoulder and they prepared for battle.

Chapter Twenty One

JET

Jet's legs led him down the halls of the mansion that was quickly turning to rubble. He wasn't sure how he was moving but had a feeling the shamans were helping him.

"Okay, now, don't be nervous," said Kieran, standing on his shoulder. "Remember what we talked about. These shamans can help protect you until you are ready to face her, but can't hold on forever. Take deep breaths, concentrate as hard as you can and think of only the form you desire."

Jet focused on his voice as he finally reached the outside where Natalia was waiting. Her gigantic scaly size made his heart beat faster than a hummingbirds. His entire body was covered in sweat and he wanted to faint. "I changed my mind. I can't do this!"

"Focus, Jet," Kieran spoke steadily. "There's no backing out now. Remember why you're doing this!"

Jet shook his head as much as his hands, like autumn leaves.

"Just close your eyes," instructed the fairy.

Jet did as he was told and just as he did, Natalia took the opportunity to breathe fire directly on him.

"FUCK!" he yelled as he could hear the roaring flames around him, but the sphere around him protected him from the heat. The shaman summoning the sphere chanted louder.

"Come on, Jet! Think dragon!" Kieran cheered.

Jet took a deep breath and nervously closed his eyes again. He thought about movies and images he's seen before of dragons. A different shaman began to chant a language he'd never heard of before, different from the one casting the protective bubble. The first feeling he had was his fingers and toes tingle, like almost a tickle; but soon grew more intense. Soon, the tickle turned painful as he could feel the inside of his body changing. His bones were growing and shifting, nails were turning to claws, skin popped out golden scales. Jet wanted to scream out in pain as he fell to the ground and writhed around. It was so unbearable he prayed that he would pass out so he wouldn't have to feel it any longer. But just as he thought it couldn't get worse, an insane rush of adrenaline hit him like a tidal wave and the pain he felt transformed into pure rage.

At last, Jet opened his eyes and he was no longer laying on the grass curled into a fetal position, but standing on four, scaly paws, twenty-feet above the ground. The protective shield that once protected him from Natalia was gone but Jet had no fears anymore. Kieran had transformed at the same time and stood next to him. He was red and black, just like his wings and was already challenging Natalia. They both stuck their enormous wings out as far as they possibly could to appear larger and Jet did the same. He looked to Kieren to help him with his new body.

Natalia took her first attempt to attack Kieren who was taking the lead and chomped down on one of his wings. Kieren roared out and tried biting her back. But she was quick. She had already been in the form longer than them and seemed to be learning quickly. As Kieren fought with her on the ground and used his fire breathing, Jet figured out how to move his wings and took to the sky. He wanted to come at her from another angle. His massive wings flapped over the nearby ocean as he learned how to control them. For a moment, he looked down at the ocean and saw his reflection. The flashes of lightning would occasionally catch some of his golden scales and he could see it in the water. His wings were black and he had even larger scale-like growths on his back and tail that matched his wings.

"If only Devon could see me now…" he thought to himself.

Taking a sharp turn back to land, Jet saw the red and black dragons fighting viscously. He swung around to the back of Natalia and she happened to raise her wings up. At that exact second, Jet opened his massive jaws and bit down on her right wing as he flew above her. She roared out and he even managed to lift her off the ground slightly. As she fell back down the ground, Jet lost his grip and left her wing bloodied. He circled around them and Kieran no longer kept her attention. Jet seemed more of a threat so she ran as fast as she could to the cliffside, and extended her ripped wings. He didn't have the advantage anymore and the chase was on. Jet immediately ascended higher into the clouds where thunder boiled and the clouds were moist with rain. The vision the dragon had was incredible, not needing to shield himself from water or hindered from the foggy clouds. Everything was crystal clear and he waited for Natalia to reveal herself.

Seconds later, she poked through from underneath at full speed, almost colliding with Jet. He roared loudly at her and she instantly snapped back at him. Using his large wings to keep him steady in the thin air, he attempted to bite her long neck. Even though one of her wings was damaged, she still evaded him, and did the same thing and clamped down on Jet's neck. He roared in pain and could feel every tooth of hers piercing through his scaly body. Jet moved around as much as he could to loosen her grip, but she only dug in more. The pain shot up and down the length of his body. Just when he was going to attempt to shake her off, he noticed Kieran flying toward them with his jaw wide open. A stream of magma hot fire spewed from his throat, directly onto Natalia, but it only made her more upset. The next thing he tried was grabbing the end of her black, spikey tail and using all his might to pull her off. After some struggle, Natalia let go of Jet's neck and roared loudly. She spun around to face Kieran, but he kept his mouth full of her tail, making it difficult for her to steady herself.

Jet shook his head and refocused himself, trying to ignore the searing pain in his neck. He couldn't see the blood, but his sensitive dragon nose could certainly smell it. His confidence grew as his backup arrived. Natalia was much more powerful than he anticipated. Just then, she whipped her tail from Kierans' jaws, covering her tail and his muzzle with blood. With barely any time to prepare, Natalia viciously grabbed one of Kierans wings with her claws and shredded it with ease. The stormy winds made it hard for Kieran to keep a float. Rain swirled around them like a hurricane in the making. Jet couldn't help but watch Kieran struggle to stay with them in the clouds. And as Kieran's wings flapped hard, his focus was more on not falling out of the sky and less on Natalia's next move. In just a blink of an eye, Natalia bit down on Kieran's neck, as close as she could to his head so he couldn't move. He roared out in pain, but it sounded more like a whimper than a growl. A sinking gut feeling took over Jet and he tried doing what Kieran did which was grabbing her tail. But before he could even open his jaws, Kierans' red eyes rolled back, exposing the whites covered in red veins. Soon, his wings dropped and the fight that burned inside of him was gone. Natalia resembled a dog with a play toy. She glared at Jet, with her mouth still around Kierans' neck. Jet felt the adrenaline rush back through his veins and let out a blast of fire that grew like a volcano in his belly. Natalia moved back a little, but let Kieran go. He watched as the limp dragon body fell through the clouds and disappeared from sight.

The black and gold dragons floated above the clouds, staring at one another, catching their breath. It was just Jet left to defeat Natalia. Without his backup, he wasn't sure how to defeat her. The pain from her bite was still fresh, but he couldn't dwell. He had to kill her, now. If he didn't, all the lives waiting in the doctor's mansion would surely be lost. If two dragons couldn't defeat her, nothing would. Unsure of his next move, Jet took a sudden dive back toward the ocean, hoping to lose her in the clouds and rain. As the ocean and cliffside came back into view, he flew toward the mansion again. But the large house that once sat on the hill was completely gone. He wasn't sure how the magic affected his brain, but he knew where the mansion was. It must have been pixie magic helping to hide everyone. As he briefly thought of the house, he thought of Devon. He knew he needed to defeat Natalia but also wanted to see him one last time. Though, Devon seeing him as a dragon might not be the best idea.

Before he was able to reach the cliff, Natalia was already on his tail and she breathed fire at him. The flames hurt his wings slightly and landed on the rocky beach below. He didn't want to put everyone at more risk by fighting next to the house. His claws sunk deeply into the sand and he positioned himself to where the cliff was behind him so she couldn't sneak up. Natalia landed clumsily in the water and walked up to the shore, not taking one eye off Jet the entire time. They roared at each other again. Wanting to finish her off, Jet took the first swing at her with his claws as he stood on his back legs. He swiped her face and made contact. He had scratched her eye and it bled. It must have hurt because she backed away. Now was his chance while she was injured.

Jet spread his wings fully out and breathed fire at her again. She roared back, but was clearly distraught. He tried to swipe at her again, but she was too far to reach. As he tried walking toward her, he noticed his back two feet were buried far in the sand. With all his might, he made a huge effort to free them, but as he got one out, the other became even more sunken in. The rain was only making it worse. His heart began to race as Natalia seemed to be getting back into position. Jet tried again to pull his feet out and used his wings to help leverage him out. He flapped as hard as he possibly could. Every second counted as his mobility was disabled. Natalia quickly noticed that he hadn't moved and made her move. Jet breathed fire at her to stay away, but she countered him with her own fire, making a cocoon of flames in the center of them. So hot it made the rain dissipate within milliseconds. He held it as long as he could, but only had so much he could breath at a time before needing to take a breath. Natalia stopped too and took the moment to bum rush Jet while he was still stuck.

Natalia lunged at him with both claws. She was so strong and had such an advantage, she was able to flip him over onto his back. So quickly in fact, one of his wings got caught underneath him and felt something break. Worse than that, she pushed his neck down and his head went right into the ocean water. Jet's back legs were still in the sand, while Natalia practically stood on the rest of him, forcing his head underwater. The waves were irregular due to the storm and he only had seconds to gasp for air. She was so heavy there was no way just his two front legs could get her off.

Jet could see death. The pain in his neck was blindingly painful with the help of another dragon standing on it. There were no fairies or pixies around to help. He didn't blame them as Natalia could eat them in one quick bite. The only thing he could think of as he exhaled his last few breaths was that Devon had finally forgiven him. It wasn't in the way he wanted but he hoped he had meant it. He pictured Quinn's face, soaked in tears right before he left. He wished he had more time with her. It made him smile to know she wouldn't forget him.

He hoped even though he didn't kill the monster Natalia, that he at least damaged her enough. He doesn't know why he was chosen or why he had this rare ability, but if it helped put an end to the senseless war, it was all worth it.

Chapter Twenty Two

SYDONA

The scene in front of Sydona's sapphire eyes shook her to the core. The doctor's entire home no longer resembled a house, but reminiscent of a tornado. While there was still enough to walk on, large sections of floor were missing and books littered the remains. Sydona heard John mutter "Pryah" as he shoved his way through people. He jumped over a section of missing floor and shimmed his way over bookshelves and falling drywall. Flames engulfed some of the house, but most of it had been burnt and extinguished. Sydona wondered if Kieran and Jet helped with that. She knew much more would have been destroyed if he weren't out there.

Sydona threw caution to folks coming up the stairs. And they didn't have much time to adjust to the hazardous site before the dragon roared from behind them. Sydona glared straight at Virgil who looked like he was still protecting them.

"I don't think it's working, Virgil!" she shouted
through people running past her, chanting.

His purple eyes flew open, then brown when he
discovered the scene above. "She can smell us…"

The dragon screamed louder and it became obvious
that they were no longer hidden. "Go!" she screamed
at everyone below. "Get out now! Come on!"

Sydona knew they had to redirect it. Silas,
Giovonna, Raoul, Jubilee and herself took flight
away from the base, toward the dragon. There were
no signs of Jet or Kieran; Natalia was the only dragon
left. Her heart sank as she feared the worst for his
fate. As they flew past, they caught Natalia's attention for a minute, but as more people flooded out, she
whipped her scaly neck back around. It appeared one
of Natalia's eyes was badly damaged and red blood
soaked half of her face. Sydona hoped it would be
to their advantage. Without having to tell Giovonna,
she already set up an arrow in her crossbow, aimed
and shot it in the back. It bellowed in pain and immediately pivoted back around. Silas took one of the
ropes and tugged in the opposite direction as hard as
he could.

Giovonna loaded another arrow and flew around
to the other side and Sydona grabbed the rope on
that side. They both just nearly missed the breath of
fire in the chaos. Soon, more of them joined, including Knox, Avani, Quinn and more Vultures. More
ropes hung off the dragon and several people were

now pulling it toward the forest. For a brief moment, Sydona thought they would actually be able to do it. Waves of Vultures who couldn't fly approached with automatic guns and pistols. Fire power exploded from every direction and the dragon seemed overwhelmed.

From the corner of Sydona's eye, she saw the shining glimmer of John's glasses from the thunder in the distance barreling toward the dragon. He was running at them with a large sword in both hands, pointed straight ahead. With a loud war cry from the man who walked with a cane and never hurt anyone with his own hands, raised the broadsword above his head, preparing to kill the dragon with one deadly blow. John swung his sword around, and bated the dragon who kept snapping at him. He was surprisingly quick on his feet. From a distance, it seemed like he knew what he was doing and was able to cut the dragon's muzzle a couple of times. But, suddenly, John slipped on the wet grass and the dragon took advantage. Like a snap of a finger, Natalia grabbed one of John's legs and yanked him off the ground. He screamed out in pain, but kept a tight grip on the sword. Even with his leg being crushed, he still waved the weapon around, hoping to still inflict some damage. Sydona's heart sank. The dragon then shook him violently from side to side, knocking the sword to the ground, rendering him defenseless. With a quick flip, the dragon let him go, and he went flying into the air several yards away from everyone. He landed somewhere in the forest and Sydona's first action was to check on him. He cried out in agonizing pain, his entire leg covered in blood and part of it bending in an unnatural way. Sydona didn't quite know what to do and bent down next to him.

"Syd," he groaned. "Why are you here?"

She shook her head. "I'm not sure."

He coughed a few times, and blood stained his teeth. "Please—please find my wife and daughter. And tell them I'm sorry."

"Sure," Sydona said out of sympathy. She knew she would never be able to find them. But as his dying wish, she could only give him hope, even if it was false.

As she watched the same man die that killed so many of the people she loved, she knew if she didn't say it now, it would eat her alive. "I forgive you, John."

John squeezed his eyes tightly as tears rolled down his face. He grabbed her arm gently and mouthed the words 'thank you.' He then rolled his head to the side and his arm fell to the ground like a dead weight. Sydona closed his eyes and wiped away a tear from her own cheek. She finally felt all the anger and resentment that had been building inside her for so long disappear. It filled her with a new purpose and she composed herself.

The dragon roared again and she flinched. Suddenly the barking orders from Knox echoing in the trees brought her back. She ran out of the forest and back into the chaos of the battle.

"The mouth! The mouth!" Knox yelled. "We need to close its mouth!"

Sydona rushed back into the fray and grabbed the extra rope from her waist. She tied a slipknot quickly and sprinted the length of the dragon and flew up into the raining sky. Hollering orders and throwing her loudest voice into the wind, she had a few fliers strategize to hold the dragon's head so she could wrap the rope around its head. She only had a couple of seconds to do it perfectly. Sydona took her only shot and threw the loop around its jaw, and with the help of Raoul and a few other fairies, they were able to line it up perfectly. She pulled it tight and snapped the dragon's mouth tightly shut. It whipped its head about violently. Smoke rose from its nostrils as it struggled to remove the binds. Its massive claws were desperately trying to reach its mouth and take it off, but they were pulling it away with a rope, frustrating it even more.

At one last attempt to free itself, it began to flap its enormous black wings. Flurries of wind from each flap blew people away from it, making it taxing to hold on to. Little by little, the dragon freed its limbs from ropes and the wings flapped harder. Sydona and Knox tried their best to control everyone and to stay strong, but it was no use. The dragon lifted itself off the ground and hovered over, getting higher and higher. Soon, it turned toward the ocean and took off.

Their entire group, including Quinn, Dani and Virgil set out after it before it got too far.

"What do we do now?" Giovonna yelled to the group from the back.

"It's retreating!" said Virgil. "We've worn it down, just gotta keep at it until it can't take anymore."

Sydona looked back at the group and panicked. "Knox, where's Devon?!"

"He went into the forest. But there are a few pixies with him in case he runs into trouble."

"Virgil!" Avani yelled in front of her. "Why don't you stay back? Help protect the base, or find a way to hide everyone?"

"Okay!" Virgil agreed. "I have no idea who you are, but okay." He tilted his stubby body sideways and made a U-turn back to the destroyed mansion.

Sydona then noticed the dragon getting further and further from them. From the looks of it, it was still trying to get the rope off. Land was but a speck now and it was leading them as far off into the ocean as possible.

"We need to turn back! There's nowhere to land out here. We'll be too vulnerable," shouted Knox.

Sydona hesitated because she wanted it to be over with and knew if they went back, they would be back at square one, with fire breathing and everything. She was already exhausted and assumed everyone else was too. To have it come back around after recovering, they would have a very small chance to survive.

"I'm finishing this! You can go back if you want," yelled Sydona. Her heart was practically in her throat.

"Dios mio, Syd," yelled Avani. "Are you crazy? You can't do it on your own!"

"She's right, Syd," Silas added. "We can go back and prepare as much as we can for it to come back. But if it hits you at all, you only have water to land in. You can't run on water, unless there's something I don't know about you."

"Yeah," Quinn said. "And I don't know about you, Syd, but I never learned how to swim. Just come back with us, rest a bit."

Dani also joined. "We can get more pixies, too."

"I know it's crazy, believe me," Sydona snapped. "But I don't think we can stand a chance if it comes back even more upset than before. I just can't risk it."

No one said a word, except for her trusty friend Raoul. "I'll go with you, Syd."

"Me too!" shouted Jubilee.

"Come on, guys," said Knox and he turned back to the mainland. It hurt that Giovonna and Silas didn't want to come, but understood their reasoning. She couldn't live with herself if they died because of her.

The dragon turned and was now heading west. Rain still poured and the waves crashed viciously below. It was dark, making the dragon only visible when lightning struck in the distance. The rain stung her eyes and had to constantly wipe her hair from her face. An automatic rifle stuck to her back and she flung it forward, keeping it ready. She sped up, doing her best to catch up to the dragon. Raoul and Jubilee stuck by her side as they quickly gained on it. Either they were just that fast, or it slowed down.

Once Sydona felt a safe enough distance away, she took aim and shot close to its head. She missed but the dragon stopped in mid air and spun around to face them.

"Shit," said Sydona, feeling her face turn white.

The dragon faced her head on, and Sydona grinned when she noticed the rope still wrapped tightly around its muzzle. It stayed hovering and just stared at Sydona. Smoke rolled out of its nostrils again. The sharp green eye of the monster wouldn't turn away from her and it made her think Natalia was still inside. Sydona flew around it, keeping eye contact, feeling almost hypnotized by its only eye. For a split second, she felt sympathy toward it, almost as if it knew it would die soon; by her hand or another way.

Sydona quickly snapped out of it when Raoul and Jubilee yelled at her to shoot again. Aiming as best she could, she shot the dragon again, right below the spiny neck. The eye contact broke as the dragon screeched internally. It was at that second it flapped its wings and outstretched its neck toward them. They buzzed away from it as fast as possible. The gunshot definitely took a toll as it fell behind, and struggled to stay afloat. The sounds of the flapping wings got closer and her heart beat faster. It was determined to knock her out of the sky.

"Shoot it one more time, Syd!" yelled Raoul.

It was easier said than done. In the midst of the unrelenting thunderstorm, the rain made it incredibly difficult to grip, aim and shoot in while flying away. But she had to try something. She sped ahead as fast as she could, so she could turn back around to give herself just a few more seconds to aim. Goosebumps covered her arms, down to her trigger finger. With both eyes wide open as she possibly could, she pointed the rifle in the same area she shot before, using it as a bullseye. With a squeeze of the trigger and the dragon almost within arms reach, a bang echoed off the cliffs ahead.

She had squeezed her eyes shut from the sound, but when she opened them, she realized she had shot near its muzzle and the ropes fell loose. Her body numbed. With a growing chest of the dragon, the fire in its body almost visible to the outside, it shot out an enormous spray of white hot flames. Sydona felt the intensity of the fire and began to lose her grip and fall from the sky. Luckily Raoul dusted her and she came back to feeling normal again. She had no more advantage and with a split-decision made, she turned back to the mansion for help. Expecting to see pure ocean ahead, she feared but was also grateful to see a helicopter approaching. She squinted her eyes and realized it was Willow and Harold.

Willow was on the passenger side, holding a very large automatic gun and lit the dragon up. Hearing screeching from behind her, adrenaline pumped through her veins. The dragon refocused on them and immediately breathed fire at them, Willow was hollering like crazy, along with Harold who kept her encouragement up. Even through the dragon, thunder and raging ocean below, she could hear them both with ease. While Willow took the focus of the dragon, Sydona flew to the back side and shot it from the back. It worked a bit, but then only wanted the helicopter and no matter what Willow and Sydona did to trick it, it honed in.

Harold weaved in and out of the dragon's flames. Sydona continued to shoot it from the back, but her ammo was running low and she needed to make every shot count.

"I'll put it to sleep while its back is turned!" Jubilee told Raoul and Sydona.

"No!" Raoul shouted. "It's too dangerous!"

"I got it. I just need to get a good shot," Sydona explained.

Sydona gained on the dragon to give her a better advantage. With one swipe of its tail, the black spines scraped deep into her right arm and she screamed out in pain. Unable to grip the gun after the blow, she had to switch it over to her other arm. Raoul and Jubilee covered her in orange and yellow dust to help. Blood dripped down her fingers rapidly and her arm felt like it was on fire. Using the little strength she had left, she aimed as best she could, with a very shaky arm. Willow was able to shoot again and the dragon floated in front of the helicopter. Now was her chance. As Willow was reloading, Sydona could see it was about to incinerate them, she squeezed the trigger but then quickly paused as Willow was in the line of fire. So the dragon did what it did best and aimed its lava flames at the copter.

Harold dodged it, but in the same action, caused Willow to drop her gun and watched it fall into the ocean. Sydona shook as both of them were running out of options.

Willow held on to the bands on the copter and yelled out to her. "I'm gonna jump!"

"What?!" everyone shouted, including Jubilee.

"Willow! Don't be stupid!" Sydona cried.

"I owe ya one, remember?!"

Sydona felt her stomach drop and her heart break. This was not at all what she had in mind. But, with her mind already made up, Willow waited until Harold had the helicopter level. Harold was strongly against it, but knew there was no way to change her mind. With a running jump, Willow leaped onto the neck of the dragon.

"Willow!" Sydona screamed as she circled around their struggle.

She moaned and groaned, but seemed to be using a sharp object to stab at the creature. The dragon roared out, but she wasn't sure if it was from pain or frustration. Willow, screaming and cursing, used a voracious stabbing motion but the dragon took off flying, trying to get her off. Sydona kept hearing Harold cheer her on, but when the dragon rotated its entire body suddenly and Willow fell right off.

"Aahhh!!" she bellowed as she free fell.

With a quick swipe, the dragon grabbed her in mid air with its massive claws.

"No!" Sydona screamed. She quickly tried to aim the gun again at the head to make it drop her. She feared it would crush her in its powerful talons.

Just then, a high pitched whistle echoed nearby and Virgil quickly flew past them. For a man of his stature, he was very elegant in flight. Not soon after, a wave of glowing followed up, and a dozen pixies went straight to work on the threat. It was hard to see what each of them were doing, but one made the atmosphere around them blisteringly cold. So much so, Sydona could see her own breath through the rain drops. The pixie used the rain to make ice balls and spears and threw them at the dragon as hard as she could. In the chaos, Willow's screams were getting weaker and Sydona'a heart raced.

"Jubilee! Put it to sleep!" she yelled.

"But, you said it was too dangerous!" she cried.

"She's gonna crush Willow, we need to put her out!"

Jubilee hovered around, searching for a place to enter, but there was so much commotion. Sydona heard her whimpering and crying. Her hands began to shake, afraid that Willow would die in the dragon's claws. She took another chance to shoot it. Now with the frigid cold around her, it was even harder to steady her aim.

"Everyone back!" she hollered as loud as she could. When some of the pixies kept going, she had to yell again, her voice cracking in the process. "Get *back*!"

Raoul sprinkled her with his orange dust, hoping to relieve some of the strain. It made a very small improvement, but she focused on it as much as she possibly could. Harold was out of the line of fire, but still hung around. As she quickly let out a large huff of air, she closed one eye and aimed right for the dragon's heart. The belly slowly turned red as it was brewing up more fire, but Sydona squeezed the trigger on the rifle.

The dragon cried out along with Willow, her voice brash but fading. She hit the right spot as the dragon began to fall out of the sky. Willow was still in her talons, and from what Sydona could tell, was squeezing her even tighter. She followed the dragon down and observed Willow's face. Within a split second, Willow quit fighting and her neck and arms went limp. The waves consumed them both and Sydona's heart leaped out of her chest.

Pointing her arms straight out over her head, Sydona dove into the water. Once the bubbles cleared up around them, she was able to see the dragon struggling badly. It finally let go of Willow and she started to sink. Hoping the shot and the water would finally off the dragon, she only focused on Willow. She swam as fast as she could in the raging waters and finally reached her. She was much heavier than she'd anticipated, but Sydona used all the strength she could muster. Her other arm still hurt from the dragon's spines but she kept thinking of how Willow would do the same for her. With each push of water to the surface, her heart pounded.

She soon broke the surface and gasped for air. Willow's head bobbed above the surface and Sydona dragged her to the shore. The same shore the dragon, or what was left of it, already beached. Once Willow was securely on solid ground, she started doing mouth-to-mouth resuscitation.

"Come on Willow…" she said in between breaths.

"Oh no…" said Raoul as he and Jubilee met them.

One, two, three, four, five, six, pinch nose, and breathe. Sydona repeated this several times and no response from Willow whatsoever.

"Come on, Willow! Please breathe!" she pleaded, choking between tears.

Raoul dusted her as well, but she didn't so much as move her eyelids. As Sydona leaned back, not seeing any improvements, she saw the rest of her body. Lifting her shirt up slowly, the damage done by the dragon couldn't be fixed by a simple CPR method.

"Holy shit…" Sydona said, horrified. "See if the pixies can help her…"

Virgil was nearby and landed on shore next to them.

"Virgil! Can you take her?" asked Sydona, now noticing the pixies hovering around.

"Yes ma'am!" he said promptly. "Are you going to be okay?" he asked, looking at her bloody arm.

"Yeah, I'll be fine. Just take her, please."

He nodded as some of the pixies veiled her in dust, so much so, she levitated slightly. Virgil took her by the arm and flew back to what was left of the house.

Raoul and Jubilee started to follow them, but Sydona had unfinished business.

"Aren't you coming?" Raoul asked.

"I need to make sure this is done."

As she made her way over to the once twenty-foot long, fire breathing dragon, the wind carried Natalia's screams to her ears and the scene in front of her could only be described as nightmarish. For a second, the full sized dragon wings protruded from Natalia's entire right side. Eventually, the wing crumpled like a dead leaf and left only a fraction of the person within naked on the shore. As she got closer,

Natalia was barely crawling to dryer ground, moaning and crying. She coughed up blood and it pooled around her. Her once smooth, caramel skin, was now red or covered in black spots from embedded dragon scales. She watched the woman who caused her so much torment, suffer and writhe in pain. It seemed fitting. Raoul watched too, from her shoulder. But Jubilee held Raoul's hand and looked the other way. Sydona bent down and leaned over Natalia, who had stopped moving, aside from her lungs taking in air. Even the sound of her breathing was cracked and jagged.

Sydona curled up her fists so tightly and with a swift kick from her boot, she kicked Natalia in the stomach as hard as she possibly could. She recoiled on the ground with each kick. Eventually Raoul had to tell her to stop.

Once Sydona calmed down enough to stop hurting her, she spoke. "I swear to God, if Willow dies because of you…"

Natalia soon looked up at her, and curled up a malicious smile, teeth covered in blood. It appeared she tried to laugh, but hardly any noise came out. It was clear she could hear what she said and it made Sydona's blood boil. Her fingers found the handle of her knife and held it in front of Natalia. She expected some kind of regretful expression, but the smile only got wider.

"Jubilee, you might want to look away..." Sydona said as she crouched down next to Natalia.

The engraving on her blade reflected for just a second before she inserted the pointed end directly through her throat. With widening eyes, her smile faded and blood began to pour from her mouth. Sydona kept the blade inside until her head fell to the sand and the life left her eyes.

She stared at her for a while longer, then removed the blade and cleaned it off on her pants. Eventually standing up, she turned around to see Raoul with wide eyes. She listened to the crashing waves and the pouring rain, now letting up. She heard Jubilee cry after she saw what she did and Raoul's sighs. But to hear nothing from Natalia, the infamous one known for running her mouth, felt deafening.

Sydona put her dagger back on her hip, briskly walked away from the body and spoke. "Let's go home."

Chapter Twenty Three

SYDONA

The helicopter's propellers peeked over the top of the hill, right next to the destroyed mansion. As Sydona's feet touched the scorched ground, cries from Giovonna rang out. A large crowd gathered around and she fought her way into the middle where Willow was lying lifeless on the grass. Sydona clasped her good hand over her mouth and tried to prevent herself from falling apart. Harold and Giovonna sat next to her while the few medical pixies flew away slowly, unable to bring her back.

"W-Why are they leaving?" Sydona asked, confused. "She needs help!"

Virgil was in the crowd and spoke up for them. "They tried everything, my dear. I'm very sorry."

Sydona shook her head. "No, they didn't do enough! Come on!" She knelt down next to her and attempted CPR again, but Virgil and another person forced her back on her feet. "Stop! She can't… she can't be dead. She can't!"

Giovonna immediately squeezed her tight and tried to calm her. "Willow… Not… not Willow," she cried out.

"I know," whimpered Giovonna. "I know…"

Sydona soon felt more arms around her, including Silas, Avani and Devon. After they pulled away, and Sydona cleaned her face, she noticed Harold standing alone, solid as a statue, staring at Willow.

She slowly approached him as most of everyone else left the area. "Harold… I—"

He closed his eyes and shook his head.

Sydona didn't push, but just stood next to him.

After only a minute, he spoke up. "Why she gotta be so goddamn stubborn?"

"I don't think it was stubbornness… But I do know if the roles were switched, I would've done the same for her."

He didn't say anything, but refocused his attention to a small rock he kept rolling around in his palms. "That day that you found Willow's and I came a knockin'… I never seen her defend someone she just met as much as she defended you. I didn't get it… until now."

Sydona squeezed her eyes. "She saved my life… and I'll never be able to repay her."

Harold wrapped an arm around Sydona's back. "You helped us find each other again, kid. You done more than enough. You saved my life, too."

An overwhelming need to embrace Harold took over and she went in with both arms. He responded back with a tight squeeze. As she let go, she stood up and thanked Harold for everything.

"No problem," he said.

"Oh, and I didn't know you could even fly a helicopter," Sydona said, trying to lighten the mood. Harold grinned.

"I reckon there's a lot you don't know about me."

Harold walked over and covered Willow up with a blanket laying nearby. He then took it upon himself to sing *Amazing Grace,* the same song that Giovonna sang when her mother died. Harold carried Willow's body and laid it next to Ian, in a row of all the fallen souls. The words of the song made Sydona even more emotional as she gazed at her late father's face.

As the song ended, everyone began to disperse and figure out what they were supposed to do next. The rain finally let up and the clouds dissipated. A sliver of the morning sun broke through and sprinkled down on the cliffside. Knox, Avani and Devon stayed behind with Sydona.

"Can I see her?" asked Avani.

Sydona could only nod. The sight of Avani brought back the terrible feelings. She never noticed, until now, how much they looked alike.

"Thanks…" said Avani with a mournful face. Before she turned to walk away, Sydona spoke up, but softly.

"For the record, I made her suffer as long as I possibly could."

Avani stared wide-eyed at her but Sydona didn't look at her at all. After several tense and uncomfortable seconds, Avani could only turn away and go find her sister. With a heavy sigh, Knox ran behind her and they flew down to see what was left of Natalia. Sydona's eyes followed them until they disappeared behind the cliffside, then her fists unclenched. She knew it wasn't Avani's fault, but she hated what just happened so much that it was hard to hold back her feelings.

Virgil caught her eye and he made his way over with a grin plastered on. The moment of silence to herself was gone. His arms stuck out as if he were coming to hug her, but luckily he stopped just short.

"My goodness, child, you did it!"

Sydona nodded with an expressionless face.

His smile started to fade as he waited for some kind of reply. He then looked at her arm and gasped. "Your arm! Doesn't that hurt?"

Sydona glanced down at the blood running down the bicep to her bruised fingers. "Not really."

Virgil whistled and several pixies flooded over and began to do work on her arm.

She wanted to shoo them away, but it was helping the pain.

As they swarmed around her arm like a hive of bees, a smile grew back on his wrinkled face. "Well, I for one am just overjoyed to be a part of this history. To witness a dragon slaying by a flier who lost everything. Trust me when I say, Sydona Wilder, you won't be soon forgotten. We must stay in touch so I can drink up every detail of the epic journey." He wiggled his brows and waved his hands around, unable to contain them.

Sydona wanted to be more excited that everything was over. But she never felt more empty in her life. She did her best to stay positive and she lifted her chin and changed the subject. "What will you and the pixies do now?"

"To live in peace, darling. Why, isn't that why we came?"

Sydona swallowed and gave him a small smile. "Thank you, Virgil."

Virgil gave her his phone number and she promised to call as soon as she bought a phone. The pixies did quick work to her arm and while she had a lot of scarring, the bleeding stopped and the pain level lessened. He then waddled away, whistled loudly and in a flash, they flew away and disappeared into the morning fog above the trees.

Wanting to clear her thoughts and show others she wasn't up for chit-chat, she decided to check out the forest where the beginning of the battle began. She soon walked past the broadsword and tilted her head. As she took a closer look, she realized it was the same one she remembered seeing in Malik's office. But more importantly, why the sudden use of violence? The man who had other people fight his battles, or who used bargaining chips or a taser. A sword seemed barbaric to her. Thinking back to what he told her on the steps about his family, she thinks he was finally done being a coward and wanted to prove that he could protect them with his own hands. She also thought that maybe he was trying to be the hero, which seemed like the doctor she first met. There were two sides of him and while she still forgave him, she was glad he was gone.

Soon after, she made her way back out of the forest. Knox and Avani had returned from the cliffside as well, but with extra bodies. Devon was walking with them as well. Avani held her sister in both her arms, wrapped up in a jacket, while Knox had Jet in his. Devon was also holding something and as they got closer, it was clear it was Kerian back in pixie form. Devon stayed close to Knox and was crying so hard it could be heard across the way.

"Oh my God… Jet," Sydona uttered. The sight of him, blooded up, scorched, bruises and scales that were still embedded in his skin was heart-wrenching.

"We—We, we found Jet in the water with, with, the pixie next to him," Devon cried, his words shaky and timid.

"Come here, Dev," Sydona said as she crouched down with open arms. Devon jogged to her, still carrying the pixie and let Sydona hug him tightly. "She killed him, Syd. She did…"

"I'm so sorry, honey!" Sydona held back her tears as much as she could to stay strong for him. Just then, Quinn and Dani rushed over. As soon as Quinn saw Jet though, she cupped her hands over her mouth and dropped to her knees. Dani stood on Quinn's shoulder and did her best to comfort her, although she was not doing well herself. The tears surrounding Sydona made her want to cry as well but pushed it down.

Sydona walked over to the girls while holding Devon's hand.

"I think Jet really cared about you, Quinn," she said softly.

Quinn wiped her nose with the length of her arm. Mascara ran down her pink cheeks and she shook her head. "He was a special guy. I could tell from the first time I saw him. He went through a lot and pretended like he hadn't. I wonder if his dragon form was almost like his true identity. So misunderstood, hiding behind those tough dragon scales. I just hope he's in a better place now."

Devon let go of Sydona's hand and hugged Quinn. She left the three of them to mourn and caught up with Avani and Knox. They laid Natalia's body next to all of the other fallen people. Sydona didn't think Natalia should be placed next to those she killed, but Avani was mourning. It wouldn't be right to say something. Sydona only paid attention to Avani and Knox.

Avani finished laying her down and fixed the blanket to cover all of her. "Did she say anything to you, Syd?" Her face was snotty and tear stained.

Sydona clenched her teeth. "Sorry, no…"

Avani sniffed loudly. "Just wish I could've been there for her, you know?"

Sydona forced herself to take deep breaths.

"Raoul told me… that it was her who killed Willow. Is that true?"

Sydona knew that it was hard to know if the person was still inside the dragon form, but deep down she knew Natalia was still in there. "I'm sorry for your loss, Avani. Willow didn't deserve what she got, but Nat, well…"

Avani shook her head. "I know she was a tyrant and Willow was a strong person. Neither of them deserved that fate. Jet either—" she paused to compose herself. "I just can't believe she's gone. There's so many things I wish I could've said to her before she left me."

Sydona swallowed hard. Instead of letting her anger surface, she pulled Avani in for a hug. Avani let herself go and cried harder. Sydona stroked her hair and Knox stood close by but didn't join them. Knox caught her eye and she could tell he couldn't empathize with his wife. He wanted to be there for her but he didn't shed one tear.

Avani pulled away and put her arm around Knox. Sydona changed the subject. "So, now that Jet is no longer here, I'm wondering what's gonna happen with Devon?"

"That poor kid," Knox said as he glanced over at him and the girls. "He's been through way too much shit for his age. Wish we could do something…"

Avani looked up at her husband with wide eyes. "Why don't we take him?"

"Oh," Knox rubbed the back of his neck. "That wasn't *quite* what I meant—"

"Elias, this is perfect. We have known him for a long time, so we're not some strangers and we could give him a nice home to stay in. Something steady. He needs some kind of stability, don't you think?"

"Dear, we're not really equipped to adopt right now, are we?"

"You wanna let him live out on the street?! No, we will talk to him, Sydona. I'll convince him," she winked at her. She seemed to be over her sister already.

"Who, Knox or Devon?" Sydona smiled back, glancing quickly at Knox who looked less than thrilled.

"Exactly. Come on, let's see how he's doing."

Avani took the lead with Knox trailing behind, over to Devon, Quinn and Dani. Sydona let them have their talk and she made her way over to the rest of the group. Giovonna, Harold, Silas, Raoul and Jubilee were gathered around the bodies under white sheets. It took her back to Eagle Lake and an overwhelming feeling of dread swept through her. But at least their deaths were not in vain and the killing had finally ended. The thought of a normal life ahead began to cheer her back up.

Giovonna could not stop crying. The sounds of her sniffling and weeping were soft and soul-crushing. Sydona rubbed the girls back and brought her in for a hug.

"I can't believe she's gone, Syd. I can't..." her tears soaked into Sydona's shirt. Giovonna pulled away and suddenly realized the blood on her shirt and all the scars on Sydona's arm.

"Oh my god, what happened to you? Are you okay?!"

Sydona smiled. "Yes, I'm fine Gia. The question is, are you?"

Giovonna cleaned her face off with her hands and nodded. "I will be."

Silas spoke up while he grabbed Sydona's hand and squeezed. "So what are you gonna do now, Gia? Go back home?"

Giovonna let out a snotty laugh. "Yeah, sure. Let me just go back home after I ran away from there twice. They'd probably just kick me out anyway."

"Well why don't you come live with us then?" Jubilee asked in her painfully squeaky voice.

Raoul pushed Jubilee aside, but Sydona replied. "While I would love nothing more, she's only a teen."

"Maybe I could change their minds? Dr. Malik did say I am quite the convincer," Giovonna said proudly.

"Uh, Syd…" Silas pulled her aside and whispered. "So, uh, I wasn't quite sure how to bring this up, but seeing as we're on the subject." He cleared his throat. "I was kinda hoping that maybe you and I could try this living together thing?"

"Oh," Sydona hesitated. "I hadn't really given it much thought, yet."

"I know, it's a strange thing to be thinking about after all this. But I promise I will help out around the house. Feed chickens, water the plants and stuff. You'll never want to live alone again."

Sydona couldn't hold back a grin. "Okay, yeah. Let's do it! And Gia," she turned to her, "If your parents allow it, you should come by. At least to visit."

"Really?!" Giovonna squealed and Sydona watched her tears dry right up.

Raoul cleared his throat. "Syd, what about Harold?"

She had forgotten he was standing nearby, lost in his own thoughts. She wandered over to him with Raoul on her shoulder and Silas and Giovonna celebrating behind them. "Hey, um, if you need some place to stay, Harold… You're always welcome."

His brown eyes met her and he nodded with a small smile. "Thank you…" He then walked back to the group and they invited him in with open arms.

As they let go, Avani and the others walked up.

Quinn was the first to speak. "It was so great meeting you all, but me and Dani gotta bounce."

"Yeah, very nice to meet you," Dani said. "Wish it was under different circumstances, but at least we can all go home now, ya?" she chuckled, clearly trying to lighten the mood.

"Where are you two going now?" asked Silas.

Quinn shrugged. "Not really sure but, we'll be fine. As long as we have each other."

"Speak for yourself, mate! We deserve a castle after all this!" Dani bellowed, elbowing Quinn.

"I'm happy to find a cardboard box and I can draw a door and some windows. Does that work for you, princess?" Quinn laughed loudly. Sydona wanted to laugh, but hearing the word princess only made her think of Willow.

"Whateva!" Dani crossed her arms.

Quinn rolled her eyes. "Again, really great working with you all. Maybe we'll see each other again sometime. Hopefully with less killing."

Sydona nodded. "It was a pleasure meeting both of you. Safe travels."

Quinn nodded, pulled down the goggles on her head, and took off running. Dani trailed dust behind as they reached the clouds above.

Avani, Devon and Knox were next in line. Devon held Avani's arm.

"Devon will come with us," Avani smiled and stroked the back of his head. "We have a house with a spare room that I think would be perfect for him."

"Yes," Knox answered from behind them. "And a big backyard, too. We might even have a big tree we can build a treehouse in."

Devon glanced behind him. "You do?"

Knox bent down so as not to tower over him. "Yup! I'll even show you how to build it."

Devon released a big smile, forgetting about all the tears. "Can we fly there?"

Knox grinned and let out a laugh. "Of course, kiddo."

Devon let go of Avani and gave Knox a hug so strong, he almost fell backward.

"Before we go, we gotta stop by the IDF where they kept all those kids while their parents were in camps," said Avani. "You wouldn't mind helping us with that, right?"

"No, I don't mind," said Devon. "Are the kids my age?"

"Oh, I'm sure there is," assured Knox. Devon replaced Avani's arm with Knox's. Sydona could swear she saw his heart grow.

They all hugged each other goodbye and soon, the new family flew up into the air and Sydona watched until they disappeared.

Sydona walked to the edge of the cliffside, overlooking the vast ocean that sparkled in the rising sun. Seagulls flew past singing joyfully, ignorant of the recent events. She couldn't help but to focus on the sounds. The crashing waves below, washing away everything from yesterday. She glanced down at her wrist still wearing the bracelet. With a smirk, she unhinged it and held it in her hand. She thought back to the first time she ever saw the wretched thing. Images of her mother and father appeared in her mind when she found them again at Eagle Lake. All she had left were memories of them now. A gust of salty wind kissed her face and she looked back out toward the sea. She ran her finger around the bracelet a few times and her teeth clenched.

"Hey, there you are," Raoul said from behind her and landed on her shoulder. He noticed the bracelet in her hands. "What are you doing?"

Sydona shook her head and let out a deep sigh. "I spent all this time thinking flying was what defined me."

She clutched the bracelet in one hand, swung her arm back as far as she could and threw it out into the ocean. As she watched it splash into the unknown, a warm sensation rushed through her body. Never in her life did she think she would be getting rid of the one thing she thought made her special. She would live a grounded, normal life she never knew she wanted, until now.

Raoul buzzed out in the direction she threw it and turned back to her with a smile. Soon, her friends joined her and they sat down and stared out, admiring the sunrise. Silas sat next to her and kissed her gently on the lips, while Giovonna sat on her other side and rested her head on Sydona's shoulder. It was finally time to start living her life and live free.

The End

Epilogue

FOUR YEARS LATER

Sydona shut the medicine cabinet in the bathroom and caught herself in the mirror. She brushed her short blonde hair a few times and straightened her bangs out with her fingers. Adjusting her lips and pouting them, she finally felt satisfied enough to go down stairs. She looked down the hall covered in vines and braided twigs to look for any messes. A pair of black boots were thrown about in the hallway and Sydona rolled her eyes. Whispers from a fairy, hanging out in a tiny house embedded into the twigs told Sydona they were Silas'.

"Oh, I know. Thanks, Grimley," she said with a smirk.

Sydona went to her bedroom and peeked outside of her window to find Silas. Where the burnt tree once fell, was now a full, lush area of flowers, bushes and a few new trees, held up by stakes and strings.

Most of the fairies were outside, getting ready for the party. Silas stood on a ladder at the edge of the nearby forest, setting up lights.

"Silas! You're still messing with those lights?"

He turned around and protected his eyes from the sun with his arm. "I'm trying to make it perfect!"

Sydona grinned. "Well, hurry up! Everyone will be over soon."

He waved his hand at her and continued setting up.

Sydona shut the window and accidentally pushed Raoul's little bed off the sill. She grabbed it and set it back up, fixing the cloth blanket. With a happy sigh, she headed out of her room and went to grab the boots.

"When is everyone coming over?" asked Giovonna.

"Six," Sydona said, then admired Giovonna's new head wrap, purple with white lilies and decorative swirls. "That's really cute."

Giovonna touched it and smiled. "Oh yeah, Valerie gave it to me on my birthday and I forgot about it until today."

"Valerie, huh? Is she coming tonight?"

Giovonna giggled. "Nah, we've only been on like three dates. I think it would be too soon, ya know?"

"You mean, going to a party to celebrate a fairy's wings is going too fast? It would be an interesting story for the future though." Sydona lovingly pinched her side.

"She's still getting used to the fact that I can fly, Syd. I think it's best to wait to show her a thousand fairies," she laughed.

Just then, a ding went off in the kitchen and Giovonna excused herself. The house was filled with sweet smells of fruit, cakes and pastries. Ever since Giovonna moved in six months ago, Sydona's kitchen has been taken over by Giovonna's cooking experiments. Sydona made her way downstairs and straightened up the living room, fluffing pillows and dusting off areas with her hand.

A knock at the door startled Sydona, but she composed herself and opened the door wide.

"Hola, chica!" Avani exclaimed. She leaned in for a hug and squeezed Sydona. But soon they were torn apart by two little boys running into the house with Devon chasing after them. Sydona let them and turned to Knox. He was wearing a suit and let his hair grow out. His image was a lot less intimidating and she smiled at him.

"Good to see you, two! You told me you had kids, but I wasn't expecting them to be this old, already!"

Avani went to tame the boys and Knox shut the door behind him. "They are brothers whose parents were part of the Sparrows. We took care of them for a while, but eventually decided to adopt them. They really got along well with Devon."

"Aw, I'm sure Devon is enjoying having some siblings, huh."

Knox chuckled. "He's a hell of a kid, Syd. He's 15 now, and spends so much time with his brothers.

"How old are they now?"

"Deegan's eight and Colton's five."

"Eve and Colton would probably get along really well, then!"

Giovonna came over after giving the boys hugs. "Everyone's here then, yeah?"

Sydona answered. "We're still expecting Quinn and Dani, too."

"Oh, that's right! What about Virgil? Will he be with them?"

"He couldn't make it, but he sends his love."

"Well, it's gonna be a full house, that's for sure!" said Giovonna.

"Yes, it will," Sydona said with a nervous laugh. "Good thing we have most things set up outside. Let's head out that way, shall we? Plenty of space to run and fly."

Knox, Avani and the boys went outside and greeted Silas, still messing with the lights.

Another knock at the door and Sydona answered it. It was Harold, holding a casserole dish in his hands. Within seconds, Quinn and Dani landed in her front yard.

"The gang's all here!" said Sydona with an elated smile.

Harold handed her the dish and hugged her with one arm. He was dressed up more, too. His hair was combed back and wore slacks in replacement of his usual jeans. He smiled, but it looked insecure. The death of Willow hung over him, and possibly the sight of Sydona and everyone brought it back for him.

"How are you doing, Harold?"

He shrugged. "Oh, ya know. Takin' it one day at a time."

"That's all we can do, right?"

"I s'pose…" he gave her another smile, but she wasn't convinced.

"Everyone's in the back, if you want to see them."

He nodded and moved to the back door. As soon as he opened it, he heard Giovonna call out his name and his smile grew.

Quinn walked inside after Harold with Dani hovering next to her. Quinn didn't wear the goggles on her head and her hair was blonde now. Dani looked the same and they both smiled as they hugged her.

"You have a super cute house here," said Quinn after she examined what could be the strangest house most people have seen. "So, do the fairies live inside your house?"

Sydona scratched the back of her neck. "Yes, yes they do. And, thank you. It probably looks pretty bizarre to everyone else."

"I fuggin' love it!" said Dani with wide eyes. She buzzed around the living room and dining room, peeking into all the houses the fairies made.

Sydona grinned. "Well thank you! So how have you guys been? Where are you living now?"

"We went back to my hometown. Found a cute apartment for me and Dani. I'm workin' in a book-shop right now, pretty boring. Especially coming after battling a dragon," she laughed.

Sydona returned the laugh. "Yeah, I can't imag-ine! Although being surrounded by books all day sounds like a dream come true."

Quinn nodded. "It's peaceful, and it's exactly what I needed…" she paused and stared off. After a few seconds she shook her head. "Sorry, being here, and seeing you all again just reminds me of Jet."

Sydona's stomach twisted.

"Anyway, sorry," Quinn perked up and she shook off the negativity. "Where's the VIP?"

"It's in the backyard," Sydona replied. Quinn nodded timidly and headed to the back. Dani soon flew close behind her.

As she began to close the door, she glanced out-side for just a moment. Her heart leaped as she spot-ted Annie and Joseph walking up to her house. Annie timidly waved as Joseph stood close beside her, wearing a half smile. Sydona rushed down to them and stopped them in the middle of the yard.

"I didn't think you'd come out," Sydona said.

Annie clasped on to the strap on her oversized bag, "We weren't sure what to think after… all of that came to light." She said softly and looked over at her son, who was almost two feet taller than when Sydona last saw him. "We were *scared*. Scared that you might come after us since we knew you. They were saying a lot of terrible things about you. I mean, I didn't want to believe them but you also never told us you were a—"

"Yeah, I'm sorry about that," Sydona interrupted because she didn't want to think about all of that right now. "I thought I knew how you'd react if you found out I was and I really did enjoy coming to your booth. I considered you a friend, but I don't know… I just didn't trust people in general back then. And I didn't want you too close to me, because well, I'm a crappy friend."

Joseph spoke up in a deeper voice that startled her. "No, it makes sense, Syd. I ended up reading all about Fliers and the fairies, it makes sense why you hid. Humans have not been that great to people like you."

Sydona gave a half smile. "I appreciate your understanding, Joseph. So, you know *all* about us now?"

"Yeah, they actually started teaching it in schools about two years ago! They said since they live among us, we should know more about them. Told us about the pixies, too. Hey, you'd tell me right?" Joseph leaned in. "Are dragons actually real?"

Sydona looked over both shoulders and then looked him dead in the eye. "Do you think I'd be standing here right now if dragons existed?" He stared at her back, wiggling his lips as he tried to understand what she meant. He eventually grew a smile and gave up. "Alright, I guess you're right, it *is* pretty ridiculous!"

Sydona winked and looked back over at Annie. Her eyes were wide but Sydona didn't clarify further.

"Well, party is out back if you want to join everyone!" Sydona said cheerfully and began to lead them back.

Annie spoke up and Sydona turned back around. "I brought some fruit from our farm and I thought you might like some!" And as she opened her large bag to show her what she brought, Raoul buzzed over within a blink of an eye.

"I heard someone say 'fruit'," he said as he buzzed around in the air, sniffing. He paid no attention to the mother and son, but Joseph noticed him immediately and his eyes grew with wonder. "A fairy!"

The young boy seemed much more mature than last time, but it all came crashing down at the sight of Raoul. He glued his eyes to the fairy and Raoul only cared about the fruit. Joseph noticed his obsession and offered to take the bag to the backyard. Annie agreed and Raoul flew to the party with Joseph running happily behind.

"Thank you, Annie, for the fruit. And for coming," said Sydona with a nervous laugh.

"Is everyone back there…" Annie began.

"Like me? Mostly, yeah. But I promise, no dragons."

Annie chuckled slightly and made her way to the backyard.

Sydona walked back up to her house and shut the front door. As she looked around the now empty house, she smiled at the simple fact that she could joke about dragons. It took such a long time, but she just realized that all of that was in the past and wouldn't be haunting her anymore. Soon, she heard children giggling from the back yard and screaming playfully, and decided to join in on the fun. Her feet inched their way out of the living room, through the messy kitchen and the back screen door.

Her bare feet touched the soft, cool grass. Wind gently blew her emerald, floor length dress, filling her with goosebumps. The smoke from the growing bon-fire tickled her nose as it mixed with the pastries wafting out from the kitchen window. Lights began to grow brighter as the sun tucked underneath the trees. The lights Silas set up around the forest lit up the yard and illuminated the area softly. It was at that time, a little girl with long, dark hair caught her eye and filled her heart as she came running.

"Mommy!" she yelled as she jumped into Sydona's arms.

Sydona twirled her around while she giggled with glee. "Eve! Did you wish Finn a Happy Vila Prah?"

"Yes I did! He's so excited, he couldn't sleep!"

"He couldn't? Well I bet he'll get some good rest tonight, huh?"

"Yep!"

"Hey, can you do me a big favor?"

Eve nodded her head enthusiastically.

Sydona reached into a pocket on her dress and pulled out a photo.

"This is a picture of a very special person that I would like you to hold on to. Can you do that for me?"

"Yeah," she nodded and examined it. "Who is this?"

"This is Willow."

Eve gasped. "She has my middle name!"

Sydona smiled. "She sure does. So don't you think you would be the best person to hold it since you share the same name?"

"Yes, yes, of course mommy!"

"Good. Since she can't be here, this will be like she is here, you see?"

"Okay," Eve agreed.

Soon, Silas and Raoul joined them and Raoul landed on Sydonas's shoulder.

"Hi Raoul! Mommy gave me a picture of Willow. See? See daddy?" She pulled it back out and showed them proudly.

Silas grinned and nodded. "I do! You know, she was the bravest person I've ever met, and you wanna know a secret?"

"Yeah!" Eve jumped in excitement.

"Because you have the same name, that means you'll be super brave, too." He winked.

Eve blushed and giggled. "Really? That's so cool!"

At that time, Jubilee flew over to them and landed on Eve's shoulder.

"Hey, Ilee, I'm gonna be brave like Willow!"

Jubilee matched her high pitched laugh. "I knew Willow! She was your mom's best friend and she saved her life."

The four year old's violet eyes lit up. "She saved your life, mommy?" She asked as she pivoted around toward her.

Sydona nodded her head and held back tears. "She sure did, baby."

"What happened?"

Sydona took a second and swallowed hard. "I'll tell it to you when you're a bit older, okay?"

Eve shrugged. "Okay."

Silas chimed in, "Eveyln, why don't you go play with Devon and his brothers?"

Eve nodded, and tucked the picture in the front pocket of her jean overalls. "Come on, Ilee!" She ran off with Jubilee floating by her side and trailed golden dust.

Silas then saw a string of lights fall down and he sighed heavily. "Dammit. Took me hours to put those up! Be right back!" He slapped Sydona on her behind.

Sydona and Raoul watched everyone as they got settled in.

"Wow," spoke Raoul. "I can't believe everyone actually came."

"Really?" Sydona asked with a raised brow.

"I mean, I know why they came, because I'm the glue that keeps us all together. But, I don't know why else…"

Sydona laughed out loud with a large sigh, "Oh, shut up, Raoul."

"It is good to be back, though."

"You said it, buddy."

The entire gang gathered around the large fire and sat on stumps and hand-made chairs. Fairies and even pixies joined the celebration of the new fairy getting his wings. As the shaman came out and cleared his throat to thank everyone like he always did, Sydona couldn't help but take a look around at all of her friends and family being together in one place again, in complete peace. She glanced down at the tattoo on her forearm and read the words that got her through every minute of the last few years. She lived and loved, without fear.

More about the Author

Laura Mae is a Tucson, Arizona resident and lives with her boyfriend with their two pets. This is her third and last book in the *Fliers* Series novel. She plans to continue her writing journey with short stories, with maybe a possible prologue to *Fliers*.

Follow her on social media by visiting her website at www.lauramaeauthor.wordpress.com

Thank you for supporting indie authors!

Don't forget to review if you enjoyed this book!

www.ingramcontent.com/pod-product-compliance
Lightning Source LLC
Chambersburg PA
CBHW030834110726
47900CB00006B/1889